The Earl and His Lady

by Sally Britton

OTHER TITLES BY SALLY BRITTON

The Branches of Love Series:

Book #1, *The Social Tutor*

Book #2, *The Gentleman Physician*

Book #3, *His Bluestocking Bride*

Book #4, *The Earl and His Lady*

The Earl and His Lady

Cover design by Blue Water Books

Sally Britton
Visit my website at www.SallyWritesBooks.Wordpress.com

First Printing: August 2018

ISBN 978-1-947005-11-2

Dedicated to my husband, who keeps me going, and to my children. They are my inspiration.

Chapter One

Virginia, Baroness of Heatherton, crushed the letter from the barrister in her hand, hating each word it contained. She harbored no ill will toward Mr. Olivier for writing the abhorrent thing, but that did not lessen her dismay and fear.

"Mother?" The sweet voice of her elder son drew her from her dark thoughts. The two boys played inside today. The weather had turned gray and cool, considering it was the month of May.

"Yes, Phillip?" She looked down at the carpet where her two boys played together with wooden horses.

"Can we live with Cousin Christine forever?" His green eyes sparkled hopefully, round and wide beneath the dark curls inherited from his father. "She said she'll teach me how to ride *and* drive a cart if we stay long enough."

"Me, too!" Little Edward, only four years old, paused in his construction of stables he'd formed with books borrowed from the library. "I want to ride a pony, please."

"That would be exciting, wouldn't it?" Virginia smiled at both of them and her hold on the letter relaxed. For the time being, she and her sons remained safe. The threat of her brother-in-law's actions remained far enough away to give her time to think. "But Cousin Christine and Cousin Thomas might grow tired of us eventually."

"Never," a voice said, drawing Virginia's eyes to doorway. The woman in question entered the sitting room. "I would keep you here forever if I could." Christine Gilbert, formerly Christine Devon, walked with a fluid confidence most women worked years to achieve. Her time spent in the saddle had given her a different sort of grace than one learned on a ballroom floor.

Christine sat next to Virginia and leaned down to the children. "I came by way of the kitchen with news for you. Cook has shortbread out on the cooling racks. Should either of you wish to sample it, I think she would be happy to oblige."

Both boys came to their feet and turned pleading eyes to their mother.

Virginia attempted to maintain a serious expression but trying to repress her smile gave her away. Her sons were the center of her world. They'd lost so much with their father's death. How could she deny them a small treat? "Go on. And take some to Nurse Smythe. You know shortbread is her favorite."

The boys charged out of the room like pups intent on the scent of their treat. Christine laughed and Virginia bit back a laugh before she spoke.

"They are getting spoiled living here with such an indulgent cousin." Her shoulders relaxed and she shook her head ruefully.

"I love having them here, and I'm glad you came too." Christine's wide smile attested to the honesty of the statement. She possessed no guile, saying what she thought, by turns entertaining and horrifying Virginia. Thomas Gilbert, Christine's husband, took it all in stride and with good humor. He obviously adored his wife.

Seeing their happiness made Virginia feel the loss of her husband more keenly. When Charles left her behind, he took a large piece of her heart with him. Virginia feared the ensuing hole would never be filled again. Charles had been ill for months before he passed away, giving Virginia ample time to learn to hide her grief, to keep her emotions safely behind a wall. The letter discomposed her, however, bringing her emotions nearer the surface.

"Is something amiss, Virginia?" her cousin asked.

Virginia forced a smile, but it felt shaky at best. "I have a letter from Mr. Olivier."

Christine's eyes narrowed. "It doesn't sound like he's sent pleasant news."

"Not at all, I'm afraid. My brother-in-law is pushing through with his suit to obtain guardianship of the boys, and the court is sympathetic. I worry leaving Bath as abruptly as I did made me appear unstable." She sighed and held the crumpled paper out, not even caring that its ruined state showed her frame of mind so clearly. "What am I to do? I thought Charles had taken care of all of this."

"He never dreamed his wishes would be overturned." Christine took the paper and smoothed it out in her lap, her eyes reading the tidy script of the solicitor. "But Mr. Olivier is advising you to remain in the country?"

"Yes. He says that so long as I am in mourning the Court of Chancery may be reluctant to act. It would be indecent to pull sons away from a grieving widow." She put her hand to her temple and rubbed a circle over the steady pulse beneath the skin, hoping to stave off a headache. "But what am I to do? I cannot hide here forever. I will have to go back to our estate, and once I am there, Mr. Macon will know where to find me. The vulture." She couldn't say a kind word about him, not after he made her last days with her dying husband a knot of worry and fear.

"Did you read the whole letter?" Christine asked abruptly, frowning down at the missive in her lap.

"What else is there after receiving news such as that? No. I have little patience left to read whatever consoling words Mr. Olivier sends." Although she truly appreciated the gentleman's help, the case was hopeless. She hadn't read beyond the first paragraph he'd penned.

"Maybe you ought to read the rest. At least the part where he tells you how to avoid giving up the guardianship of your sons." Christine lifted the letter, placing it in Virginia's lap and pointing. "There."

Virginia refrained from casting her eyes heavenward. Dramatics were hardly necessary, but sometimes she rather wished to give in to them. Instead she focused on the words her cousin pointed at and read them aloud.

"*I believe there are only two ways to keep your sons under your care, given Mr. Macon's aggressive suit. You must either find a male relative whose protection could be extended, thus making him the guardian of the boys, or you need to remarry, preferably a peer.*" She stopped reading, her mind going numb.

Christine plucked the letter up and continued where Virginia left off. "*With a peer as husband, your brother-in-law would have to prove a member of the nobility as an unfit guardian. Chancery would not do so without an extreme amount of evidence to support such a stance.*" Christine shook her head. "I think the male relative option the more likable of the two. But you only have your dreadful brother and my father, correct?"

Virginia forced herself to answer, though her words sounded hollow to her ears. "My brother, since becoming the Earl of Vinespar, has never shown an interest in my mother or myself since he inherited. I sincerely doubt your father would show any inclination to aid me either, after I encouraged Julia's match to her delightful husband."

Christine sighed. "And Thomas and I hardly count as near enough relatives to do the trick."

"What am I going to do?" Virginia asked.

Christine shook her head. "An impossible choice, to be certain. Your brother is a lout."

"Turning to Vinespar is impossible," Virginia said evenly. "He would be worse than Mr. Macon, I think. I love my sons, and they are dependent upon my protection. Neither of their uncles have their best interests at heart." Virginia slowly came to her feet and walked to the window, looking out over the gardens that Mrs. Gilbert, Thomas's kind-hearted mother, said would be in bloom any day. "What will I do?" she whispered, more to herself than her cousin.

"Would you even consider finding a husband?" Christine's words came out nearly strangled, and Virginia understood why voicing the idea was difficult. She herself could hardly think it.

Christine fought for a love match to her husband. She wouldn't understand how Virginia could contemplate marriage only three months after her heart's mate had died. Yet people married for less compelling reasons, without ever considering love.

But how could she ever wed another with her heart still attached to her late husband? Charles had been everything that was good in the world. Though she had prepared for his loss, when the night came that he left her behind forever, her heart had shattered.

Phillip and Edward had to be considered. If Gerard Macon won guardianship of them, he would not permit Virginia to raise them. He made it clear the boys would be sent to boarding schools and she would be left to live on her allowance, with only the unkempt dowager house as a place of residence. What he would do to Phillip's inheritance until the boy came of age was uncertain, but Virginia doubted the funds would remain as sizable as they were at present.

"I'm—I'm not certain what to do," she said to the gray May skies. Marry? How could she—? Virginia wouldn't find love again. Love like she'd shared with Charles was difficult to obtain even once in a lifetime.

Christine's skirts rustled, and the younger woman came to stand beside her. Her arm wrapped around Virginia's waist in a sisterly embrace. "I will help in any way I can, Virginia. Tell me what you need."

Virginia felt the weight of responsibility on her shoulders more heavily each day, and the baroness knew she must bear up for the sake of her sons. The time for weeping had passed with her husband. The time for mourning would have to come to a premature end. And the business of life was left up to her.

"As soon as I have some idea of that, I will give you your orders." She spoke the words shakily, the strength she desperately needed slow to come to her aid.

"I will do my best to think of answers with you," Christine said, her words firm and kind.

"Thank you, Christine," Virginia said with all sincerity. "For everything."

Christine only nodded and gave her cousin another half-embrace before she walked away, leaving Virginia to stare out the window, wishing for a little sun to shine through the clouds.

¤

Lucas Calvert, the sixth Earl of Annesbury, never did anything by halves. When he liked someone, it was with the full force of his personality. If he supported a venture, he threw his considerable influence forward to ensure success. Should he make an enemy, the man would never know a fiercer opponent in business or politics. His reputation as an eccentric but shrewd member of the peerage was well known, and people often watched his behavior and dealings in order to determine what their own should be.

Riding across the country roads to Annesbury, Lucas knew he ought to be more satisfied with his life. Yet every day that passed left him less and less able to enjoy his successes. The passing of his wife nearly six years ago had left him numb to all but the most exceptional experiences. When she died, she took all the color of the world with her.

London, with all the *ton* posturing and jockeying for favor, remained nothing but a gray blur before his eyes. Which was why, despite Parliament being in session, he decided to retire to the country. He had no desire to sit and listen to bickering peers all day while nothing of importance was decided.

Parliament almost ignored the American problem after the Tippecanoe incident. They hoped a declaration of peace would end the irritation of the United States' hostilities. They had greater problems on their hands when Napoleon's decision to build an empire brought violence and pain to all of Europe. Then the Luddites at their own front door hardly helped matters, stirring up unrest.

Frankly, Lucas was done with all of it. The world could keep its problems and he would see to his own.

Lucas rode for his favorite estate, knowing he could not go on in this manner forever.

"But what is there I have not tried?" he muttered to himself, glaring at the road. The scenery became more familiar with each passing minute.

Annesbury Park remained a place of comfort; it held all the best memories of time spent with Abigail within its walls.

When he and his mount rounded the gates at the foot of the drive, the chestnut trees lining the carriageway made him sit straighter. He'd loved climbing those trees as a boy and had always been grateful to whichever ancestor planted them. Chestnut trees were hardly the tall, stately variety that lined many a road. They were round, comfortable trees, reaching outward as well as upward, like the arms of a parent ready to embrace a leaping child.

After passing beneath the shade of their leaves, he was home. At last.

His careful eye took in the grounds of the estate, noting the sheep grazing on the wide lawns. He smiled to himself, remembering how aghast his mother had been that he kept barnyard animals where they might be seen. But he liked the woolly beasts and they did their share by keeping the grasses manageable.

When he came to the house, he waited for the groom to collect his horse. He hadn't sent word ahead of his arrival, but the butler came forward quickly.

"My lord," Gresham said, his face more lined than Lucas remembered. "Welcome home."

Lucas studied the man more closely. The butler had been part of the household staff for as long as Lucas could remember. How old must he be? He ought to retire to one of the pension cottages on the property, but Lucas wouldn't dare mention the idea to the butler.

Gresham had been there when he brought home Abigail, throwing the door open, proudly welcoming the new countess seven years ago.

Lucas no longer felt the sharp stab of pain Abigail's memory used to cause. Instead, an empty sort of feeling entered his heart, echoing with his memories.

"Thank you, Gresham," he said, trying to push the strange sensation from his mind. He stripped his gloves and hat away, handing each to the old man.

"London not to your liking, my lord?" the astute old man asked, raising a pair of bushy white eyebrows. "Or is it business that brings you home?"

"Oh, just wanting a change of scenery." Lucas froze when his words rang through the empty hall, reverberating back to him. He took a few steps further inside, hearing the click of his boots on the marble. "Where is everyone?"

"We weren't expecting you, my lord," Gresham reminded him, the faintest note of disapproval in his tone. "There is a fair in Rothwell and many took their free day to attend. The grounds staff went yesterday, the majority of the house staff today."

Lucas nodded, taking in the darkened hall and closed doors of the downstairs rooms. "But you didn't go, Gresham?"

"My lord," Gresham said, making his way to the cloakroom to lay aside Lucas's things. "I am hardly at an age for fairs that require more than a short cart ride to attend."

Darting a glance at him, Lucas saw a good-natured smile on his butler's face, but the truth of the statement still gave him pause. "How old are you, Gresham?"

"Sixty-nine, my lord." Gresham bowed at the admission, then straightened back up as tall and proper as ever he had stood. "And grateful for every day of it."

Lucas didn't think he could say exactly the same of his own thirty-three years. "Good. Good." He took a step toward the stairs but stopped. There would be no room ready for him. Barton, his valet, was still hours behind on the road with Lucas's carriage full of luggage. Lucas hadn't been patient enough to wait and travel in the loaded conveyance.

"Is Cook out, too?" he asked, his eyes following the staircase to the dark hall above.

"I'm afraid so. She left some cold ham and pickles, bread and cheese, for anyone who remained to have a pleasant repast. I could see to it you have tea and some refreshment, my lord. One of the kitchen maids remained."

An empty house did not feel at all welcoming. Lucas shook his head. "No. No, that is not necessary. You said the grounds staff is present? I assume that includes those at the stables?"

"Yes, my lord."

Lucas turned and held out his hands. "Then I must ask for my things back, Gresham. I think I will pay a visit to Gilbert. I'll return later this evening and eat whatever can be found."

"Very good, my lord." Gresham handed the hat and gloves back to Lucas, and the earl hurried out the front door and into the open air of spring.

He let out a tight breath and looked up to the sky, noting the only clouds to be soft, gentle wisps of white that meant the day could be depended upon to remain pleasant.

Lucas went down the steps two at a time and walked at a fast clip to the stables.

Cutter, the stable master, came forward quickly. "Welcome home, my lord."

It was his second welcome, but while the stables were much more full of life and sound than the manor, the hollow, empty feeling stayed with Lucas. "Thank you, Cutter. Could you have Zephyr saddled? I'm taking a ride to the Gilbert estate."

"A fine day for it, too, my lord. I'll see to it myself." Cutter bowed and disappeared further inside the stable while Lucas stepped outside of its doors.

He'd set the household on its ear, returning without warning. He knew Gresham was displeased, despite his matter-of-fact behavior. It really wasn't fair of him to arrive unannounced, but Lucas did have standing orders that the staff were to be permitted holidays when the family was not at home. It was lax of him, he supposed, but he'd never had a problem until today.

"Zephyr, my lord."

He thanked Cutter before mounting his favorite gelding, a chestnut beast tall enough to make Lucas comfortable. At just over six feet, it wasn't often that Lucas found either horses or furnishings sized to his comfort.

Zephyr had obviously been well exercised in Lucas's absence, as the animal did not become over-excited at the prospect of a ride. Lucas adjusted his hold on the reins, a little disappointed. A bruising ride would've done him good, but since he intended to visit Thomas Gilbert, he supposed it would be best to appear as presentable as possible. Especially if he hoped to be asked to tea.

Travelling always left him hungry.

Putting aside his other concerns and focusing on that alone, Lucas nearly succeeded in telling himself visiting a friend would improve his state of mind.

The butler at the Gilbert home did not act surprised to see the Earl of Annesbury on their doorstep without any warning, but Lucas supposed that was more a sign of good training than any actual lack of the emotion. As the highest-ranking gentleman in the county, Lucas's visits caused a stir in every house he entered.

Hopefully, the Gilbert servants would grow more used to him. He liked Thomas Gilbert and his wife and intended to further the acquaintance when he was in residence at Annesbury.

"The Earl of Annesbury," the butler announced at the door to the parlor.

Lucas fixed a pleasant smile on his face and stepped through the doorway, prepared to greet whichever members of the Gilbert family were about this afternoon.

But the only person inside the room, standing in its center, was a tall and stately woman he could not ever recollect seeing before. She wore a gray dress, trimmed in black lace, but the lack of color did nothing to detract from her beauty. Golden curls framed her lovely face, and her cheeks pinked as he stood gaping at her. Green eyes stared steadily back, and he realized she must be as lost as he, given the disappearance of the butler and no one to introduce them.

As the gentleman, and the interloper, Lucas decided it should fall to him to fix the situation.

"I do apologize, I did not know the family had guests." He dropped his most respectful bow, usually reserved for higher-ranking nobility, and offered his most contrite smile to the lovely woman before him. "If you like, I'll take myself off again until they've returned?"

Surprising people with his presence was obviously something he would have to avoid in future.

"Oh, no. That isn't necessary, sir. My lord. Lord Annesbury?" On his title her voice went up slightly and he couldn't decide if she was uncertain of the title or asking him a question.

"My friends call me Calvert," he said, trying to do what he could to help her relax. "When I was a boy, I said I never wanted to be Annesbury. Sounded too much like a girl's name."

The tiniest smile lifted her lips. "That would be a difficult title for a young man, I suppose."

"Very." He wanted to step closer, to take the woman's hand in his and bow over it properly, but he still didn't know her name or relation to anyone in the house.

She took a small step forward. "Do forgive me. With no one here to introduce us I will have to take that duty upon myself. I am Virginia Macon, Baroness of Heatherton."

The title, an obvious mark of her marital state, deflated him.

Which was ridiculous. It shouldn't matter to him what her marital state was.

"Ah. It is a pleasure to meet you, my lady."

"Please, do sit down. I imagine Mr. or Mrs. Gilbert will be in shortly." She gestured to a chair and after she sat he did the same, several feet away from her. "I have heard a great deal about you, my lord."

"Oh?" Really, what did one say when people began a conversation that way? Many years ago, he might have had a witty phrase at his disposal, but he'd discovered that letting other people fill in the gaps taught him more than trying to be clever.

"Yes, my cousin and her husband have told me of your investment in them." She raised her eyebrows and the smallest glimmer of amusement lit her eyes.

Lucas leaned forward, hands on his knees. "Ah, their stables. Yes. I have been very impressed with how expertly they've put their plans into action."

She gave a brief nod. "The stables, yes, but also your investment in their marriage. They believe they owe a great deal of their happiness to you."

He sat back, less interested in this topic of conversation. He supposed someone like her might think it a romantic gesture, but he had no wish to discuss his motives on that score.

"Nonsense. They are responsible for their own happiness. Where might they be at this time of day?"

"Where else?" she asked, folding her hands together in her lap. "They are at the stables."

He nodded and stood, causing her to rise as well. "Then I will search them out, since it is the stables I have come to talk to them about. But thank you for your hospitality."

The smile faded from her lovely face, making it less warm and more polite. "Of course. It was an honor to meet you, my lord."

"My pleasure." He bowed, then swiftly made his escape.

Admiring an attractive woman, while a fine enough pastime for some, was not something he wished to do for himself. Especially if she was married.

Lucas shook his head as he went down the hall, ignoring the startled expression of a passing maid, and out a side door to the stables.

It is not because she is married, he told himself. *Not just because she's married*, he amended. *I have no need to look at an attractive woman of any sort.*

When was the last time he had even applied that adjective to a member of the opposite sex? He could not recall. His scattered thoughts only disconcerted him and he picked up his pace in an attempt to leave them behind.

Chapter Two

"Calvert." Thomas Gilbert's voice rang across the paddock nearest the stables, greeting Lucas as he approached. Lucas made his way to the fenced area and noted horses being exercised inside its confines.

The stable yard was full of activity. The stable itself was at a distance from the house, with a stretch of grass between the two. The stables were in a fine, imposing structure, a paddock attached at the side furthest from the house, and beyond that were more fenced in areas for the horses to exercise.

Gilbert slipped through the railings of the paddock and came forward at a jog, raising his hand to clasp Lucas's. "I didn't know you were in the neighborhood," the gentleman said, a broad smile in place. "I would've invited you for dinner."

"I just arrived, so please don't dismiss all thought of such an invitation," Lucas said, returning the warm handshake. "How goes it, Gilbert?"

"Very well. We have mares in foal, stallions on loan, and new investments." Gilbert put a hand on Lucas's arm and gestured with the other to the paddock. "And we're now giving riding lessons to young gentlemen," he said, tone not at all serious.

"Are you?" Lucas asked, puzzled as he turned to look more carefully at the people mounted behind the fence. He saw Mrs. Christine Gilbert sitting atop a handsome gelding with a small boy in the saddle before her. On a Dartmoor, a creature only slightly bigger than a pony, another boy rode in a slow circle around the pen.

"Your home must be positively overrun with guests," Lucas said, crossing his arms and studying the children with interest. They both had dark hair.

Gilbert chuckled and moved to rest his forearms against the rail. "Not at all. It's just the three, and I don't think any of us want them to leave. Christine dotes on those boys."

"Ah." Lucas's mind went back to the woman in the parlor. "Are they any relation to the baroness?"

"The baroness?" Gilbert met his eyes and then straightened. "You've heard of her?"

"Met her, in fact. A moment ago." Lucas shook his head and chuckled. "It was quite the predicament, with no one to make introductions." He raised his eyebrows and affected a shocked expression.

"We can rectify that shortly," the other man promised him. "The boys are nearly done with their riding lesson."

Mrs. Gilbert approached them, a bright welcome on her face. The boy sitting before her on the horse looked as if he was having the time of his life. It made Lucas smile. He well remembered his father putting him on a horse for the first time. The lad was still small enough that a pony might be too much for him.

"Lord Calvert," Mrs. Gilbert said, her voice full of cheer and energy as always. "Please, allow me to introduce my little cousins to you, Master Edward Macon. Edward, this is Lord Calvert, Earl of Annesbury."

The little boy nodded, his face contorting into what he must think to be a polite expression, his eyebrows pulling down low and his mouth pursing into a serious frown. Lucas nearly laughed aloud but instead offered a short bow. "A pleasure, Master Edward. Are you enjoying your riding lesson?"

The boy nodded, his face still serious. "It's a lot of fun. Cousin Christine says I'm nearly ready for a pony."

"I am not surprised," Lucas said, just as serious. "I cannot imagine a finer instructor than your cousin."

The other boy came forward, his face screwed up in concentration, his little horse moving sedately.

"And this is Lord Phillip Macon, Baron of Heatherton," Christine said, a touch more solemnity in her voice.

The boy glanced up, still frowning, and nodded once. "Hello."

Lucas's mind whirled. The boy was the baron? Then the woman inside, his mother—? His mind attempted to catch up while he bowed to the child. She had been wearing mourning colors. Was she a widow?

"If you will give us a few minutes, my lord, we are nearly finished and then we may all go inside for tea and biscuits."

"I'd ruther have milk," little Edward protested with a child's hasty pronunciation. "Please."

Christine shot a grin over his head at Lucas and her husband. "I think we can accommodate that, Edward. But let us finish one more turn about the paddock so we can tell your mother how well you did today." Lucas saw her wink at her husband before beginning the round once more, Phillip following on his horse.

"They've never been on horses before," Gilbert explained, offering Lucas an apologetic smile.

"They've not been here long, surely?"

"Three months, actually. But riding was not deemed an appropriate activity until recently." Gilbert sighed and shook his head. "It was no small thing, the two of them waiting patiently for this day."

Lucas took in the somber coloring of the boys' clothes. They were both in gray suits and wore black armbands. "They are in mourning? And they've been here three months?"

"It's a long story," Gilbert said, his voice softer and less likely to carry. "They lost their father three months ago. Virginia, Lady Heatherton, came here to be with family during this difficult time."

That gave Lucas still greater incentive to banish all thought of the attractive woman from his mind. A woman recently bereaved should not be thought about. At all. Except when offering condolences. She had nine months of mourning ahead of her, after all, and would necessarily live a half-life during that time period. Spending part of it with family doubtless helped.

"It's kind of you to open your home to them," Lucas said at last.

Gilbert nodded, but a troubled look remained in his eyes. "Truthfully, I would let them stay forever, but I fear Lady Heatherton will take her leave of us soon."

"Why is that a concern?" Lucas asked, his curiosity getting the better of him.

"It really isn't my place to say more," Gilbert said, glancing at Lucas from the corner of his eye. "The last time I confided a matter in you, I wound up engaged to be married."

Lucas couldn't help the bark of laughter that escaped him, though he quickly muffled the sound and looked to ensure he hadn't startled the horses. The smaller animal flicked its ears at him but remained walking at its plodding pace.

"I cannot see that it ended badly for you," Lucas said. "But is this issue as serious as the other?"

Gilbert clapped him on the shoulder before slipping through the rails again. "Perhaps worse." Then he went to the horses where he helped first Edward, then his wife, slide from the saddle. Phillip bravely tried to dismount on his own, and only stumbled a little after sliding to the ground. Lucas watched as the party made their way back to the fence, while a groom appeared in order to take the horses in hand.

"Tomorrow, we will brush them down ourselves," Mrs. Gilbert was saying as they grew nearer. "It's important you know how to care for a horse if you're going to ride one." She flashed another wide grin at Lucas as she walked past him, an arm around each boy.

"Your wife is positively smitten with those two," Lucas said when Thomas rejoined him. They followed the woman and boys, a few paces back.

"Christine will love anyone who loves horses." Gilbert shook his head and gestured to the two dark-haired boys. "It helps that she feels protective of them, too."

The prick of intrigue returned. What need did Christine Gilbert have to be protective of the children, given their mother's presence in the home? Though it wasn't of any consequence to him, he nearly asked about the situation again.

Ahead of them, the boys took off running while Mrs. Gilbert called after them, "Please remember to wash!" She shook her head and turned to cast her husband a crooked smile. "They couldn't wait for their biscuits. I suggested they go ahead and leave the old people behind."

"Old people?" her husband protested, as though affronted. "I am not old."

"If you are, then I must be ancient," Lucas returned. He was older than Thomas by seven years. "I suppose, in the eyes of a child, anyone old enough to be their parents would be wizened creatures."

Christine Gilbert, on her husband's arm, abruptly turned her head to fix him with a severe look. He stopped walking, meeting her eyes with some confusion.

"I was not implying that you are at all old, madam," he said, wondering if he had given offense in his jesting. Lucas couldn't think so, given the woman's playful nature.

"I realize that." She looked up at her husband then back to Lucas. "But you are certainly old enough to be a parent."

The comment didn't hurt as it would have only a few years before, though it struck him as odd. "Indeed. That happy blessing has yet to come my way." Lucas tried to speak with lightness, her continued stare made him uncomfortable. He could practically see the woman's thoughts whirling about behind her eyes.

"Christine," Thomas said, drawing her name out slowly, as if in warning. "You shouldn't meddle in your cousin's affairs."

Lucas looked between them, not understanding the relationship between Christine's intense stare and the baroness. He did recognize Gilbert's exasperated expression, having seen it before in their business dealings. But the man's ire was no match for whatever wild thoughts his wife now had.

"Thomas," she said, without looking at him. "Virginia needs whatever help we can give her, and since our influence is limited we ought to apply to friends who may be able to do more for her."

"Please," her husband said, a note of real pleading in his voice. "It isn't our story to share."

Christine sighed and finally turned to her husband, her expression changing from determination to soft persuasion. "Tom," she said, her voice gentle. "Lord Calvert could help. He knows people, he has influence, and after that letter Virginia received...." She let the phrase fade away into the quiet of the morning.

Lucas took a single step away from them, raising his hands in a placating gesture. "I have no wish to intrude, Gilbert. If you two need to discuss something, I can go ahead and wait for you in your study." Though he had not been married long before becoming a widower,

Lucas could easily recognize a battle of wills between husband and wife, as well as the obvious affection they held for each other. A private moment might be all they needed to come to an accord. And though he was curious, he could live without knowing what troubled the beautiful guest in their home.

"No." Thomas shook his head and reached up to rub the bridge of his nose. "She's right. I trust you will be discreet with whatever information we give you, Calvert?"

"Of course. If I can assist your family in any way, it would be my pleasure." Lucas half-bowed to seal the promise, looking between them with mounting interest. "But what could my influence, as you called it, do for your cousin?"

Christine Gilbert kept her husband's arm but came forward to loop the other through Lucas's. Together, they continued the walk to the house, though much more slowly than before.

"Virginia lost her husband three months ago. She sought safety by living here, at the suggestion of a barrister in Bath. You see, in his will, her late husband left the guardianship of his sons in her hands."

Lucas nodded. "That makes perfect sense. But she is worried for her safety?"

"For theirs," Thomas Gilbert answered. "The boys. The late baron has a younger brother, Mr. Macon. He's appealed to the Court of Chancery to remove the children from their mother's care."

Lucas's eyebrows shot up, as well as his indignation. "On what grounds?" he asked, his voice flat. Though why he immediately believed the baroness a perfect model of motherhood he couldn't say. He didn't even know the woman.

"On the grounds that a woman is incapable of raising a baron or seeing to the proper education and rearing of her noble sons," Christine said, each word dripping with disdain as she spoke. "But it is only an excuse. Virginia is perfectly capable. She believes her brother-in-law wants control of the estate and can achieve it through control of the boys."

"Sounds nefarious," Lucas murmured. "Though I could certainly believe it. Rank and wealth is everything to some." He looked away from Christine Gilbert's concerned eyes and to the house, realizing they were nearly there. "What does being here accomplish for the baroness?"

"Her brother-in-law doesn't know where she is, for one thing," Gilbert said.

"Is he dangerous?" Lucas asked. "Does she need protection?" No woman of genteel birth ought to have to hide away in fear.

"Virginia's barrister friend thinks there is danger in him knowing her location," Gilbert explained with a lift of his shoulders. "He also believes keeping her far away from Bath, and the county's courts, will delay a decision against her while he tries other avenues of argument. But the court is leaning on Macon's side."

"Which is why I think you might be able to help," Christine put in at last, stopping them before they entered the conservatory's door to the house. "The barrister believes if she had the protection of a peer the courts would be less likely to act against her. She needs someone of influence as an ally."

"Of course. Would she accept my help?" he asked. "Is there no one else to whom she can turn?" He released her arm and folded his, looking between the couple. Lucas liked them both immensely; he counted them as his friends, though they might be surprised his regard was that personal.

Thomas Gilbert moved to put his arm around his wife's shoulders, looking like a man ready to do battle, so grim was his expression. The woman met his eyes briefly and then folded her hands before her in the demurest posture Lucas had ever seen her take on.

"My lord, it is not that easy. She's been told she needs the personal protection of a male relative. Her brother has no interest in coming to her aid and she has no other close connections. The only other suggestion her barrister has shared is that she might find the protection she needs with a husband."

Lucas stared at her, uncomprehending for a moment. His mind sorted through all the information given and came to its conclusion on the matter. Then, his honor rising to meet the challenge presented, he said, "I need to marry her."

His heart sped up at the thought, though from fear or excitement he couldn't say. Abigail had been gone for years, but he'd only begun thinking on the possibility of remarriage in the months since his younger brother found a wife. Accustomed to saving people, the idea of offering the protection of his name did not immediately repel him. If anything, the idea intrigued him. Could he do it? Could he marry a stranger, albeit a very beautiful stranger, to save her and her children from the cruelty of another? It would bear some thought, but why not?

The reactions of the two people before him did not match the emotion of his declaration, as they both went pale. Gilbert's jaw dropped open as though its hinges had fallen off. Mrs. Gilbert's eyes grew large and she covered her mouth with a hand.

"Oh no," she said through her fingers, stepping forward and making an odd, flapping motion with her hands. "No, that isn't what I meant at all. I only thought, with you being the right age, and knowing people, you might know someone who would be willing. I didn't mean to imply that you—"

"Please, Calvert," Thomas said, reaching out to take one of his wife's hands. "That isn't what we want. We would never expect it of you. If you knew someone who could be persuaded, or even a court where the opinion might be different—"

Lucas stepped back and regarded them with a critical eye. "Neither of you thought to suggest I should marry the lady?"

"No—"

"Not really—"

He raised one eyebrow at that and smirked at the blushing woman. "Not really?"

"It occurred to me briefly, but I didn't think to suggest it," she admitted, then bit her lower lip and looked up at her frowning husband. "I think you were right, Tom. I shouldn't have said anything on the matter." She turned penitent eyes on Lucas. "Can we please forget all of it?"

Thomas groaned and raised a hand to pinch the bridge of his nose again. "Yes. Please, Calvert. Forget the whole mess." He took Christine's arm. "And join us for tea."

Lucas tried not to smile, but his amusement over the situation could hardly be helped. It was not all together a rare thing, to be approached by others who wished to use his influence in one matter or another, but this was most definitely the most absurd and ill-conceived attempt to win his support on a matter.

"Tea would be appreciated. Thank you."

They led the way inside, Christine still blushing and Thomas's expression pinched enough that Lucas felt sure the man had a sudden headache. Though tempted to laugh, he shook his head and followed, his mind already at work on the baroness's plight.

Chapter Three

Virginia and the elder Mrs. Gilbert, Thomas's mother, were putting the finishing touches on the tea table in front of the sofa when the door to the parlor opened. Christine and Thomas entered, arm in arm, with the strangest expressions on their faces. Virginia stood slowly, a question rising on her lips to ask what ailed them, when the earl walked in behind them.

She stilled, watching him with interest. His expression looked less ill and more amused than her cousins'. Looking from the couple to the earl, she could not imagine what would set all three of them in such strange humors, but decided it would be best to ignore it.

Mrs. Gilbert curtsied. "Oh, Lord Calvert, it is wonderful to see you again. I only just learned you had returned from London."

He bowed to her, lower than necessary, his respectful behavior setting Virginia more at ease. "Mrs. Gilbert, it is good to see you again. I hope you do not mind my intrusion."

"Not at all. You are always welcome in this home." She gestured to the chair he had used a half an hour before, when he'd sat awkwardly with Virginia for less than five minutes.

"Thank you." After the ladies sat, the gentlemen followed suit. Mrs. Gilbert poured out for each of them. "How is your garden this spring, Mrs. Gilbert?" he asked after receiving his cup.

Virginia watched as the matron's expression went from politely pleasant to pure joy. Those who knew her well knew that Mrs. Gilbert adored her flower beds and orangery more than anything. Virginia thought only Christine's love of horses came close to Mrs. Gilbert's dedication to her beautiful blooms and soil beds, yet it had taken her nearly a month of being in the home to discover how deep the attachment went.

"It is positively the envy of the neighborhood," the woman answered proudly. "My roses are already bursting out everywhere, like fireworks. Now that I know you are home, I will send some to you."

"The big yellow blossoms, if they are ready," he said. "My mother always had them in our entry and it wouldn't be right to go without them."

The older woman's cheeks pinked and she nodded her agreement. "Yes, Pamela did always like those. I made a present of a cutting for her once, but she claimed hers never blossomed as mine did. I cannot think why."

"Because she did not pour half so much care into them," the earl answered. "My mother's great love is being a hostess, not a horticulturist."

"And she excels at that," Mrs. Gilbert answered. "Her parties are talked of, before and after, as the highlight of everyone's year. How is Lady Pamela?"

Virginia listened politely as she drank her tea, noting her cousin and Thomas had collected themselves and both were intent on their teacups and sandwiches. She turned her attention back to the earl, who was speaking of his family in warm tones.

She really had not expected him to be so young. The way Thomas and Christine spoke of him, with such gratitude and admiration, she had pictured someone older, with gray in his hair. But Lord Calvert, Earl of Annesbury, didn't have any silver to be seen. His hair was more like burnished gold, cut close in the Roman style. He held himself well and she imagined he would fit with the Corinthian set if he were just a few years younger. The first thing that struck her, when he entered the parlor earlier, was his height. She thought he must be of a height with her late husband, though with wider shoulders.

There was no other comparison to make between the two. Where her Charles had been dark, Lord Calvert was fair. His eyes were blue-gray, and his bearing full of confidence. He was a man who knew his worth to society and wore his consequence with ease. Did anything ever unsettle him? She couldn't think so.

He caught her looking and she resisted the desire to look away. Instead, Virginia smiled and tried to remember what they had been talking about. But he spoke first.

"Lady Heatherton, I had the good fortune to meet your sons. They look to be very bright lads. What are their ages?"

"Phillip is six," she answered, surprised he would bother to ask. "And Edward is halfway to five. They are wonderfully bright, I think, though I have a bias as their mother."

"Nonsense," Thomas said from the sofa where he and Christine sat, holding hands. "I cannot think I was half so clever. Phillip has a good head on his shoulders. He was telling me about the life cycle of the frogs in my fishing pond."

Virginia's heart swelled and she smiled at him. "Thank you for taking him fishing yesterday. He talked of nothing else last night or this morning, until the horses were brought up."

"Fishing cannot hold a candle to riding," Christine interjected with a lofty air and everyone in the room laughed.

Virginia attempted to keep her attention in the present moment, but her mind continually turned to the letter from Mr. Olivier. She lost the thread of the conversation, staring out the window without seeing the lush gardens humming full of bees.

"—wouldn't you say, Lady Heatherton?" Christine's voice asked.

"I beg your pardon?" Virginia turned to find all in the room with eyes upon her, including Lord Calvert's. "I am terribly sorry. I'm very dull company today. My thoughts are elsewhere."

Mrs. Gilbert reached out and put her hand on Virginia's arm, giving her a sympathetic pat. "You are perfect company, my dear. Christine appealed to your taste for riding upon horses or in boats."

Grateful for the understanding, Virginia allowed herself to smile and answer the question. "I am afraid I much prefer a rowboat on a pond to a side-saddle."

"But would you do the rowing?" the earl asked.

Virginia turned to Lord Calvert, her brows drawing together. What sort of a question was that to put to a lady? She started to answer in the negative, but then considered again her situation. She had no gentleman to row her upon a pond, as her husband had done in the summers before his illness overtook him. Soon enough, she would have only herself to rely on. She could not depend upon the hospitality of the Gilbert family forever.

"I would." She met his blue-gray gaze steadily. "I have always loved being on the water. If the only way to achieve that is to take up an oar, I will certainly do so."

The earl regarded her with a contemplative expression. "Should you and your sons wish it, my property is nearby and we have a substantial lake for rowing, fishing, and the study of frogs."

Was he teasing her, or extending a true invitation? Whatever the case, Virginia responded appropriately.

"Thank you, my lord. That is kind of you."

The door to the parlor opened with a crash and little Edward came flying across the room. "I didn't do it, Mama! I didn't." He launched himself from the carpet into her arms and not a moment later Phillip came storming into the room as well.

"Mother, Edward broke my horse." Phillip brandished a three-legged wooden horse, gifted to him from Christine. He had hardly let the toy out of his sight since receiving it.

"Oh, darling." Virginia, her arms around Edward, looked from her elder son to the other adults in the room. "Please, forgive us for the disruption."

"Nonsense," Mrs. Gilbert said, her warm brown eyes softening in a distinctly maternal way. "Tend to your children, my dear."

Virginia nodded and stood, keeping one arm about Edward's back and gesturing for Phillip to precede her from the room. This event showed every indication the boys would either dissolve into tears or an endless round of argument, and she had no wish to share that display with the other adults. She briefly met Christine's eyes as she walked out, the other woman gave her a commiserating smile. Virginia's gaze passed over the earl, whom she realized was watching the scene with at least mild interest.

Phillip contained his ire long enough for them to reach the hall. He rounded on Edward the moment the door to the parlor was closed. "I told him not to play with it," he half-shouted, half-sobbed. "He wasn't supposed to touch it, but he kept sneaking it away."

Edward buried his face in Virginia's skirts at her hip, shaking his head in denial. "I didn't, Mama! I was only looking—"

"Looking doesn't break things—"

"I hardly touched it—"

Had they been smaller, Virginia would've whisked them both into her arms and to another room. As it was, she was trapped in the hall with them until the matter was sorted out.

"Boys, enough." Her voice was firm but her tone low. "Phillip, hand me your horse." She reached out and Phillip put the wooden figure in her hand. The finely crafted toy was missing a foreleg, but the wood was cleanly broke, not splintered. "Have you the leg?"

"I cannot find it," Phillip said, his anger giving way to a more mournful tone. "I looked and looked. The horse was on the floor, by our bureau."

Virginia crouched down, her hand on Edward's shoulder. "Edward, do you know where the leg is?"

The four-year old's lip stuck out and his eyes swam with tears. He met Virginia's eyes and she saw the hesitation in them, sensed his temptation.

"Darling, tell me the truth. Do you know where the leg for the horse has gone?"

His brown eyes darted briefly toward his brother, then came back to hers. He reached into the pocket of his trousers and pulled out a piece of wood.

"I didn't mean for it to happen. It was an accident." He held the tiny foreleg, painted white, out to his mother.

"See," Phillip yelled, and Virginia looked to see his hands balled into fists at his side. "I knew he did it. He broke it and now it's ruined." Angry tears leaked from his eyes.

"Edward, what happened? How did it break?" A heavy weight settled deeper in her chest. At moments like these, she missed Charles. While the argument between children was not dire, it helped to have another parent to balance out the mood, to assist in settling disputes and restoring good humor.

"I was looking at it." Edward trembled and stared at the rug. "Then Nurse Smythe called. I had to get a clean han'kerchief from the drawer. When I closed the drawer, Phil's horse fell. I didn't mean for it to happen." His gasped on the last word and raised his hands to cover his face.

Virginia's heart squeezed tight. "The horse must've been near the edge of the bureau." She looked at Phillip, standing like an avenging angel ready to mete out justice. "Phillip, I think the horse's balance must've been upset when Edward closed the drawer. It sounds like an accident."

"He wasn't careful and it broke," Phillip said, his eyes flashing. "It's broke and it cannot be mended."

"But darling, he—" Virginia was interrupted by a voice from behind.

"Perhaps it can be mended."

She rose and turned, her cheeks turning warm. Had they been loud enough for the others in the parlor to hear every word of the childhood tragedy unfolding? Standing outside the closed door was the Earl of Annesbury. He took two long strides and bent his tall frame in a polite bow.

"May I, Lady Heatherton?" He reached out to her.

Virginia looked from his hand to Phillip, whose anger had faded to a dull upset, and then to Edward, who looked curious.

"I would not wish to trouble you." She held the horse out with one hand and the foreleg with the other. He took the horse and his fingers grazed her palm when he took the broken appendage.

"No trouble." He gave her the barest of smiles, though an amused light twinkled in his eyes. "I have a younger brother and the two of us were forever repairing our damaged toys." He turned the leg over in his hand, then the toy horse, and shook his head. "Ah, I see the problem. Phillip, let me compliment you on the fine horse and assure you that it can be mended."

Phillip took a step forward, his eyebrows lifting. "It can? How?"

"We will need a very special pot of glue I keep at my house. As you can see, the break of the horse's leg is a clean one." He bent and held the broken toy for both boys to see, Edward creeping closer.

"You can fix it?" Edward asked, his voice a near whisper. "Really?"

Virginia's heart lifted and she looked from one hopeful boy to the other.

"I can provide the glue," the earl answered. "But as you can see, this toy is small. My hands are too large to do the necessarily delicate work. I think, if you are willing to help, the two of you can have it mended in no time. What do you think, Lady Heatherton?"

Frankly, she thought him a positive genius for suggesting such a thing. "That is a very sound plan. If you are willing to provide the glue. What do you say, Phillip? Edward?"

"Yes, please."

"We can mend it."

"Excellent." The earl stood and held the horse and leg out to Phillip. "I can bring the glue back with me tomorrow morning. You need to keep the horse safe until then."

Phillip nodded and turned to his brother. "Come on, Ed. Let's find a safe place to keep it in the nursery."

Virginia watched Edward's expression change to one of absolute joy. His brother had forgiven him, and since she knew Edward's world revolved around Phillip at times, a sense of relief filled her.

"Take your leave politely," she reminded them when it seemed both boys would dash off.

They bowed, said their "good afternoons," and then turned and ran for the stairs.

She nearly called after them to correct their speed, but she caught the earl staring at her and closed her mouth over the admonition.

"Thank you, my lord," she said instead. "You've made them friends again."

He lifted one shoulder in a shrug and folded his arms across his chest. "As I said, I have a younger brother. Marcus and I were nearly always in argument over something, but my father made us work together to solve our problems. He offered up the same solution, the same glue, when I hurt my brother's favorite toy boat. We're both lucky I remembered the occasion."

"Yes, we are." Virginia remained grateful, but had to ask, "What brought you into the hall, my lord?"

He looked from her to the parlor door and back again. "I thought to offer my assistance is all. I understood the situation before you left the room." He cleared his throat and adjusted the cuffs of his coat. "Would you care to rejoin the others, my lady?" He offered his arm.

Virginia considered his escort, hesitating. But why? It was a considerate gesture. Normally even small altercations between the children drained her of late. Each argument, each childish hurt, chipped away at her self-possession. But today, with this man's assistance, she did not feel the need to collect herself before facing the others.

"Yes, thank you." She took his arm. He led her back into the parlor, releasing her after a few steps inside, and she retook her seat.

"Is everything all right, Virginia?" Christine asked, her eyes darting from the earl to her cousin. Her smile, Virginia thought, was uncertain.

Hastening to reassure them, Virginia began relating the story of the broken horse and the earl's gallant offer of glue. Mrs. Gilbert praised his quick thinking.

"It was nothing, ma'am," he insisted, taking up his cup. "I am happy to be of service in any way I can."

If only all our problems could be solved as easily as applying a little glue. Though Virginia did not voice the thought, when she met Christine's sympathetic gaze, she knew her cousin was thinking something similar.

Chapter Four

L ucas arrived home after dark, having taken his evening meal with the Gilbert family. He had been grateful for their lack of formality, the warm welcome of Thomas Gilbert's parents, and the easy conversation to be found at their table. In London, much of his time was divided between the heavy talk of politics or the inane babble of society. Here, in their quiet corner of England, they spoke of apple harvests and spring foals, gardening, the needs of their village. It was also more comfortable to be among people who were not trying to persuade him to their way of thinking on political matters.

He admitted, though only to himself, that he'd enjoyed observing Lady Virginia Macon, Baroness of Heatherton. The woman's troubles revealed to him, she became an object of interest. In mourning, and experiencing great personal hardship, she still carried herself with all the grace and gentility of a duchess.

In the candlelit dining room, made intimate by the smaller table employed by the Gilberts for family meals, he'd studied her carefully from the corner of his eye. Had he not known of her circumstances, it would've been difficult to guess that her mind was not fully engaged in the present. But he saw her gaze turn inward a time or two, watched her smile falter into an uncertain frown. He had seen the weariness in the slight drop of her shoulders before she would remember herself, her posture straightening again.

Did her family at the table see it, too? They must, knowing her situation. But no one spoke of it with him present.

The boys had appeared before the adults had their supper, the two of them showing no evidence of their prior argument. Edward did venture, albeit shyly, to ask when he might expect Lord Calvert to visit the next day.

"First thing after breakfast," Lucas had promised. It would be an easy thing to send the glue over with a servant, if the Gilberts didn't have their own, but Lucas meant to be there for the repair of the toy.

Might there be a way he could assist in repairing the family as well?

In the years since his wife's passing, Lucas had attempted to fill the hole she left in his heart with other things. He discovered, after trial and error, the best way to mute his grief was in helping others. Though he would not discuss it, knowing it would sound trite to people who did not understand, Lucas knew the truth of the matter. When he put aside his personal hurts and instead alleviated the pain of others, his peace returned.

Thomas and Christine Gilbert's marriage was the latest of his victories. Through his quick-thinking and maneuvering of Christine's father, Mr. Devon, he had made it possible for the young couple to wed.

Congratulating himself on their account, he'd next turned his attention to his younger brother. Marcus had married in order to obtain his inheritance, not realizing the woman he chose loved him deeply.

Marcus had asked him, months ago, if Lucas would ever remarry.

Lying in his bed, alone in the house apart from the servants, Lucas considered the question anew. His younger brother had no wish to be his heir. Marcus was happy to remain a country gentleman and avoid the snares of society and rank, as was his wife.

Sleep eluding him, Lucas rose and pulled on his robe. He lit a candle and left his room, going to the family gallery on the floor above.

He walked with purpose, his thoughts spinning through the memories of the day. Again and again, the image of Lady Heatherton kneeling before her crying son came to his mind. Her blonde hair, piled atop her head in a curling crown, gave her a regal air. Green eyes, a shade reminding him of fields in the summer, had looked by turns uncertain and determined. She was tall, for a woman, but still shorter than himself. The gray of her gown, her fair skin, gave her a rather somber look.

Lucas stopped in the gallery, standing before his wedding portrait. Raising his candle higher, he met the hopeful, happy eyes of the young groom the artist had captured. The man in the painting had the whole of England at his feet and a bright future before him. He did not know that the woman at his side would not be long in the world with him.

Abigail's beauty could not, Lucas told himself, ever be captured by earthly mediums. When he looked upon her portrait, studying the lines of her figure, he knew there were details his memory must make up for where the artist's skill had lacked. The laughter in her blue eyes was hinted at, but impossible to truly see. Her light brown hair, strewn with pearls, brushed her shoulders in elegant twists.

The years since her passing had dulled the ache in his heart. Lucas accepted her death, but he missed her companionship still.

I loved her with everything I was, he thought. *What would she think of me remarrying?*

She would not wish him to be alone forever. He knew that. Had he been the one to go, he would hope for her to find happiness again.

"I don't think I can love again," he said aloud, staring up at her oil-painted eyes. "But Lady Heatherton might understand. She lost her husband recently, you know." He was not really speaking to Abigail so much as thinking out loud. But it helped. When the one person in the world you could confide everything to vanished, it was hard to go back to keeping your own counsel.

He put the candle down on a table, allowing the shadows to conceal most of the painting. Lucas sat down beneath it, on the ground itself. He rested his forearms across his knees, allowing his hands to hang limply.

"She's in trouble," he said to the darkness. "And her sons. They are too young to suffer more loss." He'd been a grown man when his father died, leaving him the title and responsibilities of an earl, and his pain had been acute. How did children cope with such a loss?

"I could help them."

As he'd helped many people over the years. He'd whispered in the right ears sometimes or boldly extended his protection at others. It had become his habit to save people, to see them happy, to spare them pain.

Why should this case be any different? Assisting the baroness would be practical as well. Someday, he would need an heir. He could give her time to mourn, treat her with all the respect and deference a woman in her position deserved, and someday have a son of his blood to inherit the title.

The baroness's sons would benefit from a stepfather like him, too. He could see them well trained for their futures, ensuring Edward received an education and entered a profession wherein he would thrive.

If she must marry to keep her sons, why not marry me?

Lucas constructed the plan in his mind, tipping his head back against the wall. The more he thought it through, the more at peace he felt in his decision. He closed his eyes and relaxed, preparing the proposal he would put to Lady Heatherton.

Virginia, he reminded himself. *Her Christian name is Virginia.*

¤

"My lord? Your lordship?"

The summons drifted through the fog of sleep, startling Lucas awake. He opened his eyes to a blur of shadow and light. He reached up to rub his eyes, disoriented. He tilted his head up and a terrible crack sounded from his neck. He bit back a curse and forced his eyes open again.

Gresham stood over him while Randal looked over the elderly man's shoulder. "My lord," the butler said, stooping. "Are you well, sir?"

"Perfectly well." Lucas glanced about him, realizing he sat on the floor in the gallery. The night's restlessness came back to him and he groaned. "Fell asleep in the wrong place is all."

Randal and Gresham exchanged a look before Randal reached down. With his help, Lucas came to his feet and then leaned heavily on the table where his candle had burnt itself out. He chanced a look over his shoulder at his wedding portrait. He sighed and gathered his robe more tightly around him.

Sunlight blazed through the windows across the gallery, giving all his ancestors on the wall a most excellent view of his disarray. He wondered what they would make of him.

"What time is it?" he asked, raising his hand to cover a yawn.

"Half past nine, my lord," Randal answered, fidgeting with the end of his coat. Lucas recognized the agitated movement. Randal thought something was wrong with him and wouldn't be satisfied until he'd fixed it.

"We came looking when you did not come for breakfast, my lord." Gresham fixed him with a sterner expression than most servants would dare. Perhaps he was less patient in his old age.

"Breakfast. Yes." Lucas's memories of the night before, of going to the gallery, finally coalesced. He did curse aloud then. "I've no time for that. I'm going to be late to an appointment at the Gilbert home." He strode down the hall, his robe flapping behind him, and didn't look back until he'd gained the doorway. "Randal, are you coming or shall I shave myself?"

Randal, who remained standing where he had been, started and then came running down the hall to catch up. "Coming, my lord."

Lucas tried not to laugh at the man's startled expression and hurried to his room. If they could get the business of shaving and dressing over with quickly, he might make it to the Gilberts' a quarter after ten. That would still be later than he wished, but he could hardly help it at that point.

A man didn't present glue and a marriage proposal without being properly shaved and attired, after all.

Randal rushed through his usual ministrations. Lucas never had a reason to find fault with his valet. When he was shaved in record time, he gave the man a tip for his trouble. The glue was sent for from the work shed, then he went to obtain a horse and be on his way.

Lucas rehearsed his decision and its reasoning to himself again.

Lady Virginia Macon needed a husband to save her children from an overzealous uncle. The boys needed a man in their lives to bring them up properly prepared for their futures. He needed, eventually, an heir to his title and estate to spare his younger brother the responsibility. Marrying the baroness would sufficiently fulfill all those needs, and others besides. There would be a Countess of Annesbury again, seeing to his houses and tenants. He knew his estates lacked a woman's touch. And perhaps, God willing, she would be a good companion for him.

The echoes of an empty Annesbury Hall would not need to be borne again.

Chapter Five

Virginia watched her sons in the garden, amused by their whole-hearted concentration on their current game. They had built up an animal infirmary and gathered several toys to be ill and others to nurse the afflicted. The wooden horse started the patient roster, as it was laid on a sun-warmed brick with a handkerchief to cover its battered body. A soldier was added as doctor, but then more toys filled sick beds. A wooden lion, a clay dog, a paper bird, were all abed with scraps of cloth to keep them from catching a chill. Tin soldiers were the primary nursemaids, but Edward had found a doll in the nursery and set her as head nurse.

Having breakfasted some time before, the boys had thought the earl would show up immediately after they finished their toast.

"But Lord Calvert cannot come until he has finished his own toast, and we know not when that will be," she had explained. They decided to wait in front of the house, in a small garden.

Virginia accompanied them with a book, though she found it difficult to concentrate on its pages. Her mind remained consumed with the problem at hand. Phillip's voice, raised fearfully, interrupted her thoughts.

"—not consumption. None of them can have that."

"But it's a real sickness," Edward, innocent and trying to be clever, argued. "We can have a doctor come and—"

"The doctor didn't save Papa." Phillip's young voice, heavy and somber, cut off his brother's words. Then Phillip turned away from their make-believe hospital, folding his arms. "This is a silly game anyway. I don't want to play anymore."

What could she say? As his mother, what could she possibly do to comfort his heart? He missed his father terribly. Phillip's words touched a tender spot in Edward's heart, she could see, as her younger son's face began to screw up, as though he might cry or shout.

"Now then, what have we here?" she asked, keeping her tone bright as she left her bench and came to kneel in the grass. "What a very fine place for creatures in need. Tell me, Edward, what ails the lion? Has he a toothache?"

Edward's expression changed back to one of easy happiness. "No, Mama. He's like the lion in the story with the mouse. He has a thorn in his paw."

"But where is a mouse to help him?" she asked.

Phillip, slumped over and glaring at the grass, said nothing. Edward began to spin a tale of the missing mouse and talked of an expedition being mounted to find him.

"He must remain in hospital until a mouse can be found to do the job," he said at the finish, nodding emphatically. "But it's all right. Someone will come save him." His complete faith in a miraculous rescue, however imaginary, made Virginia smile.

She had given up on expecting someone to save her from her troubles. That very morning, she'd woken with the conviction that she must act. Her heart was torn between two possibilities. She must find someone to marry, preferably a man with enough of his own wealth to leave her sons' inheritance alone. Or she could flee to the Americas, where the British courts could not touch her. But that scheme was fraught with its own danger and more unknowns than she cared to think upon.

Either decision required a great deal of study and fortitude on her part.

The sound of hoof beats on gravel brought the boys' attention to the road. Virginia turned to see the arrival of the Earl of Annesbury atop a large chestnut horse. He waved when Phillip leaped to his feet.

"He came, he came," Phillip shouted happily.

"Hooray!" Edward jumped up and down, throwing his little fist in the air.

The earl dismounted and gave the animal a pat. A groom appeared from the side of the house, where he must've been stationed to wait upon the earl's horse.

"That is a hero's welcome, if ever I heard one," Lord Calvert said, his words laced with good humor. He thanked the groom for taking his horse and came to the boys, a drawstring bag in his hand. "And what is all this?"

"We made an animal hospital," Edward answered.

Phillip went to the horse's brick-bed and pulled back the handkerchief. "But the only one really injured is the horse."

Virginia watched, surprised, as the earl lowered himself to the ground between the boys, studying the horse carefully.

"Mm. I see. Just as it was yesterday." He glanced up at her and winked, which made her smile. His consideration to her sons, his willingness to enter into their game, gave her reason to be kindly disposed to him. "I have just what the poor fellow needs."

"The glue?" Phillip asked, his eyes dropping to the bag in the earl's hands. "Will it work?"

"It should. But we must make doubly sure it holds, so I've brought a special bandage as well. It is careful work, mind you, and you will have to do it together." The earl opened his bag and removed a small pot of glue, putting it on the brick nearest the horse. Then he withdrew a brush, a thin strip of white cloth, and scissors. "Here are the necessary tools. Phillip, as the elder brother, it falls to you to glue and hold the leg in place. Edward, you are to carefully wrap the bandage and trim the ends."

"We can do it," Phillip said, and his younger brother gave a firm nod.

"Excellent. I leave your patient in good hands then." The earl stood and stepped back to Virginia. She was grateful to him and impressed. He gave the children the tools they needed to repair the horse and their argument.

It was something like what Charles would've done. She had the feeling Charles and Lord Calvert would've gotten along well, had they known each other.

"My lady," he said, half-bowing. "Would you do me the honor of a walk along the lane?" She looked from his gloved hand up into his eyes, more gray than blue in the light of the morning sun and holding a somberness in them she did not understand.

Virginia looked from her sons, working together with frowns of concentration, back up to the tall earl. What could he wish to speak to her about? Was it only common courtesy? Did he think she expected to be waited upon?

The manners bred into her demanded she accept him, especially given his attention to her sons. She put her hand in his and allowed him to help her stand.

"If you wish it, my lord," she answered, glancing at the boys again.

"They will be fine," he whispered, giving the hand he held a gentle squeeze before offering his arm. "And we will not go far."

She met his eyes, taking in the confidence she read in his expression, and nodded her agreement. He stepped in the direction of the gravel path and she followed, her pace even with his. He did not walk with hurried steps, but his movement was measured as though he had a destination in mind.

"Thank you for aiding them, my lord," she said after several seconds of silence. "They are the best of children, but the injury of that toy would've made them enemies for days."

"I well understand," he answered, his voice quiet and his eyes fixed ahead. "And there is more to it than the toy, isn't there?"

Virginia swallowed and turned her eyes away, fixing her gaze on the trees lining the path. "They have suffered a great deal of loss. Phillip seems to feel it more keenly than Edward, but I find both children are given to express more emotion than before."

"I understand. Grief is difficult enough for those of us with years of experience in life. I cannot imagine how it would color the world of a child."

She glanced at him, curious, and saw he was studying her profile with careful eyes. What did he see when he looked at her? A grieving woman? A concerned mother? She knew she was not in the bloom of good health anymore, and she'd hardly felt like eating. Did she resemble a specter, or a tragic character from a novel, thin and pale, with hopeless eyes?

Not given to flights of fancy, Virginia drew away from those thoughts and forced a polite smile upon her face.

"It is a lovely morning. Wouldn't you agree, my lord?"

A sigh escaped his lips and he made a show of looking about them. "A fine spring day. Yes. But it is not the weather I wish to discuss with you, Lady Heatherton."

"What do you wish to discuss, Lord Calvert?" she asked.

He stopped walking, necessitating she do the same. They had gone just far enough down the lane that she could only glimpse her sons through the trunks of several trees, but she could see them playing happily where she'd left them.

"I have something particular I wish to speak to you about." His words brought her back to him. His lips were turned up in the smallest of smiles, though his brow was drawn down in a more serious manner. "I think what I have to say may be considered shocking by some. I ask that you listen with an open mind to what I am about to propose. Will you do that for me, Lady Heatherton?"

"I think I can promise that much, my lord." And her curiosity demanded it. What could this man, a stranger, have to say to her that could be shocking?

He took a deep breath and the tension in his face actually eased, as though he'd already said the most difficult part. "I have learned of your present difficulty in regard to your brother-in-law. Mrs. Christine Gilbert told me of it," he admitted.

"Oh?" Virginia raised her eyebrows and mentally made note to speak to Christine about that later. The servants sharing information amongst themselves she might understand, but her cousin telling this man of her private affairs? That did not sit comfortably with her.

"Yes. She thought it possible I might know of a solution to the situation." His lips twitched as though he tried to hide a smile, though Virginia saw little of humor in the situation.

She stiffened her posture and lifted her chin. If they were going to discuss her private business, she had no wish to show him more than a strong front, a good line of defense.

"And have you a solution, my lord?" The sooner he spoke his mind, the sooner they could end the conversation.

When he spoke, his voice dropped an octave lower and his eyes shone earnestly. "I do. I think you ought to marry me."

For the space of two heart beats, Virginia only stared at him, uncomprehending. Then a laugh squeezed its way from her lungs and she dropped his arm. "Marry you?"

He nodded firmly. "I am unmarried, with title and influence. My name will protect your sons and they will not be taken from you."

Virginia's heart pounded heavily against her ribs. She stood, gaping at him like a fish, and he kept talking as though it was not at all extraordinary to propose marriage after less than a day's acquaintance.

"I have thought it all through, my lady, and I feel I must make a few things clear at once. If we marry by special license, we need not wait for the mourning period to end or have banns read where your brother-in-law will learn of it." He spoke rapidly, perhaps sensing her rising disbelief. "It will be a marriage in name only, until the full mourning period has passed. I respect your right to grieve a husband who was a good man. I lost my wife—" Here his words took on a choked quality, but he cleared his throat and continued.

"I lost my wife years ago, and I understand the importance of grieving. I do hope, someday, to have an heir of my own, but that can be addressed at a later time."

Virginia's cheeks warmed but she felt herself nod.

Am I actually considering this madness? She could hardly believe it.

"My lord," she said, forcing the words out before he could say another word. "What are you suggesting? How can you be certain? You have only known me since yesterday."

Lord Calvert spread his arms as he spoke, gesturing with his hands. "And? Many a marriage has been founded on less and been successful."

"Many a marriage has been founded on more and been a disaster," she quipped, folding her arms across her chest. But she had not closed her mind to the idea. She knew Lord Calvert by reputation and her cousin's glowing praise of him. "I would want a legal contract in place," she said. Dear Lord, what was she doing? "Assurances that you would not touch my sons' inheritance or my marriage portion."

For how demanding she sounded, he only looked solemn.

"Easily managed." He stepped forward, close enough that she could see the blue in his eyes again. "And more. I swear to you, on my honor, to treat you with kindness and respect. I also swear I will do all in my power to care for your sons as if they were my own. You and they will want for nothing. Your concerns will become mine, their successes a priority. I do not enter into this agreement lightly."

"Only hastily," she said, tilting her head to the side as she regarded him. Virginia's heart had slowed as she listened to his earnest words. Could she trust him? He had a reputation of being fair and decisive. He'd done what he could to ensure her own cousin's happiness. She knew he had influence and power, even in London. And hadn't she just been thinking that Charles would've liked him?

Charles had often told her it was more important to look to the actions of a man than his words. Hadn't the earl already given her some evidence of the sort of man he was in his treatment of her children?

Lord Calvert mirrored her, tilting his head and studying her with his blue-gray gaze. "Would you like time to think on it?"

It would be sensible to ask for time, to discuss the matter with others, to consult Mr. Olivier in Bath. But the fact remained that no one could make decisions for her anymore. As a widow, all responsibility fell to her to care for her family and her future. Though a more cautious mind would step back from the proposal, would scoff at the absurdity of it, Virginia's instinctive reply was the one she must make.

Taking a deep breath, assuring herself that her heart was safely tucked away behind the fortress of her making, Virginia gave her answer.

"I do not think more time will change my mind. If you are certain, I am as well. Yes. I will marry you, Lord Calvert."

His eyes brightened and he bowed, keeping his gaze on her face. "I am honored to have your trust, my lady."

Virginia waited for a feeling of dismay, for regret to settle in her stomach, but instead it was as though a weight had gone from her. When he extended his hand again, she took it, the warmth of his grasp comforting.

"Please," she said, watching his expression as she spoke. "Allow me to tell my family and my sons."

"Of course, my lady. Would you like me present?"

Virginia shook her head. "I am not afraid. I only wish to handle their questions and concerns on my own. And I must contact Mr. Olivier. He is a barrister in Bath and has been helping with my case."

"I will see to the special license." His eyes flicked away and he shifted his weight from one foot to the other, and then looked down at the ground. "There will be at least one line of inquiry put to me, since you have not completed the year's mourning period."

It took Virginia a moment to realize he was uncomfortable, perhaps even embarrassed. "What might that be, my lord?" she asked, puzzled. The man could say all he had to her with a straight face, and now his ears turned pink?

"Is there any way," he began, speaking slowly and mostly to the ground, "that you could be with your late husband's child?" His ears were redder than pink by the time he finished his question.

Virginia felt warmth explode in her cheeks. To discuss such intimate details with a near stranger—! She told herself not to be ridiculous. They were both mature, had both been married. Swallowing the discomfort, she started to shake her head. But he was still looking down.

"I am not with child," she answered, her voice soft. "My husband has been gone three months. And in his last months of life, he did not have the health to engage in activity which might've made me so." She released his hand and turned, going back down the walk, her arms wrapped around her waist. It was a strange thing to discuss, of course, but the loneliness in her heart, the longing for what had been lost, caused her heart to ache.

How she missed Charles. Missed being held by him.

Lord Calvert was by her side again, keeping pace with her easily, keeping his hands tucked behind his back. "I am sorry to intrude on your privacy," he said, his eyes forward, trained on the house. "I will not do so further."

"I understand the need." Virginia's eyes found her sons, playing happily in the garden, their place in the world less secure than they knew. She was doing this for them, for their safety and security, to keep them from the influence of a man who cared nothing for them.

"How soon can you secure the special license?" she asked.

"I will leave tomorrow, if you wish it," he said.

"That will do. Thank you." The words were too trite given the extremes he went to on her behalf, but Virginia could summon no greater enthusiasm. Shock held her in its grip.

Virginia hoped she'd made the right decision, but her well-protected heart did little to reassure her.

Chapter Six

L eaning against the paddock's rail, watching Phillip canter around its edges on his horse, Virginia did her best to commit the moment to her memory. Edward was doubled-up with Thomas, riding at a slower pace while Thomas called instructions to Phillip.

Her sons, in this precious point in time, were happy. They were in the midst of an adventure, trusting Thomas to lead them, trusting her to keep them safe. They knew nothing of how their lives would change in a few days' time. The earl had taken his leave of them, accepting his crock of glue with a bow. He had extracted a promise from her to send a message if he was needed, then he'd gone on his way.

"They are fine boys, Ginny," her cousin said. Virginia looked to her side, meeting Christine's warm brown eyes and wide smile with a smaller one of her own.

"I know. I hope they grow into fine men."

"Under your influence, they will." Christine, not usually a demonstrative woman, surprised Virginia by putting her arm around her cousin's shoulders. "And we will help where we can."

"You have already done more than I have any right to ask. We have lived in your home for three months, we have overtaken your house and gardens, not to mention the biscuit trays."

Christine laughed. "We love it, Ginny. If I thought I could convince you, I would ask that you make your permanent home with us. But that will not do for you, will it?"

Shaking her head, Virginia murmured her assent. "It will not, I'm afraid. We must have a home of our own again."

"What are you going to do about Mr. Macon?" Christine asked, lowering her eyes to the grass. "I imagine you have given it a great deal of thought."

Virginia's heart squeezed. It was time. "I have. Apparently, I'm not the only one to have been troubled by making plans, either. I understand you told the Earl of Annesbury my troubles?"

Christine's face blanched and her eyes widened. "Oh, Virginia, it was such a foolish thing for me to do. I am dreadfully sorry. But he's been helpful in the past, and I wished—"

Virginia slowed her words with a hand on her arm. "I am not upset with you, Christine. How could I be? He came up with a solution, you see."

Christine stilled and a look of relief crossed her face. "Really? Will it work?"

"It had better." Virginia sighed and turned, leaning back against the rail as she met her cousin's eyes. "I've not told anyone yet, and I mean to tell the boys tonight. But I have agreed to marry Lord Calvert."

Christine stood gaping, her body still as a statue. Finally, a sound like a squeak escaped her. "*Really?*"

"Yes." Virginia closed her eyes and tilted her head back, letting the afternoon sun warm her face. It had been too long since she'd allowed warmth into her life.

"You met him yesterday." Christine sounded cautious, not disbelieving. "Are you sure, Virginia? Is this what you want?"

"I want my sons to be safe from a tyrannical uncle," she said, her voice soft. She could hear Edward giggling as he and Thomas rode by. "I want them to have days like today, in the sunlight, without worry or fear. I want to be with them, watching them grow and learn. I believe marrying a man of the earl's reputation will give me those things." She opened her eyes and took in her cousin's solemn expression.

"He is a good man," Christine said firmly. "Although I believe he is used to getting his way." Her smile appeared, smaller than before. "I am only sorry you do not love him. I understand marrying where there isn't love. I planned my whole life to do so, until Thomas convinced me otherwise." Her eyes sought out her husband in the paddock, her expression softening as she watched him.

"I have loved before." Virginia turned to wave at Phillip as he rode by, showing him her proudest smile. "Charles will be in my heart forever, and I have our boys as a reminder of his love. I think that will be enough for me."

Christine's hand sought Virginia's and gave it an encouraging squeeze. They said no more, though Virginia could feel her cousin's affection and support well enough.

¤

Nurse Smythe, an angel of a woman, readied the boys for bed as she did every night. Virginia sat in the upstairs nursery of the Gilbert home, watching with amusement as Edward became caught up in his nightshirt.

"Sweet child, your head goes *here*," Nurse said, reaching out to straighten his path through the material. She patted his head and bustled about, plumping pillows and straightening quilt corners.

The boys were soon in bed, tucked in close, and then Nurse Smythe gave Virginia a warm smile before disappearing out the door to the hall. Virginia had already told the older woman, the woman who had nursed her Charles as a child, that she needed to speak to the children alone that night.

"Are you going to tell us a story, Mama?" Edward asked, snuggling further into his blankets. "I love stories."

"I do too." Phillip rolled over in his bed and propped his chin up on one fist. His green eyes sparkled at her with interest.

Virginia's heart warmed, as any mother's would, when she took in their innocent request and sleepy smiles. For the breadth of a second, she wondered if she was wrong to destroy their contentment with her announcement. But it was a foolish thought, given the alternative to her choice.

"Perhaps we can have a story. But first, we must have a very serious talk. I have something important to tell you." She took in a deep breath, meeting Phillip's green eyes and Edward's brown, her heart aching for all they'd been through. But they would take her behavior for their own; she had to begin as she meant to go on, with optimism.

"First, I must remind you both how much I love you. The two of you are my whole world and you have my heart." She stood from the chair and came to kneel between their little beds, reaching out to each of them. "Your father loved you, too. When he left us, he desperately wanted you both to know that and to be taken care of. Do you understand that, Phillip?"

Phillip, his green eyes dark, looked down at his pillow and nodded. "He said you'd take care of us, and we'd take care of you."

Edward reached his hand out to touch hers. "I remember, too. I love Papa so much."

"As do I, sweetheart. So much." She grasped his little palm in hers and smiled, the tenderness of the moment nearly overcoming her. Virginia forced away her tears and looked from one to the other. "Because your father cared for you, and because I love you, I have had to make a very big decision. You see, we cannot live here with Cousin Christine and Cousin Thomas forever. They have been so kind to us, but we must have our own home."

"Will we go back to Heatherton Hall?" Phillip asked, pushing himself up to sit. "Back to our home?"

He had not been there in half a year, but his excitement fully showed how much he missed the old pile of stones, as Charles had called it.

Virginia shook her head. "Not yet, darling. We must make a new home for ourselves, and—and repair our family a little." How could she explain it to them? She had thought it would be an easy matter, but found herself struggling for the right words. "Part of keeping you safe, of protecting our family, means I have had to make a very big choice. But I believe it is a good choice and it will make us all happy." She prayed it so, anyway.

"What choice, Mama?" Edward asked, sitting up as well, matching his brother's worried expression.

"Do you remember Lord Calvert?" she asked.

"He helped us with the horse," Phillip answered. "I liked him."

"Yes. I did too. He was kind to you both." Virginia met Phillip's eyes, smiling into them. "He has asked me if he might continue to help our family, if he could give us a safe home. You see, dears, he has asked if we would come and be a part of his family. He does not have a wife, or children."

Edward's eyes narrowed and he looked from her to Phillip, uncertain of how to react to this news. Phillip's eyes widened and his hands curled into fists in his lap.

"Would he be our new father?" The tilt of his chin warned her how he was prepared to respond should she say yes.

Virginia shook her head. "No, Phillip. No one can take the place of your father, in my heart or yours. But Lord Calvert is a good man, and I believe he will do all he can to help you become the man your father wished you to be."

"He won't be Papa?" Edward asked. "But we'll be a family?"

"Yes." Had she muddled the whole thing? Explained it too poorly? Virginia looked from one boy to the other, her heart aching for them. It could never be easy, a change like this, but how else could she have told them?

Phillip met her eyes and he searched them, for what, she did not know, but she put on the most comforting smile she could. He folded his arms and lowered his chin.

"Would Papa like him?" Phillip asked.

The question surprised her, but Virginia could answer truthfully. "Lord Calvert has a kind heart and wishes to do the right thing. Yes. I think your father would've liked that, and would like Lord Calvert, too."

Charles believed true gentility was not something passed through blood but shown in action and held up by honor. He was a man who did good deeds, who helped others. Virginia thought Lord Calvert's actions in that regard would earn her late husband's respect, if nothing else.

"To join his family to ours," she went on when the boys remained silent, "I will need to marry Lord Calvert. I will be his wife. But I want you both to know, to be certain, that all will be well. I still love your father and I love both of you. Nothing will change that."

"I love you too, Mama," Edward responded at once, his large brown eyes more sleepy than understanding. At four and a half years old, he would accept the change best.

Phillip remained quiet a moment longer. "I don't have to call him Papa?"

"No." Her heart sunk a little. While she would not require such a thing from her children, it did not bode well that this was his first concern. "But you are to treat him with respect and kindness, as he is doing a wonderful thing for us."

Someday, when they were older, she would explain the whole of it. But she did not wish to scare them in regard to their uncle or give them greater cause for concern. They were too young to understand, to know of the difficulties and cruelties of the adult world.

Nodding, Phillip slowly slid back down under the covers. "We won't go back to the Hall?"

"Not yet."

"But we will go live with the earl, instead of with Cousin Christine?"

She nodded. "We will."

Phillip closed his eyes. "Good night, Mother."

Had she been dismissed by her six-year-old son? Half-amused, half-concerned, Virginia looked to Edward to see his eyes already closed. The younger boy was breathing deeply, his worries of the day lost to sleep.

"Good night, Phillip." She kissed his cheek and tucked his blankets in around him, then did the same for Edward.

She left the room quietly, leaving the lamp for Nurse Smythe, and stepped into the darkened hallway. She rubbed at her eyes with one hand, again questioning her ability to assist the boys through this new change.

I must be brave and show them nothing but confidence in this decision.

That thought made her straighten her shoulders and lift her chin.

It was up to her to keep her sons safe and happy, to give them their best chance at life. While her decision had been made with rapidity, it did not feel like a poor one.

"I hope you approve, Charles," she whispered to the night. No answer came, no sign was given, and she had only the ache in her heart for company.

Chapter Seven

O btaining a special license from the Archbishop of Canterbury was no easy task, yet it was one that Lucas had full confidence in achieving. He had known Charles Manners-Sutton, the current archbishop, for several years. His father had been on friendly terms with the man before he ascended to the reverential position.

Returning to London to see the archbishop took time, but Lucas had been able to call on him at his home. After a closely conducted interview, during which he learned that the archbishop had been an admirer of the late Baron of Heatherton, Lucas was granted the license.

He kept it on his person as he returned to Annesbury, pleased the whole adventure took no more than a week.

He returned home in the middle of the afternoon and immediately received correspondence from his London solicitor and Lady Heatherton's barrister in Bath.

"Gresham," he'd said, carefully reading through the contract the barrister was negotiating on behalf of the baroness. "I need you to prepare the staff to receive a new countess."

The old man froze, his usually unflappable nature giving way to a moment of shock. "A new countess, my lord?"

"Yes. I plan to marry before the week is out." He watched his butler with interest, knowing this would be a good indication of how his news would be received by many.

"I see. May I congratulate you, my lord?"

"Thank you, Gresham. You may." He turned his attention back to his papers, shuffling through them with a concentrated frown. Everything appeared to be in order, but he would consult with Lady Heatherton.

"My lord?"

He glanced up, surprised to see the butler remained in the same place. "Yes, Gresham? Something you wish to say?"

The elderly gentleman half bowed. "Might I inquire as to who the new countess will be?"

"Lady Virginia Macon, Baroness of Heatherton. Oh, and she brings two children with her, so we need to ready the nursery as quickly as possible." He put his papers in a stack and stood, tucking them beneath his arm. "They'll bring their own nurse, but we ought to assign a maid to the nursery as well."

"I will see to it, my lord. I will make certain all is in good order for the countess." He bowed and left the room, carrying the silver tray he'd used to bring the post to the study.

Lucas looked down at the papers in his arms and then at the mantel. Though still travel-worn, he decided he ought to go and speak to his bride-to-be. Combining their households was but one matter they would need to discuss.

He put the papers in a folder, tied the string tight, and went for his horse.

In a short while, he was riding onto the Gilberts' property. The month of May had bestowed another sunny day on the countryside, for which he was grateful. The green lawns and brightly colored flowers rolled out from the Gilbert house like a carpet.

After dismounting, Lucas looped the reins of his horse through an obliging pole and went to the door. He was admitted to a downstairs parlor and waited for Lady Heatherton to appear.

Lucas set his folder down on a table and paced to the window overlooking the rear gardens, noticing Mrs. Gilbert at work clipping flowers. He smiled, remembering her deliveries of fragrant blooms to his home.

The door clicked open. Lucas turned to greet the baroness, a ready smile on his face, but it faltered when he saw her expression.

She appeared as lovely as before, her blonde hair half down this time, a bandeau holding it back from her face. Her gown was muted gray, which made the somber look in her green eyes all the more foreboding. What could be wrong?

"My lady." He bowed, then took several steps forward. "Is something amiss?"

She returned the courtesy and shook her head. "Not at all." Her words did not match her expression in the least. "Please, my lord, won't you sit down?" She gestured to an empty chair.

Lucas hesitated, his mind racing across the boundaries of propriety. They were betrothed, though hardly familiar with each other, making the lines of permissible conversation and concern blur. But if she was troubled, he ought to try to help.

"Lady Heatherton." He took the offered seat but leaned forward, fixing his eyes on hers. "I can see something of a somber nature is on your mind. If you insist it is nothing, I will take you at your word, but know that I would like to be aware of your troubles."

She lowered herself into the chair nearest his, though there was still a distance of three feet between them. She bit her bottom lip, considering him and his words.

"Very well. I suppose it is silly to stand on ceremony, considering our last meeting ended with our engagement." The words, though said evenly, gave him hope she was a woman of good humor. "I have had two letters today. One is from my friend, Mr. Olivier, who has been advising me legally. The other is from my brother-in-law."

"And which letter has upset you?" In possession of his own letter from the barrister, he felt he already knew the answer to his question.

"Mr. Macon, my brother-in-law, has discovered I am staying in this house. He wrote in a most determined manner that he wishes to see his nephews. To ascertain they are being cared for." Her hands curled into fists in her lap and her face went pale. "Given his manner toward me after my late-husband's passing, this distresses me."

"I see." Lucas's first instinct was to reach out, put a comforting hand on her arm, but he sat back in his chair instead. "Did he give any indication of when he wished to come?"

"No. But it is only a matter of time." She clasped her hands before her, making an obvious effort to relax her posture. "The letter from Mr. Olivier was more encouraging. He received your letter, and mine, and advised me to go through with the marriage. If you are still amenable."

Lucas nodded. "I am. My only concern is how soon we can manage it. We have to settle the legal matters—"

"The special license was no trouble?" she asked.

"None." He leaned forward and unwound the string from the folder, laying it open on the table. The special license sat on top, stamp duty paid, the archbishop's signature on the document. "I was lucky. The archbishop had a relatively clear calendar and was happy to see the son of an old friend."

"That is good news." She reached out and picked up the document, her eyes running over it with curiosity. "I've never seen one before."

"Nor have I." He took up the next paper. "This is the marriage settlement, in a draft form. If you agree to these points, we can ask someone local to make the contract for us. Once that is signed, we only have to appear before the vicar."

She took the paper from his hand, laying the license down carefully. As she read, her eyes widened, then darted from the page to him and back. He attempted to appear indifferent, folding his arms and leaning back in the chair.

"This is—this is a great deal more than I expected. For myself and for the boys." Her hand trembled and she steadied the paper by taking it up with the other as well. "My lord—"

"It is perfectly appropriate," he said, shifting in his seat. When she looked up at him again, her eyes shimmering with unshed tears, Lucas wondered if he ought to have had the proposed document delivered instead of coming himself. "I know Phillip has the title and all associated with that, so I have not settled so much on him as Edward. I have a younger brother, as you know, and it hardly seems fair that second sons are left with few choices. Edward will be able to choose an education and profession of his liking."

The baroness nodded and lowered her head again, her shoulders rising and falling with her deep breath. "And there are provisions for me. I thank you for that. And future children."

He nodded, his cravat feeling tight, and realized she hadn't seen the gesture. She continued speaking before he could say anything.

"And everything else we discussed. Thank you. I appreciate your attention to those details." She reached out to lay the paper down before lifting her head again. "I agree to these terms. Thank you."

"I will have the contract drawn up." He shuffled the papers, drawing the larger portion of the stack out. "These are records of my holdings and finances. I gathered what I could for you to see, should there be any questions...?" He let the phrase trail away, holding them out to her.

Lady Heatherton shifted in her chair and reached for the sheaf. "Thank you." She lowered the paper to her lap, then a breathy laugh escaped her. "It is all very businesslike, isn't it?"

It was nothing like Lucas's engagement to Abigail. They had left all the paperwork to solicitors and had spent the days and weeks prior to their marriage holding hands and dreaming of things to come. But this arrangement could never be like that one. He had loved Abigail, and she him.

"It does feel very dry, doesn't it?"

She reached up to tuck a loose strand of hair behind her ear, looking away to another corner of the room. "I have told the boys what is happening. Sparing them the details of their uncle's plans, of course."

"Of course." He cleared his throat, trying to relax his posture. "What was their reaction? Did they understand?"

"I think so. Phillip is less certain than Edward. But I told them you mean to help me, as their father wished, to care for them." Her lips curved upward in a smile that did not quite reach her eyes. "They are predisposed to like you, thanks to the glue."

"Ah, yes. How is the wooden patient faring?" Talk of the children felt more natural, somehow, than talk of marriage.

"Very well. They took the bandage off this morning and it appears the leg will stay in place, barring another fall." There, at last, her smile was genuine and her eyes lit up. "They will be the best of friends until the next disagreement."

He chuckled. "My lady, they are very fine boys. I look forward to coming to know them better."

"Thank you." She paused and he watched her expression go from relaxed to uncertain. "My lord, why are you doing this for us?"

Lucas met her gaze and considered his reasons, trying to determine how best to explain them to her. She must be having second thoughts. Any sane woman would be. He decided the simplest answer would be best.

"Because, Lady Macon, it is the right thing to do, and I am in the position to do it." He spoke with firmness of mind, determined in his course.

She regarded him silently, her eyes searching his, and he wondered if she saw the doubts he'd chased away by moving forward. Whatever she saw, it must've reaffirmed her decision.

"I think you ought to call me Virginia."

A warm burst of confidence spread through him and he raised his hand to take hers, as though they were sealing a pact. "Then I am Lucas."

Chapter Eight

Virginia did not answer her brother-in-law's letter. The earl—*Lucas*—had obtained a suitable contract for her to sign the day after he returned from London. He arranged everything with the vicar and they agreed to marry in the church three days later, with only Thomas and Christine for witnesses. Even though it was not necessary to hold the ceremony in the church, Virginia had requested it. The marriage wouldn't feel real to her if it took place anywhere else.

"I cannot believe you are marrying tomorrow," Christine said from her perch on Virginia's bed. "Everything is happening so fast."

"I know." Virginia was in a dressing gown, arranging her dresses in a trunk. "Of a necessity."

Christine huffed and tugged at her braided hair beneath her tall black hat. She had only just come in from a morning ride with Thomas and had stopped to see if Virginia was awake.

"What will you wear to be married? It cannot be mourning clothes."

Virginia paused, pursing her lips. "I had not really thought of it. I only brought mourning clothes with me." She straightened and looked inside her trunk again, noting all the layers of black crepe and gray muslin. "Oh dear."

Christine slid from the bed and looked inside the trunk as well. "It is rather dismal, for a wedding *trousseau*."

Virginia met her cousin's wide eyes, then burst out laughing. Christine, at first startled, soon joined her as well. All the worry over Mr. Macon, the concern for her sons, and the anxiety over her marriage had taken its toll on her. She had barely slept and had few reserves to call upon.

It was laugh or cry, and Virginia was quite finished with the former.

Her cousin recovered first and knelt next to the open trunk. "What are you going to do, Virginia?"

"I'm not certain. We are somewhat near in size. Could I borrow something of yours?"

"A borrowed wedding gown." Christine shook her head, her expression rueful. "Absolutely shocking. Not a single member of the *ton* would condone such a thing."

"I hardly care for them." Virginia sighed and knelt as well. "And you will not think ill of me for it."

"Of course not. How would I, if it's my gown? I have excellent taste." Christine sniffed and pushed herself back to her feet. "I will be back in a moment." She went to the door and disappeared, closing it behind her.

Virginia reached into the trunk and moved a few items around, until she found the bright bit of green she searched for. It was the shawl another cousin, Christine's sister Julia, had made for her. The delicate work had been finished just before Julia's own wedding and gifted with an apology that Virginia could not wear it in mourning. She had treasured it anyway, seeing the beautiful piece as something to help her look forward to things to come.

She could wear the shawl to her wedding. It was certainly beautiful enough.

The door opened and Christine came in, gowns over one arm in a manner Virginia doubted the maid would be pleased with.

"Here we are, my most lovely gowns." Christine shut the door and went to the bed, tossing the dresses one at a time upon the coverlet.

Virginia stood and came to examine them, her green shawl in hand. Because she and her cousin had different coloring, and tastes which diverged more often than not, she worried none of the dresses would suit her. But anything was better than gray.

A sapphire blue dress was lovely, but wrong. A deep mauve looked too much like a mourning lilac. The white was out of the question—she was hardly a debutante. But there was an ivory-colored gown with green embroidery at the bodice and hem.

"This one," she said, laying the shawl beside it. "This will do perfectly."

"I thought so, too, but I wanted to give you options." Christine's wide, cheerful smile lifted Virginia's heart. Her cousin was one of the most generous people she knew. "And," Christine added, picking up the dresses not chosen, "I will make it a present to you, so it is no longer a borrowed dress. It is yours."

"Christine, it's too lovely—"

"I insist. And as you are my guest, it would be rude of you to refuse." Christine winked. "I had better to change out of this riding habit, but I will be back to help you try the dress on."

Virginia murmured her thanks. She reached down to the gown, fingering the fine cloth. To wear something other than black or gray stirred up a mix of emotions, not all of which were identifiable. She missed color at times. The world had been a very dull gray for far too long.

She took off her dressing gown and laid it across the bed. Her maid, Louisa, had already helped her put on her underthings. She lifted the gown Christine had given her and carefully pulled it overhead. The fabric fell with a swish around Virginia. The back would need to be done up, but she went to the mirror anyway to see how it looked.

The gown's simplicity appealed to her. It would make a fine wedding dress, and when she laid her mourning aside she would enjoy wearing it often.

I marry Lucas Calvert tomorrow. Virginia touched her hair, piled up on her head in a simple twist. Her hands trembled and she hastily lowered them.

When Charles died, she had not thought to marry again. The love they shared, she knew, was not easily found. But necessity compelled her.

Perhaps there was some good she could do, too, as a countess. After reading the papers the earl—Lucas—had left her, the work ahead of her became clearer. It was a man's province to care for the estate and lands, of course, but wives had their part to play.

He owned five houses throughout England, of varying size and consequence. All five had tenants, and while her husband must care for their livelihood, it was her duty to see to their well-being. And though he owned the houses and employed the staff at each, she would be the person responsible for the day-to-day instructions and interactions.

Charles's barony, while by no means poor, had not encompassed many people or large tracts of land. But she had handled her responsibilities there quite well. She would do the same now.

A soft rap on the door preceded Christine's reentry. "Oh, that will be just lovely. Here, let me do up the back." She hurried in and started on the buttons.

Virginia met her eyes in the mirror and squared her shoulders.

I can do this. For the boys, for myself, for the people I will help.

All would be well, she told herself. *For it must be.*

¤

Lucas adjusted his cravat, staring into the mirror of his dressing room. The folds did not seem right to him, no matter how often he adjusted them.

A sigh escaped Randal, who came forward immediately, his hands replacing Lucas's upon the cloth. "My lord, this is the third cravat this morning. What about it displeases you?"

"I cannot say, precisely. It looks like it has no business going to a wedding." Lucas raised his eyebrows at his valet, trying to inject some humor into his words. "Perhaps a stick-pin?"

"Yes, my lord." Randal stepped away to a small chest of drawers and pulled out a box. Lucas resisted the desire to pull at the snow-white cloth around his throat, knowing it was ridiculous to imagine the thing choking him.

"Here, my lord. May I suggest the sapphire pin?"

Lucas looked down at the box where several pins were nestled in a bed of velvet. He had difficulty swallowing for a moment.

Abigail had given him the box, and two of the pins, as a birthday gift after their wedding. He had laughed at the velvet, claiming it looked more likely to hold the crown jewels than his small baubles.

Reminders of her were everywhere of late.

"That will do, Randal." His valet took the selected pin and carefully affixed it to the cravat.

Lucas turned back to the mirror, inspecting his clothing carefully. He'd chosen his darkest blue coat and gray breeches, trying to look solemn without wearing mourning of his own. When he awoke, his wedding on his mind, he realized he had not discussed what would be appropriate to wear. His bride was a mourning widow, he a widower. They hardly had need for finery, and it wasn't a cheerful occasion so much as a necessary one.

What a way to begin a marriage.

Randal held Lucas's gloves and hat, which the earl took, then he checked the watch in his coat pocket. It was time to go to the church.

While they were being married, Virginia's small staff from the Gilbert house would move her things to his home. Then they would take the barouche to the Gilberts' to collect Phillip and Edward. At least he knew the order of things there.

The church was not far. Thankfully, it was outside of town, so there would not be any curious eyes watching. When he arrived at the church, he was relieved to find the place deserted, except for the vicar.

Lucas came in through the vestibule, going through to the stone church. His grandfather had actually built the place of worship after renovations on Annesbury Park. Every member of his family since had attended services here, when at the manor, and most had been married within its walls. Not he, though. Abigail had wished to marry in London before the season was out.

"Ah, my lord." Mr. Ames's greeting drew his attention to the front of the church, just beneath the brightly colored windows depicting the Garden of Eden. "You are early."

Lucas came all the way down the aisle, the familiarity of walking to the front of the room lost the moment he passed his family's pew.

"Mr. Ames. Thank you for doing this on such short notice." He shook the vicar's hand, but nearly jumped out of his shoes when he heard a giggle from behind.

Turning, Lucas saw two young girls sitting on the front pew, likely no more than ten or eleven years old, hiding smiles behind their hands.

"My younger daughters," Mr. Ames said, in a voice that sounded more stern than amused with the girls' shy smiles. "I thought it would be good for them to witness such an important occasion. But if your lordship wishes, they may go on their way."

"Quite all right. I believe we ought to have introductions if they are to witness my wedding." Lucas made a polite bow, which caused the girls to leap to their feet and drop curtsies.

"Very well, very well." Mr. Ames came forward. "My eldest is away at school. But here is Gabriella, eleven years old at present, and Augusta, nine years old." He looked from one girl to the other, his brows drawn down. "And they *will* behave themselves."

The girls' smiles started to falter.

"I've no doubt of it," Lucas said, keeping his tone light. When the girls glanced his way, he offered them a quick wink.

The door to the building opened with a small creek of protest; Lucas turned to watch Mr. and Mrs. Thomas Gilbert enter, both dressed as if for Sunday services. Directly behind them, a hand up as though to straighten her bonnet, came his wife-to-be. Thomas gestured for her to precede them down the aisle, which she did with a nod, and as she drew closer Lucas stood straighter.

Angels above, she's beautiful. It was thought in half awe and half prayer of gratitude. He'd thought her stately, before. Striking. Lovely. But without her blacks and grays, with a bonnet of green framing her face and a shawl of similar color around her shoulders, her eyes shone. Her hair peeked out around the edges of her bonnet, softening the sharper lines of her cheekbones, framing her features in gold.

The gown she wore, a warm color that made him think of cream, flowed over her curves better than the gray crepe he'd seen her wearing last. The color made her seem more delicate.

When she came close enough to hold her hand out, he realized he had been gaping at her with his mouth half-open. He snapped it shut and took her hand, holding it between his own.

"Are you ready?" he asked, softly enough he doubted anyone else heard him speak.

The fingers in his did not tremble, her gloriously green eyes met his without hesitation. "I am. Are you?"

"Yes." But was he? Before, he had been saving a widow and children, which struck him as an honorable and noble sort of thing to do. With the reality of an attractive woman standing in front of him, it felt less noble and more self-serving.

Lucas's unabashed staring at Virginia was finally broken when one of the young Ames girls, Augusta he thought her name was, jumped from her place on the bench and came to where they stood. Wearing a gap-toothed grin, the child held out a fistful of wildflowers.

Virginia's eyebrows raised and one corner of her mouth twitched. She reached out and took the flowers. "Thank you, Miss Augusta. I quite forgot a bridal bouquet."

"More sensible to hold a Book of Prayers," Mr. Ames muttered from behind them.

"Perhaps. But so much about today is already dreadfully sensible." Virginia made the statement lightly, before the child's face could fall. Then she selected one of the daisies from the bouquet and held it out to the girl. After the child accepted the flower, her cheeks going pink, she went back to sit next to her sister.

A sensible arrangement. That is all this is for either of us.

Lucas offered her his arm, which Virginia took, and they turned together to the vicar.

"Shall we begin, Mr. Ames?" Lucas felt her hand tighten on his arm when he spoke.

Whatever came after today, he did not think he could regret this moment. As disconcerting as he found her beauty, Lucas knew she needed him. That would be enough to begin on.

Chapter Nine

Virginia prided herself on her capabilities as a woman of society. Though she'd not had much practice in the months since her late husband's illness took its turn for the worst, she knew herself capable of conversing with all manner of people on all manner of subjects. Yet sitting next to Lord Annesbury, whom she must remember to call Lucas, she had a difficult time forming words of any intelligence.

Heavens, it isn't as though I'm a green girl. I'm a widow.

And he, a widower. They both knew what it was to be married, they both understood loss. Surely, they needn't ride in silence to fetch the boys from the Gilberts' home.

He isn't speaking either, she noted. Was he as uncertain as she?

"It was kind of Mr. Ames's daughter to pick me a bouquet." That was a safe thing to say, wasn't it? He'd seemed pleased with the child's gesture, after all. Her grip tightened around the wildflowers. White-petaled daisies, deep magenta foxglove, bluebells, and forget-me-nots. It was a simple arrangement, to be sure, tied together with a thin ribbon likely meant for the girl's hair.

Lucas nodded, though his eyes stayed on the horses. "She seems a sweet child. Do you know her well?"

"They have come to the house a few times, to play with the boys. I am afraid Phillip is most unimpressed by young ladies at present."

She idly twisted the stem of a daisy. "He said their games were too tame."

Lucas chuckled. "And the girls are older by more than a few years. I can imagine the difficulties there." He glanced at her, a sparkle in his eye. "Boys tend to prefer more daring games at his age, while those girls are being molded into young ladies. Their father is set on it."

"As well evidenced by his glares." She narrowed her eyes and attempted to frown as darkly as the vicar had when one of his daughters coughed during the simple ceremony. Her expression earned a half-smile from her new husband. "I think being so severe rarely means better behaved children."

One blond eyebrow popped up. "Do you? And how do you silence wiggling children in a church pew?" His eyes went forward again and his expression gave none of his thoughts on the subject away.

Why did he ask? Did he intend to tell her how to raise her sons? Her ire nearly raised before she told herself the question was innocent. He barely knew her, after all, or her child rearing methods. But where her sons were concerned, she would always be on the defense.

"They both know what is expected of them when they attend church. Edward is young yet and still stays home with his nurse most Sundays. For Phillip, he knows he must be a gentleman, and one day many will look to his example. I think because he knows my expectations he well fulfills them."

"Hm. My father expected me to behave, yet I distinctly remember being pinched by my mother on more than one occasion when I misbehaved." He cut her another sideways look. "Do you pinch?"

The glitter of humor in his eyes returned and Virginia relaxed. "Only in the direst of circumstances," she said, trying not to smile. "It has yet to be necessary."

He nodded and turned the horses into the Gilberts' lane. "Excellent. I shall remember to behave myself in church, to be certain it doesn't become necessary."

Virginia felt her cheeks warm. "My lord, I would never—"

"Lucas, if you please." He handled the reins with ease and didn't so much as flicker an eyelash when he interrupted her.

Was he teasing her? Already? But they barely knew one another, she thought with some dismay. It was one thing to be friendly, but a tease was nearly a flirtation.

Virginia began to wish back her gray and black attire. The moment she could change, she would put on her best gray gown. She had nearly nine months of mourning left, after all.

The boys were playing in the front garden when the house came in sight. Edward jumped to his feet upon spying the barouche and began to wave. Phillip stayed crouched among the flowers until the horses pulling the barouche slowed. He stood slowly, rigidly, a somber sight with his frown and black jacket.

Her heart went out to him. He'd gone through too many changes in too short a time. Someday he would understand, but at present he was a little boy who missed his father and his home.

"Good morning, Phillip and Edward." Lucas jumped down, his side of the barouche on the same as the boys. He bowed to them both and the boys hastily returned the gesture. Then the man turned back to her and held out his hand, ready to help her step down.

Her gloved hand slid into his strong grasp. He steadied her as she descended, her other hand keeping hold of the flowers. Lucas released her the moment she found her feet, for which she was grateful.

"Are you married now, Mama?" Edward asked, though he eyed Lucas hesitantly as he spoke.

"I am indeed. We have but to take our leave of the Gilberts and then we can be on our way to our new home." She held her hand out and her little son darted forward to take it, uncertainty fleeing in the familiar touch.

Phillip spoke with less hesitancy but lacked any sign of pleasantness. "They're all inside. Cousin Christine's only been home a few minutes." Christine and Thomas had left the moment they signed the register, while Lucas had been obliged to speak to Mr. Ames a trifle longer.

"Excellent. Then they will be prepared for us." Lucas gestured to the house. "Shall we?"

The front door opened and a footman appeared, coming down the steps to take the horses in hand. The butler stood in the doorway.

Virginia sucked in a deep breath. When she'd left this house, hardly an hour before, she had been a baroness and a widow. When she crossed the threshold now, she would be a countess and a wife.

She went first, keeping her hand in Edward's, Phillip trailing behind, and Lucas bringing up the rear of their party—their *family*. What an odd thought.

Mr. and Mrs. Gilbert, Thomas and Christine, all stood in the entryway, hopeful smiles on their faces.

"Congratulations," they said in chorus, obviously having rehearsed the single word in advance.

"Welcome, Lady Annesbury," Mrs. Gilbert said, coming forward to put her arms around Virginia. For the first time that day, in the embrace of a mother, Virginia's eyes filled with tears. Could anyone understand her better at this moment than a woman who had borne children?

Almost as if she'd heard Virginia's thoughts, Mrs. Gilbert whispered, "You've done the best thing for them, love. It will turn out all right."

Virginia returned the embrace whole-heartedly and sniffed back her tears. "Thank you, Mrs. Gilbert."

The older woman stepped back, her own eyes looking wet, smiling broadly. "Oh, you have flowers. Lovely. Here, let me take them." She took the flowers, which were beginning to show signs of wilting. "Let me press the bouquet for you, as a wedding gift."

Virginia barely had time to nod before Christine stepped forward and embraced her. "I am glad you'll be in the neighborhood for part of the year. We needn't even say goodbye."

"Not at all." Virginia laughed. "I will be a very bothersome neighbor, too, always returning to gossip with you."

Christine snorted. "As if I knew how to gossip. But we shall go on rides together, and you will have to bring the boys for their riding lessons."

Her gaze darting to Phillip, who had his arms folded and his eyes turned to the ground. Virginia nodded her assent. "Most certainly. We will come for lessons as often as you will give them." She had the pleasure of seeing Phillip look up, surprise on his face.

Had she not told him those would continue? Virginia's heart fell. Perhaps that was one reason for his surliness.

Thomas took her hand and bowed over it, murmuring his congratulations. His father did the same. In another moment, they were outside. The boys were helped into the barouche first, then Lucas climbed into the driver's seat before reaching down to lift her inside.

A different sort of conversation must now be had, for the children. The drive to their new home, though short, she hoped to pass pleasantly.

Before she could say a word, however, Lucas began talking.

"I'm looking forward to having you fine young gentlemen at Annesbury Park. I spent most of my growing-up time there, and it isn't the same without boys running about the place."

Virginia turned sideways in her seat to see how this line of conversation went over. Phillip, with his arms crossed, glared down at his feet. Edward stared at the back of Lucas's head curiously.

"Did you like growing up there?" Edward asked.

"I liked growing up at Heatherton Hall," Phillip said before Lucas could answer his brother's question.

"I'm certain it is a wonderful place. Someday soon, I hope you will give me a tour. But for now, will you allow me to share my home with you? And would it help matters if I told you there is a secret passage in the second floor?"

Edward's eyes went as round as pie tins and Phillip's gaze lifted briefly.

Virginia folded her hands in her lap and raised her eyebrows at her sons.

Phillip narrowed his green eyes. "Is there really a secret passage?"

"There is. In fact, I don't think I'll show it to you. Half the fun of a secret passage is hunting for it, after all." Lucas glanced her direction and dropped a slow wink. "I will show you everything else. We will confine ourselves to the house today, but there are gardens, stables, a lake, and a grove of the most magnificent trees."

When the boys said nothing, the earl added, a trifle absently. "There's plenty for boys to do."

"What will Mama do?" Edward asked, regarding his mother with an almost pitying expression. "None of that sounds like what she likes."

Virginia folded her hands in her lap and answered with a cheerful tone. "I will do as I always have. I will tend to you, the house, and my own amusements."

Edward looked unconvinced. But then, sewing, hostessing, and playing the pianoforte did not rank high as amusement for children.

"You'll want to pay attention now," the earl said, turning to speak over his shoulder. "We're turning into the drive."

They turned off the country road and onto a lane. There was an open gate, with a small gatehouse nearby. Though Virginia barely glimpsed the ironwork, she could see the curls and twists were intricate. The lane itself, hard-packed earth, was lined with mature chestnut trees, stretching out every which way without ever quite touching their neighbors. They created a pleasant canopy over the path.

A gradual bend in the road brought them out of the last of the trees and laid out, all at once, a sloping grassy hill. At the top of the hill sat the house, tall and stately, as though it surveyed all the rich green land around it with a sense of pride.

A very tall, rectangular brick house, reminding her of a cat basking in the sunshine. From the main building, she could just make out a slightly lower roof attached, curling away to one side. As they neared it, she counted the number of windows and saw twenty, in white panes, at the front alone. The house rose to meet them, the green lawn stretching out in every direction.

She half-turned again, thinking to see the boys' reaction, but stilled when she saw Lucas watching her. His mouth was straight, his expression nearly unreadable, but his slate blue eyes held a different emotion. Not pride. Uncertainty?

"It is one of the loveliest places I've ever seen. Which means there must be a defect in it somewhere. Perhaps the chimneys smoke terribly?"

His cheek twitched but the smile did not appear. "I am afraid not. Most of them were redone in my father's day. The house itself was built in 1756."

"That's an old house," Edward said, sounding genuinely impressed.

"Ours is older. Built in 1658." Phillip's proud tone of voice did not get past Virginia. She offered an apologetic look to the earl.

"It is, darling. But neither house needs to be better than the other. They are both lovely in their own way."

Her son grumbled something she did not quite catch and Virginia thought it best to ignore the comment.

"We are lucky to be the caretakers of such important homes, full of history." He nodded again at the house. "And see, I have many who help me to care for it, and they all wish to meet you."

Virginia saw the staff standing in two neat rows and wondered if anyone had been left inside or at the stables. There was a row of people who obviously worked outdoors, wearing browns and blacks with tanned faces and holding their hats respectfully. Then there were younger men in dark trousers and jackets, though they were not in full livery as the footmen were. Goodness, the six footmen were of equal height. Doubtless when she had a closer look, they would be close to identical in other aspects. Then there was the butler, the housekeeper, a row of maids in aprons of different colors, likely marking their duties, and kitchen staff in blue-striped dresses and white caps.

"It's like an army," she whispered.

Lucas chuckled and she felt her cheeks warm. She had not meant to speak the thought aloud. Her father had been an earl, with her unfeeling elder brother now occupying the title, but she knew they had never had so many servants at one estate.

"They are your army now, my lady." The horses stopped and a groom came forward to take the bridle of the lead animal. "And eager to meet you." Virginia nodded and lifted her eyes to take in the height of the building again.

The boys came out of the carriage first, then Lucas reached for her hand. No sooner had her feet touched the ground than introductions to the chief members of the staff were made. The head of the stables, the head gardener, the butler, the housekeeper, and the cook were introduced by name while the rest waited only to curtsy and bow in groups.

For a brief moment, Virginia feared herself unequal to the task of seeing to the needs and work of such a crowd.

You are an earl's daughter, now a countess and a baroness. You were raised for this task.

Reminding herself of those things, Virginia did not hesitate when Lucas offered his arm to escort her inside.

Walking through the large white doors, Virginia's first inclination was to stop and stare. How could she possibly be the new mistress to such beauty? The white marble floor was well polished, the walls were covered in rich tapestries and paintings, and the whole hall was filled with light from windows above and below. A staircase of stone, matching the floor, stretched upward in a graceful curve, while the landing boasted a magnificent railing where one could look down at the entry.

She took off her bonnet, her gloves, and her shawl, giving them into the care of the butler. The man appeared nearly as old as the house itself, and every bit as stately.

Virginia reached down for Edward's and Phillip's hands as the two stared in wonder at what must seem like a palace to them. When she looked to Lucas again, she realized he had offered his arm to her, as it dropped to his side in that instant.

Lucas gave her an understanding smile and knelt before Edward. "Where shall we begin our tour, do you think?"

Would he always be so kind to another man's sons? She hoped so. She felt it would be so. Time would tell.

Chapter Ten

Lucas looked up from his newspaper when the door to the breakfast room opened. His wife of four days entered, wearing her customary gray. She had taken up her mourning colors as soon as she'd gone to dress for dinner the first evening in the house. He didn't mind. Virginia showed a great deal of respect to her late husband, as was the man's due, but seeing her in colors more suited to her beauty had naturally drawn his admiration.

Which was why, of course, it was best she put the widow's colors back on.

"No tray for you, Virginia?" he asked, raising his eyebrows. "I thought at first you were merely being polite, but now this has become a habit."

Her pale pink lips turned upward. "Of course I'm being polite, but I also like to be awake with the rest of the house. I'm still learning the routines and schedules and there are the boys to look after." She went to her end of the table.

"The morning post came." He pointed to a tray and one of the footmen came forward to lift it and carry it to her. "There is something for you, sent over from the Gilberts."

She thanked the footman and took the paper, her eyebrows drawn down. "It is from Mr. Macon. I wonder if he wrote this before or after being informed of our marriage?" She did not say it spitefully, as he would almost expect, but with mere curiosity. She slid her finger beneath the seal and broke it while the footman brought dishes from the sideboard for her selection.

"Some toast and eggs please," she said absently, her eyes already on the page in her hand.

The footman served her efficiently and stepped away, just as another servant stepped forward to fill her teacup. They had already begun to memorize her preferences, he knew, and it pleased him that she accepted the attention as a matter of course.

Lucas watched as she read, not even trying to disguise it, as the contents of a letter from her brother-in-law must naturally be suspect. Watching the color drain from her face, leaving her a shade that nearly matched her dress, made his stomach clench. He almost stood. He almost went to her.

But he waited. Despite their marriage, they were still little better than acquaintances.

She looked up. "This was written before he was informed, I think. He demands to wait upon me and will be arriving at the Gilberts' home tomorrow."

"We ought to warn them."

She stared at him. "That is the first thing you can think to say?" Her tone was not upset, only surprised.

Lucas shrugged and sat back in his chair, hoping he looked as calm as he meant to. "I see no harm in his visit. Not anymore. Your sons are safe here, as my wards. The paperwork has already been completed by my solicitor and your very considerate barrister. He will come, we will inform him of what has occurred, and he will leave. Unless you wish to invite him to stay?"

Virginia shook her head. "I risk sounding petty, but I would not want him as a guest under any roof where I resided. He made the last weeks of the baron's time more difficult. They never got on. Mr. Macon is a bitter man, I'm afraid."

"Then he will not be a guest here. There is an inn down the road where he will do very well, if necessary." He nodded to her plate. "Your eggs are getting cold, Virginia."

"I'm afraid I'm not very hungry anymore."

He frowned. She hardly ever ate more than a few mouthfuls of anything. Did that account for the sharpness of her features? Had she always been thus?

"As you wish, of course, but I have it on good authority that Cook is doing her best to impress you." He gestured with his chin to one of the footmen. "She has made the most delightful French pastries you've ever seen."

The footman took up a serving tray and brought it forward, allowing Virginia to see the sampling of iced, stuffed, and custarded pastries.

Virginia hesitated, looking from her pitiful plate of eggs to the pastries. She finally took one, and though it was tiny he counted it a victory.

He well remembered the weeks after Abigail's death. He hadn't wanted to touch food. His appetite had fled completely and it was not until his worried brother brought his attention to the problem that Lucas had realized it. His valet had been taking in the waists of his trousers, without saying a word.

Virginia needed her health and strength, and as her husband he would see both restored to her.

"What have you planned to do today?" he asked, trying to distract her from the letter and the fact that she was nibbling on a pastry. "I have my suggestions, of course. The boys were all over the grounds with Nurse Smythe yesterday, but you've yet to see more than the gardens. Would you care for a tour?"

She smiled around a bite of pastry and swallowed before shaking her head. "I am conducting interviews today with the staff. I want to understand how the household works before I attempt to lead my army."

"A good plan. Gresham and Mrs. Hail will be happy to help. Gresham has been here for as long as I have memory." Lucas put extra cheer into his words as he continued. "Perhaps you will allow me to take you on a tour tomorrow, after Mr. Macon intrudes upon us?"

Though her eyes did not look entirely convinced, Virginia nodded. "As you wish, my lord."

"Virginia," he said her name with a put-upon sigh. "Please. Call me Lucas. I hear *my lord* dozens of times a day, but rarely my own name."

She laughed, surprising him. The short burst of amusement gave him hope she was not always staid and proper. Virginia covered the laugh with her hand. "I am sorry, Lucas. You reminded me of myself with that comment."

Lucas raised one eyebrow and leaned forward, folding his hands beneath his chin. "Do tell, Virginia. You cannot leave it at that."

Her eyes lowered to her plate and she lifted one shoulder in a shrug. "It is nothing important. After Edward had started talking, he must've said *Mama* a hundred times a day. Phillip, too. And the servants called me *my lady*. Charles had gone away for a fortnight and when he returned, he did not say my name once for the first hour he was home. I finally begged him to do so, that I might hear it. I'd missed being Virginia those weeks he was away." Her eyes darted up, meeting his gaze, and then lowered again. "I'm sorry. It must seem I am forever talking of before—"

"I don't mind." He couldn't let her regret her feelings. Could anyone understand them better than he? "You need never be concerned that bringing up Charles will do any harm to me or our conversation."

Virginia nodded, not looking at him again. She took her last bite of pastry and then tapped her napkin to her lips. She turned her attention to the footman nearest her, who continued looking stoically ahead. "Please give Cook my compliments. It was a delicious puff pastry, as light as air." Then she stood. "Excuse me. I had better write the Gilberts."

"Of course." He stood and watched her leave the room, then looked over his silent row of footmen. They did excellent impersonations of marble statues, but he wondered what the servants made of the relationship between him and their new countess.

He took himself away rather than stay to contemplate the idea. He had his own correspondence to see to.

¤

Virginia paced the length of the upstairs parlor. It was a comfortable place, spacious, decorated in gentle blues and ivory-hued furniture. She immediately felt at ease in such a soothing environment. But not at the moment. Nothing could've set her at ease, really, given the impending visit of her brother-in-law. She'd hardly slept the night before, for worrying over what she would say to him.

Virginia twisted her wedding band around her finger and then looked down at it. It was the band Charles had given her. Lucas had asked, when they arranged their wedding, if she would like to keep it or wished for another. At the time, she said she would keep the one she had, though she took it off for him to place on her finger when the vicar came to that moment in the ceremony.

She paused in her step and sat on the couch facing the door.

Had that hurt his feelings? Why had she not considered it before? Had she slighted him when she kept the ring from her first husband?

He hadn't batted an eye and the service had gone on, with him providing a ring for her to slip on his finger. Was it new or from his previous marriage?

With Mr. Gerard Macon at her doorstep, now was not the time to become flustered over the issue. She took in a deep breath and prepared for her brother-in-law to enter the room.

The door opened and she nearly jumped to her feet, but it was Lucas who stepped inside and shut it hastily behind him. He came striding across the deep green carpet of the formal parlor, reaching his hands out to her.

Reflexively, she raised her hands to his. The warmth of his grasp surprised her, as did the gentle way he brought her hands together to hold them securely.

"Virginia, you've turned white as wool. That will never do." He gently squeezed her hands and some of his warmth went up into her arms, then into her cheeks as a blush. "That's better. I have instructed Grisham to take his time showing Mr. Macon to this room. One of the benefits of an elderly butler is he can make a tortoise's pace look believable." He grinned at her, the boyish expression looking at home on his handsome face.

"I didn't wish to disturb you—" she started to explain but stopped speaking as he shook his head.

"You are my wife, Virginia. Your concerns are mine. I did say yesterday that *we* would inform Mr. Macon of all that has transpired, though one would hope he has realized by now you are under the protection of someone with influence."

He moved to stand by her side, retaining one of her hands in his, for which she was grateful. The contact kept her anchored and allowed her to feel his strength. Lucas wasn't an idle nobleman. She had felt it in the grasp of his hands, seen it in the way he carried himself, in the square set of his shoulders. She needed his strength at her side for what she guessed would occur.

Gerard Macon was an unpleasant man.

The doors to the sitting room opened and Gresham stepped inside, bowing slowly and formally. "My lord and my lady," he said with great slowness, voice ringing with more pomp than Virginia had heard from him thus far. "May I present Mr. Charles Macon, brother to the late Baron of Heatherton."

Virginia glanced at her husband in time to see him smooth away a smile of amusement. Clearly, Gresham knew his job well.

Mr. Macon entered, coming into the room the way a thundercloud rolled across a landscape, bringing darkness and a scowl with him. Virginia's heart picked up speed and she stood straighter.

Lucas gave her hand a final squeeze before releasing her and tucking his hands behind his back. Lucas's normally pleasant expression was gone, replaced by the cool and formal mask of a peer of the realm. She tried to follow his lead.

Mr. Macon bowed first and Lucas barely returned the gesture. Virginia's curtsy was given in equal measure to the earl's.

"I have heard a great deal about you, Mr. Macon," Lucas said before the other man could open his mouth. The statement sounded neither positive nor censuring. "What brings you to our part of the country?"

If Gerard Macon had only smiled once in a while, instead of making out that the whole world was against him, he would've resembled her late husband more. He had black hair, deep brown eyes, and a squared jaw. He might've even been considered handsome if she did not know the selfish tendencies of his heart.

"I have come to speak to my sister-in-law." He drew himself to his full height, which was still short of Lucas's by a few inches. "On family business."

"Excellent. Please, take a seat." Then Lucas looked down at her and gestured to the couch behind them. "My lady." And he sat with her.

Mr. Macon's eyes narrowed. "I am afraid it is private business, my lord."

"Family business, private business, both would involve me. Your sister-in-law, as you must've gathered by now, is my wife. If you wish to speak to her, do so now. Otherwise, you may take your leave." He said each word with complete authority, though his posture remained relaxed, as though he hadn't a care whether Gerard Macon spoke or not. He angled his body in Virginia's direction and smiled at her.

Virginia took a measure of courage from that smile. "What can I do for you, Mr. Macon?" She felt no need to be less formal in addressing him. She had rarely seen him when her husband was alive. Now that the family connection between them had been distanced, she felt no need to pretend any sort of familiarity with him.

Looking from her to the earl, Mr. Macon drew up taller in his seat. "I would like an explanation as to why a woman who has been a widow for a matter of weeks suddenly remarries. Have you no respect for my brother's memory?"

The question came nearer to hurting her than anything else he might've said. She had expected him to first speak on the matter of guardianship to her sons. Had he guessed the best way to wound her would be through her betrayal of Charles? It did hurt, knowing in the eyes of many her act would seem disrespectful when nothing could be further from the truth.

"I found it necessary," she said slowly, "to take my life into my hands and forgo the guidance of society in this matter." Virginia drew herself up, calling on a lifetime of training for putting people in their place, firmly beneath her. "I think you must understand why, though I feel no need to discuss my personal business with you on this matter."

"Charles is barely cold in his grave and you've already taken a new husband," Mr. Macon said, some heat in his words. "It is heartless."

"Have a care, Mr. Macon," Lucas said, his voice low, almost subdued. "Regardless of your relationship with Lady Calvert, she is my wife now, and I will not tolerate anyone speaking to her in an insulting manner."

Mr. Macon glared at the earl and then back to her. "You sent no word of your decision to remarry," he said next, bitterness in his voice. "I was informed of the matter by *strangers* not half an hour ago."

"The Gilberts are my family," she answered steadily. "And it is hardly needful for me to inform *you* of my doings, Mr. Macon."

His eyes narrowed still further, his hands gripped the arm rests of the chair tightly. "My nephews' future has yet to be determined. You secreted them from Bath, hid them away from me, and performed a shameful act in order to maintain your hold on the barony. I will not have it—"

Virginia stood, raising her chin defiantly, calling to mind every instance she could of her mother dressing down her victims. "How *dare* you presume to come into my home and speak to me in such a manner. We both know, Mr. Macon, you don't care for my sons. You care for nothing but money and power, trying to sink your claws into Charles's title and wealth. He would've shared with you freely during his life, if you but showed even a measure of brotherly kindness. But you are an unfeeling, cold-hearted man."

He stood as well, his hands gripped into fists at his side. "You are no better. You want the barony for yourself—"

She cut him off quickly. "I want it for my son. Phillip is the Baron of Heatherton and no one will endanger his title or inheritance while I am living. You forced my hand, Mr. Macon, when you tried to take my sons from me. You will never have them under your hateful influence."

Mr. Macon took one threatening step toward her, a foul word on his lips, but it did not escape. Before he could take a second step,

Lucas had risen and put himself between the two of them, his whole body bristling with power and purpose.

"Mr. Macon," he said, his deep voice like the growl of a tiger. "You will apologize to my wife for uttering such language in her presence and then you will leave. You have had your say. The matter is closed. Lady Calvert, as my wife, is above your reach. Her sons are now mine and under my protection. I think you will return to Bath to find your lawyer has been made aware of the situation, as have the courts, and your case against her dismissed."

Gerard Macon's eyes shone with hatred, his lips curled back in a snarl. "I'll not apologize for calling her what she is. Crawling into bed with an earl—"

Lucas's fist flew expertly into Mr. Macon's face, silencing his hateful stream of words.

Virginia covered her mouth with her hands, pushing back a scream. She'd never witnessed a physical altercation between gentlemen. Though her heart raced with the sudden burst of Lucas's energy, she remained frozen on the spot, unable to do more than watch in horrible fascination.

Mr. Macon staggered backward, falling into the chair. Silenced, at least for the moment, his shock apparent on his face. Virginia might've laughed had she not been preoccupied with her own surprise.

The doors to the sitting room flew open and three of the footmen came inside, their matched heights less important to Virginia than their broad shoulders. They took hold of Mr. Macon, who was half-growling in his anger, and dragged him from the room.

"You'll regret this, Virginia. You've made an enemy. I'll not let it go without a fight. I swear—"

Once he was in the hallway, Gresham reappeared, bowed and closed the door on the spiteful monologue. Virginia heard her former brother-in-law begin to shout a string of profanities.

Going cold all over, she moved in the direction of the door. "The boys—"

"—are in the kitchen enjoying biscuits." Lucas's hands settled on her shoulders, then gently turned her around. "I'm sorry, Virginia. I thought he might cause a scene, which is why I asked the men to stand by, but I hoped for better."

Virginia shook her head. "He's always been a bitter, cold man. I've never seen him that angry before, though." She shuddered. "He must've been sure of winning his case, of getting the boys and control of the estate."

"He must've. But there's no need to worry further about it. He will be sent on his way and I have a groom ready to follow him, until he leaves the county." He dropped his hands from her shoulders and tilted his head to one side, regarding her with a gentle look in his eye. "Virginia, you've done the right thing. That man should never come near you or your sons again. You've saved your boys from falling under his influence."

She forced a laugh, humorless though it was, and raised a hand to her temple. "You have to say that, you know, since it is by marrying you that I've done such a thing."

He shrugged and tugged at the lapels of his coat in a self-important way. "My dear lady, I will take my share of the credit. It is chivalrous, you know, to save a lady in distress. But I am very certain that you will be the hero of this story when your sons are grown and understand all you have done for them."

Is that how he saw her? She hardly felt heroic after the scene with Mr. Macon. It was, after all, Lucas and a trio of footman who had removed his latest threat.

That reminded her.

"How is your hand?" Virginia asked, reaching out to take it up, examining his knuckles.

Lucas chuckled and pulled it away before she saw more than the reddened skin around the joints. "No lasting damage done. It may bruise, but that is hardly of consequence." He offered her his other arm. "My lady, I believe you agreed to accompany me on a tour of the grounds today. Does that still suit you?"

Her nerves would likely do better if she took a nap, but her mind and heart were spinning under Mr. Macon's cruel words and his unreasonably antagonistic behavior. She would rather not give herself an opportunity to think on it.

"That suits me splendidly. Thank you." Though Lucas didn't seem to wish for her gratitude, Virginia could not help but feel it in her heart. She'd allied herself with a man willing and ready to defend her and her sons. That made what anyone might think of her hasty marriage of little importance.

Chapter Eleven

hree days had passed since his ride with Virginia, and the unfortunate business with her brother-in-law. Lucas walked slowly down the second-floor corridor, trying not to dwell on either event. He found his mind kept going to both. Mr. Macon's wild-eyed accusations, while he'd brushed off as meaningless, nevertheless disturbed him. Lucas didn't trust a man who would treat a woman, any woman, with disrespect and disdain.

Virginia's trembling hands had been evidence enough of her feelings about the man. He had thought her strong, resolute, and unshakable when he married her. But after seeing her face her brother-in-law's accusations, he added brave to the list.

His countess was quite the woman.

Lucas paused, hearing a series of light taps echoing against the walls. He cocked his head to the side, trying to determine where the sound came from.

He went to the music room and saw the door open. Lucas peered inside without moving it and there stood two little boys. Phillip's ear was pressed to the wall and Edward tapped against it with a small wooden ball.

"It doesn't sound any different," Phillip said. "Let's go over to the other one again and make sure."

Edward started to nod when he spied Lucas and immediately straightened, tucking the ball behind his back.

Lucas raised his eyebrows and pushed the door open wider. Phillip turned and his expression changed rapidly from surprised to belligerent. He crossed his arms over his chest and stepped in front of his brother.

"We were looking for the passage. You said we could." It sounded more like an accusation than anything else.

This is going to take a great deal of work. Lucas shook his head and did his best to look non-threatening. He smiled and tucked his hands behind his back.

"I did say that. No luck yet? Would you like another hint?"

"Yes," Edward blurted, peeking around Phillip's shoulder. "Please."

Phillip's eyebrows lowered still further.

Although he was on the verge of telling them which room to look in, Lucas stopped as another idea occurred to him. The boys had been kept mostly out of his way, in the nursery or outside playing, while their mother learned the ways of the house and became familiar with the servants. Had she spent much time with them? Lucas only saw her at meals. It was best, he knew, that he allow her whatever privacy she wished for, but rarely seeing another soul about the house had hardly done much to improve his feeling of being alone.

"I would be happy to share such a hint, but what will you trade for it?"

Edward's dark eyes turned at once to his elder brother. "What can we trade, Phillip?"

Phillip's gaze went from Lucas to Edward, then down to the ground. His jaw worked as he thought, but after a moment he started to shake his head. "Not much. He's an earl. He's got everything."

Lucas hummed thoughtfully, turning away from the boys to pace toward the window. "I don't have precisely everything." He watched from the corner of his eye as the boys exchanged looks. Edward appeared hopeful and Phillip doubtful.

"You two may have noticed it has been raining a great deal this spring?"

They both nodded.

"This has made more streams than you can count, flowing all down to the lake. I find myself wondering how fast those streams go. I think, perhaps the best way to time them would be to put paper boats in the water. What do you two think of that?"

"Phillip knows how to make paper boats," Edward said, his little voice soft. "Don't you, Phillip?"

Phillip started to nod, but then froze. "Don't you know how to make a paper boat?"

"*My lord,*" Edward reminded him with a whispered hiss.

"My lord." Phillip narrowed his eyes.

"It has been several years since I have done so. I'm afraid my technique might not be what it once was." Lucas issued a melancholy sigh, which might've been overly dramatic, but it seemed to press his case.

"Come on, Phillip. Will you make a paper boat? Please? I want to find the passage."

Phillip took in Lucas once more before nodding. "All right. If I make you a boat, will you give us another hint, my lord?" His eyes turned to his brother as he spoke the title.

"You must help me test the boat, too. And you had better make at least two boats, so there is a spare."

The put-upon boy dropped his hands to his side and nodded. Edward's grin nearly split his face in two.

"Excellent." Lucas clapped his hands together, allowing his smile to widen. "Then let us go to my study. I have all sorts of different papers and we must find the best for the job."

The boys started forward cautiously but by the time they made it down the stairs, Edward was chattering happily about the last time they'd had boat races and how his had won half them. Phillip said nothing, though his expression had softened from belligerent to accepting of the situation.

When they arrived at the study, Lucas opened drawers in his desk and brought forth stacks of every sort of paper he owned. There were thicker sheets meant for cutting cards, more expensive linen, a very few vellum, and the paper he used for more informal correspondence.

Phillip lifted each by turn. "Too heavy. This one won't bend." He gave judgement on each and at last decided on the middle-weight correspondence paper. He took two sheets and asked for scissors, which Lucas promptly provided.

The boy went to the floor and plopped down upon it, directly in front of the hearth where a fire was crackling cheerfully. Edward was staring at the stacks of paper with fascination.

"Do you like to draw?" Lucas asked, lifting a sheet and holding it out to the boy.

Edward stared at the sheet, his dark brown eyes round and hopeful. But he looked up at Lucas and shrugged. "I'm not very good."

"Nonsense." Lucas picked up a pencil from the top of his desk and held it out as well. "Draw whatever you like and then let me tell you how well you do."

Edward chewed on his bottom lip but his little hands accepted the paper and pencil. He looked around the room, but before he could join his brother on the floor, Lucas gave the top of the desk a pat.

"Sit in my chair and draw here. A proper desk is needed for a proper drawing."

His eyes widened and his posture straightened. "Your desk, my lord?"

Lucas nodded gravely. "I insist, Edward."

The boy's legs propelled him around the furniture rapidly and he slapped his paper onto the surface before turning to climb into the chair. Lucas moved the chair closer to the desk for him. He lifted his pencil and put it to paper without another word, though his tongue stuck outside the corner of his mouth as he fiercely concentrated on the lines he made.

Resisting a chuckle, Lucas went to see how Phillip was getting on. He'd trimmed his paper and had begun making folds, turning the sheet into something resembling a raft.

Knowing his valet would not thank him for it, Lucas sat down on the floor across from the boy anyway, mimicking the lad's way of sitting with his legs crossed beneath each other. "That looks like a fine boat."

"Not yet." Phillip sighed and created another fold, moving inward.

Lucas let a few quiet moments pass, glancing over to be sure Edward was still enjoying himself with his drawing. The boy looked completely engrossed in his work. A thought came to Lucas and he bent forward, lowering his voice.

"If Edward's paper boat beat yours in a race, why doesn't he know how to make one?"

Phillip's hands slowed, his fingers pressing a fold together tightened. "Papa made Edward's boat." Phillip didn't look up, but his fingers started moving again. "He taught me, though. Mine aren't bad."

"I should say not," Lucas said, his tone softer. Had he made a mistake? The boats might only hurt his chances of a good relationship with Phillip more. But the boy did not seem angry any longer. "And you must remember, I am woefully out of practice myself, so I am appreciative."

Phillip offered him a sideways look. "You don't really need a boat, do you?"

"I make studies of the weather, of my property. I have been contemplating hiring someone to come out and survey the land," Lucas answered carefully, and honestly.

"Survey the land?" Phillip asked, focusing again on his work. "What does that mean? My lord?"

"I would have someone who is a mathematician, of sorts, come visit. He would bring special tools and equipment, and with his things he could measure our hills and streams, the dips in the land, and then give me his calculations. I could use the information he gives me as I plan land improvements, and he could use the information to make maps that would tell others about the land in this part of Kettering."

Phillip glanced up. "What good does that do anyone?"

"It helps with planning things, like roads or buildings. It informs people of what the area is like. It can even help with planting certain types of crops. If you know the elevation of a hill, you know what you could plant there that might not get washed away by rain. There are many useful applications."

Phillip started to nod, his eyes taking on a faraway look. "Should I do that to Heatherton Hall, do you think? My lord?"

It was the first time he had asked Lucas's opinion on anything or spoken to him without suspicion or resentment. The question held weight for more than that reason. The child was thinking of his new responsibilities as baron. What six-year-old should ever carry such a burden?

Lucas's heart softened. He'd been lost after his father's death. It had taken some time, even with twenty-two years of training under the earl, for him to understand the running of things.

He had to answer as one landowner to another. Phillip did not trust him enough for anything more personal, though Lucas hoped he would one day. "In time, when you are ready to make improvements upon the land. If you would like, I will discuss the results of my surveyor with you to better inform your decision."

Phillip nodded, meeting Lucas's eyes. "Thank you, my lord."

The boat was finished and the boy held it out.

Lucas held it up, examining it in the firelight. He turned it one way and then the other. The lines were good. "A sea-worthy vessel, I should think. As you make the spare, you must tell me exactly how you go about it."

The tiniest of smiles twitched Phillip's lips upward before he bent his head and went to work on the next boat.

His heart ached for the child. He would continue to study Phillip and one day, if he was lucky, they would be friends.

¤

"My lady? Oh, thank goodness I've found you." Nurse Smythe, her graying curls hanging in frazzled clumps outside of her bonnet, was nearly panting as she spoke.

Virginia turned from her task in the still room, instantly alert. "Nurse Smythe? Is something wrong with the boys?"

The woman's eyes were worried and her brows drew together. "There's something wrong with *me*. I fell asleep, my lady, while they were playing quietly. When I woke up, they were gone. I have looked all over the top floor, and first, and the ground. I asked the upstairs maids to look and not a one of us has found sign of them. I was on my way to find you or his lordship. I hoped they would be with you."

Virginia shook her head and bit back the reprimand that sprung to her tongue. It was hardly Nurse Smythe's fault the children had gone wandering off. It was the first time anything of the sort had happened, and Nurse had been with them for years. The boys were likely somewhere inside the house, safe.

"Inform Gresham and Mrs. Hail. We will look until they are found, though it is nearly their supper time, so they ought to come looking to fill their stomachs soon. I will find his lordship to see if he has any idea where they might be."

Perhaps they found the secret passage he told them of?

They could be playing quietly somewhere just out of sight, though if they'd heard people calling for them she thought they would come out. Her boys had never been willfully disobedient before. But Phillip had been acting less like himself of late.

Virginia went directly to Lucas's study, kicking up her skirts as she went. Though she didn't run, as a lady *never* did, Virginia moved at a rapid pace. She knocked on Lucas's door smartly and waited. When no answer came, she knocked once more before opening the door and peeking in. She had only glimpsed his domain once, during the initial tour of the house.

His study was different from what she expected. The curtains were thrown wide, revealing tall, broad windows overlooking the front lawn and drive. The furniture was upholstered in rich red, cream, and gold patterned fabric, and his desk was dark, burnished walnut wood. He had shelves full of ledgers, and an enormous marble fireplace took up half a wall.

The room lacked one important thing, though. The earl was not within.

Virginia bit her bottom lip and stood, thinking of where else she might find her husband. She went to the bell pull in the room and gave it a tug.

Scant minutes later, a footman appeared.

"My lady?" He didn't even appear surprised to see her there.

"Good afternoon. I am sorry, your name—?"

"Dorval, my lady."

"Dorval. Do you happen to know if his lordship had any appointments this afternoon? I thought to find him here, but I may be mistaken in his schedule."

"He went out a quarter of an hour ago, my lady, with Lord Heatherton and Master Edward." His face remained straight and proper, but the man's eyes smiled. "They took paper boats with them, my lady."

"Paper boats? Thank you, Dorval. That will be all." He bowed and left the room, but Virginia lingered. She went to the window, noting the world outside remained as gray in the afternoon as it had been that morning. What natural light came in was not bright. The rain had been unseasonably cold when it came, their days of sunshine were few, and none of the winter things had been entirely packed away yet. Had the boys remembered their coats before going out?

She turned her back on the window, to leave the room, when a rumble of thunder sounded in the distance.

Chapter Twelve

The boys shrieked with pleasure, the cold rain pelting down on top their heads. Lucas laughed with them as they ran up the hill to the house, all getting a good soaking despite their coats. Edward toppled, halfway to the house from the stream where they'd successfully tested the boats, and landed in a muddy patch of earth.

Phillip stopped running and turned to help his brother. Lucas hurried forward too, reaching down to take Edward's arm. The boy looked up at him, his face covered in mud, and in an instant they were all laughing again.

Edward wiped his soiled face with an equally filthy hand, managing to smear everything around even more. Phillip howled with laughter.

"Let me help." Lucas reached his now-muddy hand into his jacket and drew out a handkerchief, but Edward bent out of reach to scoop up a handful of muck.

Before Lucas could halt the action, Edward lobbed the mud at his brother.

It took him some time to get them both moving to the house again, and they were in a considerably filthy state. No matter. He would take them in through the back. The servants could fetch towels and as soon as they all stopped dripping they could go to their rooms for baths. The boys were in good spirits, and that's what counted the most.

Edward sneezed.

I should see to it they both take lemon and honey. Lucas had a vague recollection of his nurse giving him a steaming, sweet concoction after being out in a cold rain. He felt certain the cook, Mrs. Grady, would know precisely what was called for.

They came to the servants' entrance at the rear of the house, the rain still falling. Lucas pushed the door open and stepped inside, immediately enveloped by the warmth of the kitchens.

"Pardon me," he said to the maids who froze in their work. "Could we have some towels fetched?"

Two maids left the room and the cook started giving orders. Kitchen towels were brought to them, a scullery maid went to work on Edward's face and Phillip saw to himself. Downstairs maids rushed forward with flapping skirts and the boys disappeared beneath feminine ministrations. Lucas took a step back from them, but his shoe hit a puddle.

Lucas barely registered the slip before he found himself on the kitchen floor, staring up at the ceiling, his backside and head throbbing from impact.

The room went silent. Lucas groaned and closed his eyes.

He heard a footstep coming across the floor toward him, slowly and deliberately.

"Mary," a calm, soft soprano voice said. "Please take the boys up to the nursery. Use the servants' stair, please."

Perhaps his fall was not the reason for such a dramatic silence.

"Yes, my lady."

Lucas opened his eyes, meeting the gray skirts of his wife before letting his gaze creep upward. Her hands were clasped before her and her chin tilted down. Her green eyes glared at him, snapping like a crackling fire.

Why was she upset? A little mud never hurt anything. Weren't boys expected to be muddied once in a while?

"My lady," he said, still not moving. His head had begun to throb. "Good afternoon."

"My lord." Her mouth stayed set in a firm line turning down at the corners. "Might I have a word with you in private?"

He supposed he ought to move, but he had the feeling the room would spin the moment he was upon his feet.

"Of course, my lady." He pushed himself into a sitting position and the world vibrated with the throb in his head. Lucas tried not to groan as he drew his legs beneath him and pushed upward, rising to his full height. The kitchen tilted but with a deep breath he was able to right it again. "Would the greenhouse suffice? I am still dripping, I'm afraid."

Virginia turned to a maid and held her arms out, accepting a stack of towels from the girl. "It will do, my lord." She turned and swept down the hall. Lucas followed, eyes on his wife's rigid shoulders.

What had he done wrong? Her displeasure with him was obvious. All the staff would soon be humming with speculation on the subject of the conversation about to take place.

They walked through one marble-floored hallway to reach the door leading out to the expansive greenhouse. Virginia pushed the door open and stood aside, waiting for him to enter before closing it behind them. The humidity of the greenhouse, though not as warm as the kitchen, kept him from shivering.

Virginia took a towel from the top of her stack and offered it to him.

"Thank you." He started drying his hair, moving carefully around the giant bump forming on the back of his skull. He watched her, trying to decide exactly what she was thinking. "You wished to say something to me?" he prompted when she continued to stare at him, her face unreadable.

"Nurse Smythe came to me in a terrible state," she said, her tone even, her eyebrows raised. "Half the staff had already been searching the house for the boys before she found me. Then I went looking for you after the other half was alerted."

Lucas's hand stilled, the towel pressed against his neck. "Searching for the—? We weren't gone very long."

She took in a deep breath and closed her eyes. Lucas had the feeling she was attempting to hold her emotions in check, but why she was so distraught—

"My lord, no one knew where the children were. They left the nursery without permission. As they are quite young, and in a new home, and the grounds are expansive, the worst was suspected."

That explanation made a great deal of sense. He brought the towel down and held it in both hands, meeting her eyes squarely. "I didn't know they weren't supposed to be out of the nursery. I found them exploring the house."

"And then you took them out of the house," she added, turning to drop the towels on a convenient bench. "Without telling anyone."

He usually did as he pleased without telling anyone.

As she straightened again, her eyes still spitting fire, it occurred to Lucas for the first time that having a family meant more than giving them general security. The rules had changed, even for him.

Virginia narrowed her eyes at him. He had the feeling she disapproved of every aspect of his being at the moment. Did all women have the ability to project such exasperation, or was it a trait singular to mothers?

"You ought to take off your jacket. You are going to catch your death of cold."

He looked down at the sopping, dripping material and sighed. The coat he'd left in the servants' hall, but the jacket had suffered as well. He began to undo its buttons as he spoke. "I did not think taking the boys down to the stream and back would cause such a panic. We truly were gone only half an hour."

"Half an hour is more than ample time for a person to worry," she said, a trifle waspishly. "And by the time I realized the boys must be with you, it was raining."

"You cannot hold that against me." He slipped the jacket from his shoulders and tossed it onto the bench next to the towels. "We were in the middle of testing our boats, and it wasn't a very cold rain. You should've seen them—"

"Edward suffers from croup." The words snapped from her like a whip. "He's had two bouts since winter. The weather brings it on, and then he cannot sleep for the coughing." She picked up another towel and nearly threw it at him, her movements jerky and fast, but he caught it. "His throat is nearly torn to pieces."

Croup. That was no small thing. Severe cases turned into worse infections.

"I'm sorry. I did not know." What more could he say? The woman before him looked torn between anger and, he finally realized, fear. "It was thoughtlessly done." He twisted the towel in his hands, uncertain what he ought to say or do.

Virginia raised her hands to her forehead, smoothing back her hair, then came forward to take the towel. He relinquished it to her, expecting she would storm away, perhaps. But instead she raised the cloth up to his face and wiped at his cheek, her eyes not on his.

"It is difficult to talk to a grown man when he's covered in mud," she muttered, scrubbing at whatever splotch must be on his face.

To Lucas's further surprise, having her stand near him, even in the midst of her upset, caused an unlooked-for reaction. Every hair on his body stood on end, his heartbeat sounded loudly in his ears, and when he drew in a breath the air held the most heavenly scent. What was it? Some sort of fruit? Oranges. She smelled like oranges, bright and fresh. It must've been perfume. They had no oranges at Annesbury Park.

They should consider getting some.

She stepped back and examined him with a critical eye. Hastily he composed his expression to one that would not reveal his strange awareness of her.

"Better." Virginia tossed the towel aside. "I understand we are not used to each other," she said at last. "But I would ask that in future you please inform myself or Nurse Smythe if you plan an excursion with the boys. It will save us a great deal of anxiety."

"What can be done about the croup?" That seemed to him the next logical thing to address, and hopefully it would take his mind off of the alluring scent of the woman berating him. "Should I send for the apothecary?"

Virginia shook her head. "No. I know what to do. Thank you." She didn't sound pleased about it. "I had better see to the boys and make certain they are behaving for Nurse."

Lucas stepped forward, not certain what to say but wanting to stop her from leaving. "How did they escape her? They were with me for some time before we went out. She never came looking." She must be concerned about the lack of attention to them, mustn't she?

His wife stilled and did not turn around when she answered. "Nurse Smythe fell asleep. The last several days have been taxing on her."

He frowned. He had provided the nurse with a maid to care for the nursery and assist with the boys. Of course, most nursery maids were young girls, usually no older than sixteen. "Have they? Are the boys giving her trouble?"

She turned at that, her eyebrows raised. "Of course not. She is only a little tired—it is all the change, I think." He didn't miss the defensive note in her voice.

Curious, Lucas prodded further. "Change is generally considered to be difficult on older people. She is getting on in years, I believe." The woman had to have been around fifty. It wasn't ancient, but it was a good deal older than any nurse he had met.

Virginia drew herself up to her full height, which would've been impressive if he still didn't have her bested by a head. "Nurse Smythe has been with the family since my husband—" She stopped and swallowed, lowering her eyes though her chin stayed at a stubborn tilt. "Excuse me. Since my late husband was a boy. She is a loyal servant and adores my children."

Her husband Charles Macon. The man for whom she still mourned. He had to remember, no matter how wonderful she smelled, how enchanting he found her, she did not truly belong to him nor did she seem to think of him as her husband. It was part of their agreement, after all.

Lucas crossed his arms and raised his eyebrows at her. "I didn't say anything against her. Only what is generally observed in people of a certain age. If she has been with the family so long, perhaps it is time to consider a pension. The boys are nearing an age for a governess, aren't they? Or a tutor?"

Her lips parted in surprise, but then her shoulders went back and she continued in her servant's defense. "It was one little mistake, compounded by *your* thoughtlessness." Her voice was raised, but it was not quite shouting.

His ire rose to meet hers. "And I apologized for that. It will not happen again. But perhaps while we are discussing thoughtlessness, whether it is mine or the nurse's, we should also address yours."

Her body stiffened. "Mine? What on earth have I done?"

"Your display before the staff was not appreciated." Indeed, and he hadn't intended to mention it at all. But he couldn't keep himself from drawing her attention to it. "You spoke to me as if I was one of your children, due for a scolding. While I appreciate you waited to berate me in private, I would ask that you refrain from showing such marked disdain for my actions when we are in front of the servants. The new countess need not be seen brow-beating their lord in public." There. He felt better for saying it.

For all of half a second.

Virginia's eyes went wide and her face turned pale. "Yes, my lord." She gave him the slightest curtsy before turning and fleeing the room, gray skirts swishing behind her.

That hadn't been the reaction he'd expected.

What had he done wrong now?

Chapter Thirteen

In the early days of her first marriage, Virginia had been astounded at how often she and Charles disagreed. They had loved each other, after all, and didn't that mean they ought to have gotten along? Her response, at first, had been to storm away, and keep away for hours, until he either came to apologize or she had calmed sufficiently to seek him out again.

Charles had been the most patient man alive, she felt certain, and was certainly a better person than any man of her acquaintance.

But she had never *fled* an argument, the way she fled from Lucas. Because she knew Charles loved her. Even at her most immature moments, when her arguments had been akin to a child's tantrum, Charles had loved her. He would never treat her cruelly or use his position as her husband to exert his will upon her.

She blushed, remembering the child she'd been when she'd first married. How had Charles loved her, given her abominable family and their influence? Her father, the fifth Earl of Vinespar, was an indulgent man to both himself and his offspring. Her elder brother, now the sixth Earl of Vinespar, had grown into a selfish and entitled fool because of it. Her mother was cold and distant, with hardly a kind word to say to anyone of lesser rank than herself.

Virginia slowed her steps, having attained the gallery floor. She needed to calm herself before checking on her sons. Though the house grew darker with the storm and evening's approach, she could still see enough to pretend to study the paintings.

Her eyes didn't really see them. But the exercise gave her time to settle her thoughts.

If she were honest, without a handful of kind people in her life, she likely would've been more like her rather unpleasant family. She'd had a thoughtful governess who tempered her. She'd spent time with her cousins, Julia and Christine, for weeks at a time before her first season in London. Their mother had been alive then, and even a self-centered child could see how much she was adored by all who knew her. Her Aunt Devon had been kindness itself.

When Charles met her, she hadn't been entirely spoiled. Somehow, he'd seen her good qualities and had loved her for them.

Wrapping her arms around herself, holding his memory close, Virginia continued down the gallery, her eyes only skimming across the portraits of the earl's ancestors.

Having experienced little affection as a child, Virginia had been astounded to recognize her feelings for the young Charles Macon as love. When he proposed to her, she had thought it as wonderful as a fairy tale ending. They would live happily to the end of their days.

Their first argument had startled that notion from her mind. It made her smile now. She couldn't even remember what they had disagreed about and she had felt certain, at the time, that she had been tricked. Her marriage would go the way of her parents', they would end as polite but indifferent acquaintances after years of bitter exchanges.

Then Charles had sought her out and apologized.

Had anyone ever apologized to her before? Had she ever heard her parents admit to wrong-doing or wrong-feeling before? No. Never. At first, she had thought him insincere. But as their marriage progressed, as she fought against his opinions or decisions, almost testing his resolve, Charles was always quick to make peace between them again.

She paused, her eyes coming back into focus as she thought she glimpsed a familiar face. Yes, there he was, her new husband. Lucas looked nearly ten years younger on the canvas before her, but it was him. His hair was more golden, his smile self-assured, and he was holding hands with the woman at his side. His first countess.

Virginia studied the young woman in the painting, taking note of her delicate structure, her petite frame. She must've been eighteen or nineteen, and she had been beautiful. The artist had captured the youthful glow of her skin and a sparkle in her eye that promised laughter and love for the man at her side.

What had the young Lady Abigail Calvert been like? Had her husband treated her with kindness and love? Or had he exerted his authority over a more submissive spirit?

"That's unfair."

It was Charles's voice in her mind, the memory of him gently reproving her when she made too quick a judgment upon one of their neighbors. He had always steered her toward mercy and compassion when she would've naturally deemed a person lesser than herself.

Am I being unfair? Her eyes went back to the young man in the painting.

Lucas hadn't really said anything terrible to her. And she had been speaking to him without the common respect she ought to show her husband, or any person she cared for. He had accused her of berating and scolding him like a child.

The argument against him rose up in her mind. He had taken her children out of the house without telling anyone, possibly endangering Edward, and then acted as though it was Nurse Smythe's fault. Or had he?

It hadn't helped the matter, of course, when she'd become flustered in his presence. But he'd been dripping wet and nearly as muddied as the children, with smears of earth across his cheek and on his knees. What had they done? Rolled in a mire?

Her lips twitched at that thought. Truly, it had been distracting and amusing to try and converse with a peer who had a wide streak of mud across his jaw. So, she'd been a daft fool and stepped forward to clean it off herself when it was obvious he'd taken no notice of it.

Stepping close to him, being near a man of his looks and charm, had startled dormant feelings from her, reminding her just how lonely she had been.

Her husband had only been gone three and a half months.

Virginia shook her head in disgust. What sort of woman was she to admire another when she still had nearly a year of mourning ahead of her?

The gallery no longer held any interest or peace for her. She turned and went down the hall, at a rapid pace, making for the stairs. It was time to see to her sons.

¤

Virginia applied the poultice to Edward's chest, listening to him cough painfully, the sound almost like a bark. His throat already ached and his chest jerked painfully with each wave of coughs. When he'd calmed, tears in his eyes, she held a cup of willow-bark tea and honey for him to sip.

Nurse Smythe sat near the door, her eyes tired and her shoulders drooping. Virginia had tried to send the woman to bed. They had already moved Phillip to a guest chamber downstairs, the new nursery maid with him, so he wouldn't be disturbed by his brother's coughing. The coughing was enough to keep Phillip awake, but it also distressed the older boy. Virginia could well imagine why. His father's

114

consumption had first manifested itself in excessive coughing. But Nurse Smythe stayed, a look of guilt in her eyes.

"If I'd not nodded off, I could've told his lordship how Master Edward is," she had said plaintively. "Or they'd never've gone outside to begin with."

"It is not your fault," Virginia had soothed. "It isn't anyone's fault."

But if she had the earl before her, she might very well say something she would have to apologize for later. Edward's body was not very strong. He was only four years old. Croup shook him to his very core and the lack of sleep made him miserable for days. In the past, once they calmed the cough enough for him to sleep, he could be restful for hours only to start up again, just before the dawn.

Edward put his hand against the cup and pushed it away. "I don't like it. It tastes like mud—" He started coughing again.

"You didn't mind the taste of mud earlier today," Virginia reminded him, forcing a smile. "You had it all over your face and I'm quite certain you swallowed at least a teacupful."

His little face scowled up at her, his brown eyes flashing. Her heart gave a little jerk when she realized how much he resembled his father. Of course, Edward's stubbornness came entirely from her.

"It tastes like grass mixed with mud," he said firmly. Then he was coughing again, his shoulders shaking. His throat sounded ragged already.

"Sounds like a truly miserable concoction."

Virginia's body stiffened and she closed her eyes. What was he doing up in the nursery? She looked over her shoulder to see Lucas standing in the doorway, his clothing in some disarray as though it had been donned hastily. No self-respecting valet would've allowed his lord to look like that.

Edward shifted and when Virginia turned to admonish him to sit still, she saw that his whole face had brightened. Even his sleepy eyes suddenly appeared more awake.

"It is miserable. And I shan't drink it." Then he turned and coughed into his shoulder.

Sighing, Virginia lowed the cup in her hands.

Lucas approached the bed and knelt beside it, at her knee, his eyes only on Edward. "That's a shame. I imagine it's supposed to be good for you."

Edward's bottom lip went out. "I don't like it."

"That's usually how we feel about things that are good for us. I myself have a very difficult time with mustard plasters."

What was this line of conversation supposed to achieve? Virginia very nearly opened her mouth to ask, but Edward began to lift up his shirt. "I have a poultice. It smells good, though." Virginia had added just a few drops of rose oil to the herbal treatment, thinking she rather detested its scents herself.

"I see. And what is the poultice supposed to do for you?" The earl's tired eyes shot very briefly to Virginia's before going back to Edward.

Edward began to explain. "Doctor Hastings, he's Cousin Nathaniel now, but he said it would help if my chest was warm. It's warm, it keeps the cough from wanting to come out so much. But what really hurts is my—" A cough interrupted him, escaping in another raspy bark.

"Your what?" the earl asked when Edward finished, as though not at all disgusted by the horrible sound.

"My throat. It hurts. And I'm tired." Edward's shoulders slumped and he leaned back against his pillows again.

"I see. What is the tea supposed to do?"

Edward dropped his eyes and looked down at his hands, grasping at the wrinkles in his blanket. Then he looked from Lucas to Virginia.

"It's s'posed to help my throat."

"Ah." Lucas began to nod and reached out to give Edward's legs beneath the blanket a pat. "Then hadn't you better drink it? It seems your mother is trying to help, not poison you with mud-water."

"Mud and grass," Edward muttered, his eyebrows furrowing. But he held his hands out to his mother, reaching for the teacup.

Virginia held the cup with him, helping him to steady it, and did her very best not to look at the earl. Would he appear triumphant? Smug? How did he know just what to say to make her sons cooperate and *why* was she lacking the intuition to do the same? Although relieved that Edward drank the tea, with no more protest than a wrinkled nose, she felt defeated.

"Thank you, Mama," her son whispered, handing her back the cup. He curled up on his pillow and coughed into his fist one more time. But he closed his eyes. "Can I have the sachet?"

Nurse Smythe bustled forward and Virginia moved out of the way so she could tuck a little pouch of dried lavender beneath the boy's pillow. "I can watch him now, my lady," Nurse Smythe said, her eyes softer. "I can come and get you if he worsens."

Lucas pushed himself up from the ground and then his hand appeared before her, offering to lift her from her place on the bed. She bent first to kiss Edward on the forehead, then took Lucas's hand.

"Good night, darling," she said to her son.

"Good night, Mama. Good night, my lord."

"Good night, Edward. I hope you sleep better now." Lucas took her from the room, lifting a candle he must've put on the table when he entered.

A clock chimed the hour from somewhere downstairs. It had to be midnight.

When Lucas closed the nursery door behind them, Virginia could hold her words in no longer. But she didn't wish to offer a rebuke.

"I'm sorry."

He turned, lifting the candle. The light illuminated his face, showing her the confused tilt of his eyebrows and the frown on his face. "You're sorry? Whatever for?"

She closed her eyes, willing the right words to come forward. It would be easier to admit her wrong-doing without looking at him. She was, after all, terribly out of practice at making apologies.

"I am sorry for this evening, when I spoke without regard of who was listening or how my tone must sound. While I do not wish to make excuses, I would like you to understand. I have a great deal of respect for your position. I will forever be grateful for your offer of marriage. But a mother's heart is often fierce in its expressions of feeling, whether good or bad. I let my worry for the boys get the better of me. I'll do my best not to let it happen again. And I—"

"Virginia." He spoke at the same instant his hand touched her shoulder and her eyes popped open, meeting his. In the dark hall, with only a small flame to give light, his eyes were a dark shade of gray that reminded her of storm clouds. But they were gentle, not fierce. "I must apologize as well. I spoke critically and defensively. I am sorry for that. It will take me time to get used to being a father. I don't have the years of knowledge and practice that you do. Please forgive me for upsetting the household and worrying you."

She stared up at him, her body gradually relaxing when she realized his sincerity in speaking. "Thank you. If you will be patient with me, I will be the same with you."

"That's a fine pact, I think." One corner of his mouth turned upward. "But come, it's late. We had better make certain Phillip has gone to sleep."

She walked next to him down the hallway. After a few steps, Virginia remembered she only wore a robe over her nightgown. She hastily tightened the sash at her waist and folded her arms over her chest.

"Phillip?" she asked.

Lucas nodded and she saw him glance at her from the corner of his eyes. "He woke me—or rather, he insisted that I be woken. I must've barely fallen asleep when a knock at my door brought me out of it. When I threw it open, expecting the house must be on fire from the urgency of the knock, Phillip and the nursery maid stood there."

"Oh, dear." Virginia winced and lowered her eyes to the floor. "I apologize. I'm afraid Edward's cough disturbs him."

"He said he was worried it might be more than croup." Lucas paused and looked down at her, holding the candle between them. She met his eyes again and saw in them a deep concern and compassion she had not expected. Why was he not irritated at the way they had disturbed his whole life and turned it upside-down? After their interaction in the greenhouse, she'd expected less understanding and more censure.

Obviously, she didn't know him very well yet.

"Your husband died of consumption?"

Virginia did not miss the way he referred to Charles. Not her late husband. Not her first husband. Just her husband. She felt a burning sensation just behind her eyes. She must be more tired than she thought.

"Yes. And he coughed a great deal." She didn't close her eyes now. If she did, she would see Charles's face as it had looked at the end. Pale, gaunt, not at all like the vibrant, handsome man she'd married. She didn't like remembering him that way.

"I see. Phillip wouldn't do well with coughing then. Is that why you sent him downstairs, instead of to one of the spare rooms on this floor?" He gestured to the doors behind them, across from the nursery.

Virginia nodded. "He doesn't sleep at all, even after Edward falls asleep. I didn't realize it until last time, just a few weeks before we met. But he sat up all night, listening. I thought moving him downstairs would let him sleep." Her voice broke on the last word and she raised a hand to cover her mouth, preventing a sob from escaping.

Why was she crying? She was too tired to cry. She had cried too much in the months before her husband's death, in the days and weeks after. She had told herself she couldn't cry anymore, that she had to be strong and firm.

But now that she'd started, she couldn't seem to stop.

She lifted her other hand to cover the first, as though she could stuff the sobs back into her throat. But they came and all she could do was try to keep them quiet, try to keep anyone from hearing. Meeting Lucas's eyes, knowing he must think her insane or ridiculous, she tried to apologize with hers. But it was too much.

Lucas's eyes had gone wide and he turned from her.

She didn't blame him. She must be a frightful sight—

His arms came around her and cradled her against his chest. She looked over his shoulder. He had only turned to put the candle down on a shelf behind them.

And he held her.

No one had held her since before her husband died. Her cousins had given her a gentle embrace now and again, but it was nothing like this. Nothing like being cradled close, nothing like being enveloped in a comforting, strong embrace meant to hold her together as much as it was meant to shield her.

Virginia dropped her face against his shoulder and cried the harder for his kindness. After the way she spoke to him, judged him, she didn't deserve his sympathy.

Her tears went from being akin to a watering pot to an all-out thunderstorm, rivaling the downpour from that very afternoon. Again and again she tried to stop, tried to get hold of herself, but then she would feel the arms around her tighten and it would begin anew.

Why were there always more tears? Why hadn't she left them behind her in Bath when she made her escape from Mr. Macon? Why hadn't she left them at Christine's home when she came to this one as a wife?

After a time, her sobs quieted, but she didn't move. She couldn't. She became aware of Lucas speaking. How long had he been talking? She listened, feeling the rumble of his deep voice in his chest.

"Cry as much as you need to," he was saying, his voice gentle, barely audible. "I am here. I understand. It hurts, but it will heal. Crying is only part of that healing."

Virginia lifted her head from his shoulder, looking up, meaning to apologize or thank him or both, when she saw the most astounding thing. With his back to the candle, it was difficult to make out the details of his face, but she saw the unmistakable glint of tears in his eyes. She didn't say a word. For a long moment, they only stared at each other.

He cleared his throat and lowered his eyes. Turning, he lifted the candle again and held it aloft before them. "Shall we?"

No discussion about her tears. No opportunity for an apology. From his body language and expression, it was clear he had closed the door on that event. It was as if that moment between them hadn't ever happened. He continued down the hall, and she followed without thought.

But she held the feeling in her heart, the feeling of comfort and understanding. The blessed feeling of someone mourning *with* her.

Her exhausted heart warmed behind its barricade, experiencing the barest measure of relief from pain.

Chapter Fourteen

Lucas didn't expect to see Virginia at breakfast, given the late hours from the night before and the emotional weight she had carried. Still, when he finished his meal and coffee, he was disappointed he hadn't seen her. How had she fared after they parted in the hall before Phillip's door? Phillip had been asleep, thankfully.

He'd stood in the doorway, watching as Virginia entered the appropriated guest room. She'd carried the candle with her, putting it on the bedside table. The soft glow had perfectly illuminated her profile when she bent to place a kiss upon her sleeping child's forehead.

Remembering the sight, his lungs constricted as they had in the moment. Watching her graceful movements, seeing the purity of a mother's love, had done something to him he couldn't explain. In conjunction with the tenderness he'd felt for her, holding her as she wept, Lucas's heart was undergoing a change he didn't know it was ready to experience.

The breakfast table was hardly a place to examine such thoughts, especially with an empty plate before him and footmen standing by to take away the trays.

Lucas left the table and made for his study, determined to get some work done. His man of business in London had been keeping him abreast of parliamentary concerns and he had letters from the stewards of his other properties to go over. He ought to go through his schedule, too, and see about meeting with Virginia to discuss the barony's needs.

He settled at his desk and opened the first letter he meant to answer, some discussion of collecting new taxes to aid in the effort against Napoleon. He hoped to share his thoughts with a member of his party still present in London. At least it sounded as though the American annoyance had been dealt with and they only waited to hear back from that country's assembled politicians.

After an hour spent penning letters, Lucas sat back in his chair and flexed his hand. He had a secretary in town, but perhaps it was time he find one in Annesbury to assist him with his correspondence and business.

He went to the window overlooking the front of the estate. The day was clearer than the day before, though a few clouds dotted the sky. He hoped it would prove warmer, too, for the crops. Perhaps he ought to use the day to visit the farmers on his land?

Virginia still hadn't met any of their tenants.

With that stray thought, he was plunged back into the memory of the night before, of holding her in his arms.

Going to the nursery the night previous, his intention had been to help, to make right what he had done wrong, and to set Phillip at ease. The boy's eyes had been enormous when he pleaded for Lucas to check on his brother. Virginia's obvious relief when Edward capitulated and took his medicine had given Lucas leave to feel he accomplished his goal.

He'd also successfully ignored the fact that his wife had been wearing only a dressing gown over her night clothes, and that her long golden hair reached to the middle of her back in its braid. As a perfect gentleman, he'd offered to escort her back to the family wing.

And then, in the darkened hall, she'd fallen apart.

He well knew the feeling. He'd had no motive other than to offer comfort when he put his arms around her. None at all.

But in the ensuing moments, through the dark hours of the night, and now in the brightness of day, Lucas knew it would be a lie to say he remained unaffected by Virginia. Her tenderness in caring for her children, her ability to remain strong when her heart was obviously suffering, and her quick mind were impressive.

He could hardly call himself a man if he pretended he hadn't noticed her beauty. The memory of holding her returned but details he hadn't permitted himself to notice in the moment came back. The way she fit against him, her more delicate structure leaning into his to find strength, called forth his instinct to protect her even more than before.

Lucas closed his eyes and groaned. Being attracted to his wife presented him with something of a problem. She still had months of mourning her late husband before her.

He had promised she could have the time she needed.

It would be the very worst sort of thing for him to act on any of his thoughts or feelings at this point.

But—he still ought to give her the courtesy and respect due his wife.

Part of that would be involving her in the care of their shared properties.

And the day was very fine.

Visiting the tenants would be the perfect way to show his appreciation for her place in his life, and it would be an excellent opportunity to come to know each other better. After all, they ought to be friends. At the very least.

Nodding to himself, Lucas ignored the rest of the work on his desk and went in search of his countess. It was noon. Perhaps they could take the midday meal together before venturing out of doors? He wondered if she would prefer to ride a horse or in a gig.

After walking through the ground floor and seeing no sign of her, he went up to the first floor. He started down the hall when he heard music.

Did Virginia play the pianoforte?

He walked in the direction of the music room, listening to the gentle melody being played. The door to the room was ajar and when he looked inside he saw Virginia seated, her left hand in her lap and her right lightly pressing the keys. Her eyes were closed.

Should he interrupt her? Or wait?

She began to play faster, her fingers using more strength to press each key, and then her left hand lifted to join in the dance. Her eyes stayed closed, but her hands moved more rapidly, drawing the music up into a daring crescendo. His breath came quicker in anticipation of the grand sounds that must follow, ready for the song to take him as a fast-flowing river might carry him away.

But the music abruptly stopped and she turned, her eyes flying open, to face him in the doorway.

They stared at each other and Lucas realized her normally fair cheeks were completely pink.

"I didn't mean to interrupt," he said, his voice echoing strangely in a room now empty of music.

She shook her head and stood. "It's quite all right. I should be going about my business anyway." Virginia closed the instrument and approached him, her hands folded before her. Today she wore a dress more black than gray, with a white fichu at her throat and gray threads embroidering the bodice.

He was grateful for the reminder of her state of mourning. Perhaps it would help him keep a level head.

"Would you like to come with me this afternoon to meet the tenants?" Blurting his invitation hadn't been his intention. It seemed the theory of keeping a level head was out.

Virginia paused, several steps from him, and considered him. Her eyes didn't look very tired. He hoped that meant she'd slept late and not that she'd avoided breakfast with him.

"That would be lovely," she said at last. "I've been thinking that I ought to start my work outside the house. Everything here runs so smoothly, I hardly feel necessary." The smallest of smiles curved her lips upward.

"Surely not." He nearly took a step forward but it would be the wiser course of action to maintain distance. "This is your home. I hope you are running things as you see fit."

Her eyebrows arched upward and she stepped closer. "I meant it as a compliment, Lucas. You have a remarkable staff. As we said, an army. But I am coming to learn their ways and they are expert at learning mine. Perhaps you and I ought to talk about a few thoughts I've had. I would not want to make any changes without your leave."

Lucas tried to sound nonchalant. "I am not overparticular in how my household is run. As long as there are few troubles between servants and my meals are on time, I am satisfied."

Virginia chuckled. Had he said something to amuse her? "That is the way of it with men. Keep them fed and unburdened by domestic concerns and they will be happy." She came all the way to the door and his new awareness of her heightened his senses.

She smelled like oranges again today. *It must be her perfume.* And her eyes no longer held the wounded look he'd seen in them the night before.

"We cannot all be so easily understood," he argued, tucking his hands behind his back. He stepped aside, giving her room to exit if she wished it. As Virginia walked by him and into the hall, he saw her look at him askance.

"Perhaps not in every aspect of personality. But it is the duty of a wife to determine such things about her husband. When would you like to make your visits?"

The change back to the original topic saved him from making anymore foolish remarks. "After luncheon? Would you prefer to ride or should I have the phaeton prepared?"

She didn't even stop to think. "The phaeton, if you please."

"Very well." He gave her a courteous bow. She smiled and made her curtsy, but as she turned to walk away, Lucas thought of one more question, one more thing to keep her standing near him a moment longer. "What were you playing when I walked in? I was quite riveted." Lucas suppressed a groan. Had he sounded inane?

Her cheeks turned a darker shade of pink. "Nothing. Something Charles used to play. That's all."

Lucas's heart fell. "Oh. Did he compose music?"

Virginia shook her head. "Just the one piece, for his music instructor when he was younger. I'm afraid it didn't earn him any praise, but it's an invigorating piece." She seemed hesitant to say more, pausing to bite her bottom lip. "I don't want to forget it. I should like the boys to remember it. The piece is humorous, really. Thinking on yesterday reminded me of it."

He had told her she could bring up Charles without fear. He knew how important her late husband would always be to her. What about yesterday would make her wish to play his music?

"How so?"

Her smile returned. "He called it *Frogs in the Mud.*" A sparkle of humor appeared in her eye before she turned and went down the hall, now humming the melody.

Lucas watched her retreating form, telling himself he was most certainly *not* admiring her figure.

At least she no longer seemed upset about the previous day's adventure or ensuing argument.

And Virginia would accompany him on his visit to the tenants. Lucas returned to his study with a lighter step, looking forward to spending time with the Countess of Annesbury.

¤

Virginia entered the yard of a tenant cottage, looking about with an approving eye. There was a row of cottages, each with its gated yard for keeping in chickens and children. They were well-thatched, the stone walls looked sturdy and the shutters thrown open to let in air were brightly painted.

The Earl of Annesbury had given his tenants lovely houses. The row of four cottages were only some of his tenants. They had already been by another nearer the village and seen the pension cottages as well. There was only one servant in those cottages, an elderly cook who had retired five years before along with her husband, a stable-master at another estate.

All of the properties she had seen were in good repair. Lucas stood, just across the lane, speaking with two of the farmers who had come in from their work upon seeing the phaeton come down the lane. It was left to her, as it should be, to speak with the wives.

Virginia had always enjoyed her responsibilities as lady of an estate but coming to know the tenants hadn't always been easy.

On Charles's land, she hadn't at first seen the need for her to acquaint herself with farmers' wives. She knew better now. These women carried loads just as important and heavy as her own. She hadn't really understood them until after Phillip was born.

Three farmers' wives had come out to see what the fuss was about, one at her window, and it was here that Virginia stood next to the flower box, conversing with all of them.

"Mrs. Carter, what is that most delicious smell?" Virginia asked, breathing in deeply. "Is that rhubarb pie?"

Mrs. Carter, who could not have been older than twenty, nodded shyly at her window.

"Molly makes the best pie," one of the other women, a Mrs. Baton, said warmly. "Her mum taught her, didn't she, love?" Mrs. Baton was closer in age to forty, with a toddling child hanging onto her skirts. "And her mum always wins the contests with her rhubarb pastries."

Mrs. Carter's cheeks went pink and she nodded again.

The third woman, Mrs. Abbott, was closer to Virginia's age. Two little boys had come from her cottage when she did, but they were standing at the phaeton, inspecting its shining wheels with wonder.

"We've seen you and your boys often in church, my lady," Mrs. Abbott said, her warm voice drawing Virginia's attention. "My boys are close in age to your own. Though I've a few above and beneath them, too. I thought it lovely when I heard of your marriage to the earl."

"That is very kind of you to say, thank you." Virginia gestured to her sons. "How old are they? And how many more children do you have?"

"A girl above them who just turned nine, and another in the churchyard. Those two are seven and five, and I've got a three-year-old daughter visitin' my mum in the village, and another on the way." She put a hand to her still-flat abdomen, her pride apparent in her wide smile. "Mrs. Carter is expectin' too."

Virginia's eyes went to the shy young woman, whose whole face had turned red. She dropped her eyes.

"How wonderful, Mrs. Carter. Is this your first?"

Mrs. Carter nodded. "We've been married three years," she said, nearly whisper-soft. "So, we'd sort of stopped expecting it to happen."

"What a marvelous blessing."

"It's why she's hiding behind her flower box," Mrs. Baton said knowingly. "She's starting to show."

"I remember those days," Virginia said, hoping to alleviate the young woman's embarrassment. "It's such a wonderful time. The sickness starts to subside and there is evidence of the coming joy. I was dreadfully shy of anyone seeing me, at least at first. But my husband was so proud, he wanted to take me about town every chance he could. Is Mr. Carter beside himself with joy?"

Mrs. Carter nodded. "He can't seem to stop talkin' about it, and I keep telling him he must reign in his pride or he'll bust the buttons off his coat when he swells so much." She lifted her chin and smiled. The other women chuckled and nodded, well-acquainted with the actions of proud new fathers.

"I wish you every happiness, Mrs. Carter, and if you will permit me, I would be honored to send you a basket when your time comes, full of things for your little one. And you too, Mrs. Abbott. Babies ought to be celebrated by the whole neighborhood."

"Thank you, my lady," Mrs. Carter said, her eyes wide and smile pleasant.

"That's very kind of you, my lady," Mrs. Abbott said with a little dip of a curtsy.

Mrs. Baton, perhaps not to be outdone, added her own curtsy and grateful words. "I hope we may soon be wishing you the same happiness, my lady."

Virginia didn't even blink, though inside she felt her heart constrict. "Thank you, Mrs. Baton."

A crunch on the walk behind her made her turn. Lucas had come to collect her, his visit with the farmers at an end. They had gone back to work in the fields.

"Madams." Lucas nodded when the women began dropping their curtsies. "I am afraid I must steal my wife away again." They each murmured their acquiescence, then their farewells. Virginia waved and offered her compliments once more before turning to her husband.

Virginia did not miss the twinkle in his eye when he took her hand and brought it to his arm.

"Did your visit go well?" he asked just before handing her up into the phaeton.

"Very. You have two tenant families increasing, likely this fall." She tucked her hands in her lap as he settled in the seat beside her. "And no complaints to be aware of, though Mrs. Baton has a second son she's beginning to worry after. He needs a trade, it would seem." And Virginia would much rather discuss an apprenticeship than the coming babies.

"Ah, Mr. Baton mentioned similar. It seems the boy hasn't shown any interest in the local tradesmen. I said I would make inquiries. I think I've seen the lad before. He tends to hover around the horses."

She tipped her head to the side and regarded him carefully. He spoke with absolute sincerity, his eyes ahead of him on the road. "You know your tenants' children by sight?"

"And name, most of the time." Lucas raised his eyebrows at her. "What sort of landlord would I be if I didn't know them? Some will go on to inherit the tenant farms, after all. Others will serve in my household or become local tradesmen. They will be my neighbors as surely as the gentlemen whose estates border mine."

"That is quite a progressive attitude, my lord," she said, unable to hide her smile. "And one that I agree with. It does make sense. That was how we were—" She closed her mouth over the words pouring from her.

"You and Charles?" he asked, watching her from the corner of his eye. "Excellent. Then you won't rebuke me for my familiarity with them."

"Of course not," she said, more quietly now. They rode in silence for a few moments, her mind going back over their time together. The night before, when he'd comforted her, allowed her to cry, without ever showing a sign of resentment for her dwelling on thoughts of Charles, was not what most new husbands would allow. Eventually, would he expect her to forget? She had not heard him speak much of his first wife. Had the years made it easier for him?

Ought she to invite him to speak of Lady Abigail Calvert?

"Lucas?" There was no time like the present to test her own bravery on the matter. He looked her way, eyebrows raised to invite her question. "What did Abigail think of your relationship with your tenants?" Virginia held her breath, hoping she had not crossed a boundary into what was none of her business.

His smile reappeared, much to her relief, as warm as the sun above them. His eyes changed, as though he looked further into the distance than the road stretched. "She was supportive. And kind. She visited with the tenants' wives, she went about the parish doing good." He sighed and shook his head. "Even when she ought to have stayed home and looked after herself."

Virginia watched as Lucas's expression changed from one of pleasant remembrance to something more bittersweet. He turned the horses off the lane, into a stand of trees near the road. Once they were under the shady branches, the phaeton stopped. Lucas held the reins in one hand and reached up with the other to remove his hat. He put the hat in his lap.

"Has anyone told you," he asked, the words spoken slowly, "how Abigail died?"

Virginia, surprised at the turn in his mood and conversation, shook her head. Had she intruded too far upon him? She only meant to give him opportunity to speak of his wife. She hoped he didn't think her morbidly curious.

"You needn't speak of it if you do not wish to, Lucas." She laid her hand on his arm to gentle her words. "Not if it causes you pain."

He covered her hand with his and met her eyes, his more ash-gray than blue in the shade. "It doesn't. Not anymore. I think I will always miss her, of course. She is part of me. But I want you to know, to see that it is possible, for time to heal the painful memories and give you leave to remember the good."

Virginia nodded, giving his arm a gentle squeeze. Would the day come when she wouldn't ache for Charles? Everyone said it would. Wouldn't she have to forget him to rid herself of pain? She had no wish to do that. Lucas's perspective gave her a measure of comfort.

"Abigail was granddaughter to a duke. She was happiness and grace, she held herself with a regal air, and yet I saw her kneel in the grass to dry the tears of a farmer's daughter." His eyes took on that faraway quality again and his voice deepened as he spoke. "She was beautiful in body and soul."

"I saw her portrait," Virginia said, lowering her voice reverently. "She was lovely."

He nodded and his hand on her fingers pressed her closer. "Very lovely. And I thought myself the luckiest man alive. Only one thing could've made me happier. A child."

Virginia's heart dropped all the way to her stomach. No one, when they spoke of the late countess, ever mentioned a child. She bit her cheeks and her eyes began to sting.

"It took time, but we had been married just over a year when Abigail told me the good news." He turned away then, dropping her hand and using it to grip his hat instead, bending its brim as he spoke.

"We didn't tell anyone. It was a precious secret between the two of us."

Lucas gripped the hat and reins, tension evident in the lines of his body. "We never had the chance to tell anyone other than a doctor. Abigail—she fell ill. At first, she thought it was her delicate state." A sound, something she'd call a chuckle if it hadn't sounded so sad, escaped him. "She overdid, she fell ill, and then the doctor came. Abigail had an excellent chance of recovery, he said. But then—then she didn't get well." He closed his eyes and held his breath for several long moments.

Virginia sat still, offering him nothing but her silent empathy. Abigail had been young, their marriage new, when he'd lost her. She had been given years with Charles, and children. Did that make one sort of suffering worse than the other? She didn't believe so. How could she even call their heart-break different? Did it matter how a heart was broken when all that was left were shattered remains?

He let out his breath at last, in a deep sigh, and faced her again. "I loved her with everything I was. The world changed when she left it."

"And you had to find a way to remake it," Virginia said, each word laced with empathy. "Without her in it."

Lucas nodded, his eyes understanding and accepting her explanation of her own feelings. "Exactly that. I cannot say when or how it happened, but I find I can accept this new world. I have a place in it, as does Abigail's memory. I still have purpose." He picked up his hat and placed it back on his head, his shoulders straightening again, his frame regathering its strength.

"I'm grateful you told me." Virginia meant it. Coming to understand him, to fit herself into his life, would be easier if she knew something of the past.

"We had better be getting back." Lucas took up the reins in both hands again and with a gentle flick, he had the horses moving onto the road. A comfortable silence remained between them.

Chapter Fifteen

"You're doing excellent, Phillip." Lucas leaned over the rail of the paddock, watching the boys enjoy their riding lesson. Christine Gilbert had put Edward on a pony and led him about on foot while Phillip was learning to guide his mount around gentle turns. Phillip was growing bored of his time fenced in. Though he was small, he handled his horse with confidence.

"The boy's a natural," Thomas said at his side. "How many lessons is this now?"

"The third since I married his mother." Lucas had brought the boys once a week. They were at the tail end of June and summer still had not made up its mind as to whether it would stay. The weather remained cooler and the skies cloudier than normal. Thankfully, Edward's cough had not lasted long, nor had it returned. Lucas had taken care to check in at the nursery nightly, before Virginia went in to bid the boys goodnight.

Thomas crossed his arms atop the rail. "I hope everything is going well. Christine's been worried about that Macon fellow. You've had no more word from him?"

"None from him or his lawyer." Lucas didn't bother hiding his smile at that. He still thought on that confrontation with satisfaction. "I don't believe we have anything further to worry about in that quarter."

"Glad to hear it." Thomas's eyes stayed on his wife, watching her give the reins to Edward. The man wore a look on his face of pure adoration every time he dropped the conversation in favor of admiring Christine Gilbert.

Lucas chuckled. "Still enamored of your wife, I see."

The other man barely cut him a glance before answering. "And may it always be so." His eyes went to Phillip. "Dare I ask how your new bride is adjusting to life at Annesbury Park?"

Raising an eyebrow, Lucas took in Thomas's careful expression. "Perhaps I ought to ask you, given that your wife visited yesterday. The two of them were in Virginia's sitting room for over an hour. When I asked how their visit went, I was told it was *lovely.*"

The other man cleared his throat. "Oh, Christine didn't say much about it. She certainly didn't say anything to give me cause to worry. In fact, she said Virginia seemed perfectly content with her situation."

Content. Lucas knew that ought to satisfy him. His wife wasn't miserable. She had no great complaints. But *content* was not the same thing as *happy.* Could one be happy while in mourning? He certainly hadn't been. Not for a very long time. He'd had no one to help him through the difficult days, however, while he hoped Virginia knew he was always ready to support her.

"You needn't look so perturbed, Calvert." Thomas chuckled and turned back to the riders.

Lucas realized he'd begun frowning while lost in his thoughts. He forced a more neutral expression. "Thank you, Gilbert. I cannot help thinking there is something more I ought to be doing for Virginia and the boys."

"It must be a great deal to take in. Adjusting to having a wife was a pleasant enough experience, but there were difficult moments. I cannot imagine adding fatherhood at the same time would make things any easier." Charles nodded to Phillip as he rode by. "And your role is the more unique because the loss of the baron is still recent. Are the boys taking to you?"

"I think they might be. Phillip still has moments when he looks at me as if I am a pretender to the throne." Lucas couldn't blame the boy. When Lucas had been that age, he'd worshiped his own father. "But Edward has been sending me drawings by way of the servants. I get a folded sheet of paper from him nearly every day. Yesterday he sent me a piece featuring a very unfortunate looking cow."

Thomas laughed, shaking his head. "What do you do with such masterpieces?"

"I can hardly dispose of them. That wouldn't feel right. My desk drawers are growing rather full." At last count, he had fifteen such drawings. They weren't all like the cow, either. The boy had a real talent for plants."

Christine led Edward's pony to them, a cheerful bounce in her step. "My lord, your stepsons are positively gifted riders. I cannot think they will continue to need lessons for long."

Lucas slipped between the rails with ease and no thought for the cravat his valet had spent too much time on that morning. He went to Edward and held his arms out to offer support as the boy practiced dismounting.

"They have an excellent teacher, Mrs. Gilbert, who allows that natural talent to shine. What do we say, Edward?"

"Thank you, Cousin Christine." The small boy bowed, watching Lucas from the corner of his eye, obviously looking for approval.

"My pleasure, Cousin Edward," Christine said, dipping a playful curtsy.

Lucas winked and Edward straightened with a grin.

Phillip came nearer and dismounted, slowly but smoothly and all on his own. He kept the reins in hand. "Should we take the horses in today, Cousin Christine?"

"Please do. The grooms will help you."

Edward puffed his little chest out when she handed him the reins to the pony. He followed after the more confident Phillip, looking over his shoulder once, shooting a grin at Lucas.

Lucas waved and watched them go, their shapes a contrast to the animals they led. Despite both boys having small mounts, they looked hardly old enough to be in the saddle. Perhaps they truly had a natural talent. At Edward's age, Lucas thought he'd been lucky to be a passenger in a dogcart.

"Look at him, Thomas," Christine's voice said from his side, stage-whispering. "He's besotted with those children."

Gilbert clicked his tongue against the roof of his mouth. "Can you blame him? You're just as wild about them."

Lucas settled his hands on his hips and regarded his friends with amusement. "I am entirely devoted to them, I'll admit it. They're good lads. But I must ask your professional opinion about something, Mrs. Gilbert."

"Please, do call me Christine. We're related by marriage, after all." She grinned and went to the paddock gate, obviously not as willing to climb through rails as Lucas had been. "What can we help you with, my lord?"

"Lucas will do." He followed her and held the gate open, the two of them walking around to where Thomas had remained. "I'm thinking of getting the boys a pony, having it live at Annesbury Park. And a dogcart. Then when you have a foal available that might suit Phillip, I'd like to add one of those to my stables, too."

Thomas and Christine shared a look that made Lucas's heart give an envious thump. The regard the two had for one another was obvious, even in the smallest glances. He missed that ability, the closeness it required, to share a look with a person and simply *know* all they thought and felt on a matter.

"It isn't a terrible idea," Thomas answered, reaching for his wife's hand as he spoke. "So long as they still come here for lessons, I think Christine will agree with me."

Christine bumped her husband with her shoulder. "I cannot lose my pupils this early on. Though I'm certain your stable master might make a suitable instructor, I enjoy my time with them too much to give them up." She narrowed her eyes at Lucas. "You aren't trying to steal away my cousins, are you?"

He raised his hands in a calming gesture. "Never, *Cousin* Christine. They will meet you for lessons so long as you and their mother deem them necessary. But practicing at Annesbury Park, learning to handle a dogcart, that can only be good for them. Yes?"

Her eyes narrowed further. "Yes," she said, drawing out the word's single syllable. "I suppose so. Very well. Where do you think you will get your pony? We only have the one and I cannot give her up. I'm too fond of Honey."

Lucas nearly asked what honey had to do with anything when he realized it must be the pony's name. He cleared his throat rather than chuckle. "I hoped one of you would know where I might find one."

Thomas thought for a moment, then began to offer names of men in the area he thought might part with a pony. It did not take Edward and Phillip long to rejoin them, however, and Lucas swiftly changed the subject when he saw the boys approaching.

"It's meant to be a surprise," he said under his breath.

Christine's eyes glittered approvingly and Thomas grinned too.

"When can we come back?" Phillip asked, tugging his coat sleeves down. It looked like the boy had gone through a recent growth spurt, given the way his wrists stuck out of the jacket.

"Next Monday or Tuesday," Christine answered. "If the weather cooperates."

The boys bowed their thanks again and Lucas led them to the gig waiting to take them back to Annesbury Park. After they were both settled, their usual chatter began. Lucas enjoyed listening to them as they took the path homeward, their serious talk amusing him.

"Did you see me dismount, Phillip?" Edward asked, his voice going higher in his excitement. "I nearly did it alone."

"I saw. Well done, Edward."

They would continue in this vein for some time, talking of what they did right, bemoaning what they had gotten wrong or forgotten to do. But it was obvious in every word they said how much they looked forward to their time in the saddle.

When they hit a lull in the conversation, nearly home, Lucas cleared his throat. "I've been thinking, perhaps you boys would like to go on a picnic some afternoon, by the lake?"

He'd been thinking of taking them for some time. Nearly since he met them. But the business of life kept him too occupied. Since his conversation with Thomas, he realized he ought to do more to show the boys that he cared about them, wanted to be part of their life. He had hoped taking them to and from their lessons would begin that feeling of harmony between them. Most men would have sent a groom to cart his stepsons from one place to another.

"I like picnics." Edward's eyes were aglow with happiness and he tucked his hands under his legs. "Let's go, Phillip. Say yes, Phillip."

Phillip considered the question, and when Lucas saw the frown on his face forming he turned his full attention back to the road. He still wasn't sure where he stood with the child-baron. The boy took himself very seriously. Lucas often wondered if that had always been in his nature or if it had become part of his personality after his father's death.

"I think," Phillip said with deliberate slowness, "it could be enjoyable. But we ought to check with Mother first."

Lucas sighed and nodded. "I think you must be right about that. Very well. I will ask your mother and let you know when she's given her answer."

"She'll say yes." Edward spoke with all the authority a four-year-old could possess and Lucas had to resist chuckling again.

He was ready to elaborate on their plans when he rounded the last bend in the road to reveal the house.

There were carriages in front of his home. Two of them. One grand and opulent, with a familiar coat of arms emblazoned upon the door. The other carriage was more modest, but new. They were both being attended to by servants who were unloading luggage.

"Gentlemen," Lucas said, raising his voice to be sure they heard him. "You are about to meet some very important people. I think you ought to go through the servants' hall and wash yourselves well before the introductions."

Edward stretched around, leaning onto Lucas's seat to see past him. "Who is it?" he asked, his voice reverential.

"Did you know they were coming?" Phillip asked, standing up to look over Lucas's shoulder and resting his hands there for balance.

The casual touch made Lucas smile, despite the anxious feeling somewhere in his chest.

"I had no idea. To answer your question, Edward, you are going to meet my mother, the Dowager Countess of Annesbury, and my brother, and his wife. I hope you're prepared to make a good impression, but even if you aren't, I have the feeling they will be impressed by you both."

At least he hoped they would. And he hoped his mother was minding her tongue. Doubtless she was already making herself at home.

He hoped Virginia was faring well.

¤

"The Dowager Countess of Annesbury, Lady Pamela Calvert," Gresham said, sounding completely out of breath, after opening the doors to Virginia's morning room. She barely had the time to stand, and next to no time to register surprise, before a tall and imposing woman swept into the room. "And Mr. and Mrs. Marcus Calvert," the butler added, his voice fading slightly at the end of the introduction.

Virginia's eyes darted to the door once more, watching as a couple entered the room, uncertainty clear on their faces.

But Lady Pamela Calvert swiftly retook her attention. Virginia curtsied deeply, as much for the woman's position as her new mother-in-law as for the respect due her title.

"My lady, welcome back to Annesbury Park." At least she didn't sound as ruffled as she felt.

"Thank you," Lady Pamela said, her tone speculative instead of offended. "And where is my son? He ought to be here to make introductions and explain himself." She hadn't removed her gloves or her hat, which bore a large red feather and an intricate purple veil to cover her face. Without waiting for an invitation, she sat upon the chair most in command of the room.

Virginia instinctively looked to the other two, searching for allies though she had no thought as to whether Lucas's brother and his wife might be for or against her.

Marcus Calvert did not resemble his brother greatly. He was red-headed where Lucas was fair and had a slightly shorter build, wider in the shoulders, too. But when he smiled at her, she recognized her husband's charm in the expression.

"Mother," he said, guiding his wife forward. "Perhaps it would be best if we waited for Lucas? You could go to your room and change out of your traveling clothes."

"Hmph. I will do no such thing, and neither will either of you. I have questions and if Lucas cannot answer them, someone must." She turned back to face Virginia. "Sit down, madam."

Although tempted to resent the woman's presumption to order her about, Virginia swallowed her pride. She looked at Mrs. Calvert. "Won't you please make yourself comfortable, Mrs. Calvert. Mr. Calvert."

They went to the two-person couch, and once they had taken their seats Virginia took hers.

"Would you like tea, my lady?" she asked, making eye contact with Gresham who still stood in the doorway. The old servant's eyes were wide and she couldn't decide if he was enjoying the spectacle or was afraid to leave her with the lioness in the purple dress.

"Yes, yes. See to it, Gresham," the dowager countess said dismissively.

The butler hurried to close the doors and see to his task.

Virginia wasn't certain they would get along if the woman continued to act as though she were mistress in the house.

The dowager reached up to her veil and pulled it upward, revealing a lovely, if a trifle stern, face. She had hair nearly as red as her younger son and eyes that snapped in a lively, intelligent manner. "I understand your Christian name is Virginia."

"It is." Virginia folded her hands in her lap. "And yours is Pamela."

The older woman drew herself up. "And before you became countess, you were a baroness?"

"Yes, my lady. I thought his lordship, my husband, wrote to you of the matter." At least she thought he must've. Virginia couldn't recall Lucas ever saying whether or not he informed the family of the details of their marriage. She had thought it odd that she hadn't received any letters of congratulations from her new kin. But surely, he must've told them? It would be cruel not to.

"I only received his letter four days past. I was not in London when it arrived."

"She had come to visit us," Marcus Calvert put in from where he sat. Virginia turned to look to him, noticing he was still smiling but in a commiserating manner. "It took a little time to get it turned in the right direction. And if Lucas wrote to me, I never saw the letter."

"Oh, dear." Virginia closed her eyes momentarily and shook her head. "I am terribly sorry for such a mishap."

"It's hardly your fault," Marcus said.

"The British post is entirely to blame and I intend to write the Postmaster about it," her mother-in-law snapped, though she seemed less agitated than when she entered the room. "But that is neither here nor there. The same hour I finished the letter, I prepared to come here and meet you. Lucas did not share many details, and your marriage has taken us all by surprise."

Virginia looked again to the quiet couple on the sofa, this time meeting the eyes of Mrs. Calvert, who had yet to say a word. The woman's expression was calm, but her light brown eyes glittered with some amusement. Her lips turned upward briefly when they made eye contact and she lifted her shoulders a tiny amount, as if to say, *she isn't so bad once you know her.*

Facing the dowager countess again, Virginia resisted the urge to smooth her skirts or grip the arms of her chair. She presented the most unaffected countenance she could manage. She didn't know this woman on a personal level. Virginia didn't know if Lucas's mother would be predisposed to like or dislike her. The well-bred manners of society were all she could count upon.

"I am happy to answer any questions you may have, my lady. I am terribly sorry for the shock his lordship's message has caused."

Lady Pamela Calvert lifted her chin and straightened her already impeccable posture. "Good. My son informed me that he had married the widow of a baron and that you had two sons by your former husband."

"Yes, my lady. I was married to the Baron of Heatherton. My son, Phillip, now holds the title. He is six years old. My younger son, Edward, is four years of age."

"Grandchildren at last," Marcus said brightly. "You've been going on about how you wanted grandchildren, Mother."

Virginia saw the first glimpse of humor in the woman when she gave her son a glance at his comment. "Marcus, if you cannot sit quietly and wait your turn, perhaps *you* ought to go change out of your travelling clothes."

He pressed his lips shut but maintained a smile.

Virginia started to relax. If Lucas's brother could be amused in this situation, it mustn't be dire.

The inquisition continued. "How long has your late husband been gone?" the woman asked, her tone gentling.

"Three months and a little, my lady."

"Dear me." The dowager put her hand over her heart and her eyes widened. "My dear lady, please accept my condolences. Lucas did not say how recent—" She stopped speaking, but in an instant her whole countenance had changed. She no longer appeared indignant, but sympathetic. "I beg your pardon, Lady Calvert."

"As you said, you were not aware." Virginia looked down at her lap, the gray fabric easily reminding her of how recent her husband had passed. But where there had been pain, she found more strength. "My husband died of consumption. My sons and I came to stay with my cousin, Mrs. Christine Devon. That is how your son and I came to meet."

"But—"

The woman's next question was immediately cut off by the door bursting open. Virginia rose to her feet, uncertain as to who would make such an entrance. It was Lucas, striding inside the room and directly to his mother's chair.

"Mother, what a pleasant surprise." He spoke with exuberance, a wide smile on his face. He bent to kiss his mother on the cheek, then whirled to face his brother and sister-in-law, still speaking. "Marcus, Ellen, it's wonderful to see you both. I'm surprised your apple trees could spare you at this time of year."

It was an odd comment, until Virginia's mind caught up with her and she remembered Lucas's brother owned a sizable orchard.

Marcus had stood to shake his brother's hand and Ellen to curtsy. Strangely, Mrs. Ellen Calvert was the first to find her voice, and it was a low, gentle alto.

"It's good to see you, brother. I hope we are not intruding."

"We most certainly are intruding," Lady Pamela Calvert said abruptly. "But it's only necessary because you are incapable of writing sensible letters and the postmaster is equally incapable of delivering them correctly."

Lucas had made his way to Virginia's side by the time his mother finished speaking. He bent, as though to kiss her cheek. Surely, that's what it looked like to everyone in the room.

Virginia's heart seized up inside her and blood rushed into her cheeks. He'd never come close to such a display of affection, pretend or otherwise!

"Are you all right?" he whispered, his lips near her ear. No one else would've heard him. She barely heard him over the roaring sound in her ears.

She managed to give him the barest nod.

He straightened immediately and spoke to everyone in the room again. "I'm terribly sorry, Mother. I did write about our marriage."

"But in hardly any detail." She huffed and sat back, glaring up at her son. "And Virginia has been telling us that she is a very recent widow. What is going on, Lucas? Why would you wed before the mourning period is concluded? What sort of match is this?"

Silence hung in the air for a long moment. Lucas stared at his mother, then turned just enough to meet Virginia's eyes. "I would say a very good one, Mother."

Virginia's breath left her in a nervous laugh and Lucas's hand, half-hidden behind her skirt, caught hers to offer the tiniest squeeze. He was leaving it to her to decide what they would share, offering his support.

"Thank you," she said aloud, releasing his hand after returning the gesture. "But you may as well tell the whole of it, Lucas. They are your family, after all."

"Our family," he corrected, smiling down at her. "Perhaps you would like to see to the boys? I sent them to their room to change, but I imagine you'd like a conversation with them before they're presented."

It was a sensible idea and filled her with relief. She needn't stay for the recounting of her troubles and his role as rescuer. And he was right. If her children were about to be presented to new family, and a formidable step-grandmother, she wanted the opportunity to remind them of their manners.

"That is a splendid idea. I will return with them shortly." She looked at their guests to see all eyes trained on her with a great deal of interest. "If you will all excuse me." She curtsied, then made her way as decorously as possible to the door. She passed the maid bringing tea but gave it little thought. Someone else could pour out perfectly well in her absence.

Lucas had arrived just in time to save her. It was obviously a habit of his, and she was incredibly grateful for it.

Chapter Sixteen

With the initial explanations out of the way, Lucas had done the other thing proper with unexpected house guests and issued his mother, brother, and sister-in-law an invitation to stay for a fortnight. But playing host meant changing his schedule. The picnic with the boys was indefinitely postponed.

Phillip and Edward took it in stride, especially when their new step-grandmother took it upon herself to start spoiling them immediately. Even her pernicious little dog, a creature of dubious descent, regarded the children as new playmates.

Lucas's mother started receiving and making calls with Virginia immediately. She could hardly believe Virginia had not begun those functions of society yet, excepting the vicar's wife and her relations. And Virginia's excuse that she was in the awkward position of mourning and being a newlywed had not been enough for Lucas's mother.

"Nonsense, my dear," she had said at the dinner table the same night of her arrival. "People will only think untoward thoughts about such things if you do not contradict them with perfectly normal behavior."

Ellen was necessarily taken along, despite being a guest herself, but Lucas was grateful for her quiet strength. Virginia would appreciate someone whose words were measured before being spoken.

Nearly a week passed before Lucas found himself alone with his wife for more than five minutes. He was working on his correspondence when a knock came at the door.

"Enter," he called without looking up.

The door opened and clicked shut quickly. "Lucas, have you a moment?"

The sound of her voice had the same effect on him as a gentle breeze on a hot summer day. He stood immediately, his eyes taking in her business-like expression and sweeping across her form. Today she wore a dress of soft, purplish-gray. He didn't know the name of it, though he guessed there would be one, and it nearly surprised him to see even a hint of color on her person other than the gold of her hair and the soft shades of pink in her cheeks and lips.

The vibrancy of her green eyes rarely dimmed.

"Virginia, come in. You may have as many moments as you wish." He bit his tongue after speaking. Had he sounded too eager for her company? He'd missed her since the arrival of his family. He still spent nearly the same time in her company, seeing her at meals and to discuss household matters once or twice a day, but it was different. They weren't ever really alone anymore.

Her expression softened with a smile. She came to the desk, a piece of folded paper in her hands. He walked around it and gestured to one of two chairs, taking the other for himself.

"Thank you," she said after sitting. "I know how busy you are." She laid the paper down in her lap and smoothed its edges.

Had he been too busy? He really ought to engage a secretary, if only to be more accessible to her needs. Not that he thought she needed him too often, but he didn't want her to hesitate to come to him for something as trifling as being busy.

"Not at all." He sat back in his chair, giving himself as relaxed an air as possible. "How are you doing this fine afternoon? Has my mother worn out her welcome yet?"

Virginia chuckled, raising a hand to her lips immediately after the sound escaped. "Your mother is a lovely person, and I'll not say anything against her for fear she gets word of it."

Lucas had to laugh at that. "She is a formidable woman, is she not?"

Her eyes brightened and she nodded. "I adore her tremendously, but she makes me question my ability to be a countess. I do not think I quite measure up to her standards."

"No one does, except her new grandchildren and her dog." He immediately berated himself for equating her sons with a pet, but Virginia didn't seem to notice or mind. Why was he forever saying ridiculous things around her? At first it had been purposeful, to make her smile, but now he couldn't seem to stop. His allies in Parliament would be rather shocked at his lack of eloquence.

"The boys are entirely besotted with her, too. I am afraid the only grandmotherly influence in their lives thus far has been my mother, and she is not well known for tenderness of feeling. We see her exactly once a year, unless we go to London." Virginia shook her head. "And when I wrote to tell her of my marriage, I received a very succinct reply congratulating me for my rise in rank and suggesting I not appear in London until I am out of mourning, lest people feel inclined to speculate." Virginia waggled her eyebrows up and down.

Lucas tilted his head to one side, inspecting her as she spoke of her mother. It was the second time she'd mentioned the Dowager Countess of Vinespar. He hadn't met the woman, though he'd heard of her a time or two in London. If anything, Virginia seemed amused by her mother's personality, not hurt or offended.

"Should we invite her to come stay with us next?" he asked with complete seriousness. "I wouldn't want her to feel slighted, or to deprive you of her company."

Virginia waved the offer away at once. "Not at present. Perhaps next month. She detests London in August, but dislikes my brother even more, so she usually visits me then. I warn you, she is not nearly as pleasant a companion as your mother."

He wanted to continue the conversation, learn more about her family and why she spoke of them so rarely, but she had sought him out for a purpose. It would be rude to continue a topic without seeing to her needs.

"Is there something I can do for you today, Virginia? If you won't let me invite your mother to stay, that is."

"There is something I would like to consult you about. It concerns the barony." Virginia lifted the paper and held it out to him. "I received this letter from the steward. It has been some months since I've been to Heatherton Hall and, while I trust him, with the strange summer weather I worry for the tenants and the land. I thought I might ask the steward, Mr. Ferris, if he would come visit here and bring the accounts with him."

Lucas took the paper as she spoke and started reading. It was a short, formal letter, no more than a note, assuring her all was well and giving her a very basic accounting of expenditures and estate income.

If he were to receive such a note from one of the stewards at his holdings, he would be most dissatisfied. There was no word about the tenants, the state of the land, the expected harvest, or any indication the weather would cause problems. There was nothing about household matters. No questions. The whole of the note was less than three paragraphs long.

"Having him visit wouldn't be enough, in my opinion." Lucas glanced up at her, over the edge of the paper. "Though you trust him, making a personal inspection of the property would do more to reassure you, and your tenants, that all is as it should be." He handed the letter back and steepled his hands together in front of him.

Virginia's eyes fell to the letter which she folded, slowly, then ran her fingertips over the creases. A thoughtful frown brought her eyebrows together and turned her lips downward.

"That was my initial thought, but I cannot see how it would be possible. The trip would take at least two days, as it is some eighty miles from here. Then I would want two or three days to see to everything before my return here. I would be gone for a week or more." She pressed her fingers to her temple. "I wouldn't wish to take the boys. The journey would already be long and difficult, depending upon the state of the roads, and there is no reason to pack up all their trappings and Nurse Smythe for such a short visit."

Lucas nodded, mentally going through the preparation with her. She could likely need more than a few days to see to everything, especially given her lack of knowledge on the running of the estate. It was rare a woman knew all the business dealings of her husband, because their duties were so divided.

He didn't like the idea of her going alone for more reasons than that. But would she want him to come?

"May I offer my services to you, my lady?" he asked, concealing his hope for her answer in the affirmative. "I'll gladly make the journey with you, as protector, and see to Phillip's estate. I will advise you with all the care I use in my own dealings." He watched her, waited for her to speak, his heart rising in his chest. The chance to be of service to her was not his primary motivation, though it was a close second. He would have time alone with her, for several days. While he would conduct himself as a complete gentleman, of course, he wanted very much to understand his feelings for her.

Virginia's cheeks went pink and her eyes widened. "Oh, Lucas, I couldn't ask that of you. It would take too much of your time."

"You aren't asking," he said, wishing to reach out to lay a hand on hers. Instead, he put all his sincerity into his voice. "I am offering. Insisting, in fact. When we entered this agreement, I promised to do all in my power to help you in raising your sons and preparing them for the life ahead. I promised I would look after Phillip's estate, too. I will happily lend you my abilities."

She chewed on her bottom lip, meeting his gaze. He kept it steady, focused on her, willing her to accept his help. Accept him.

"Very well. I would appreciate it, thank you. When do you think you would have the time?"

He bit back a triumphant grin. "As soon as the arrangements can be made. It will not take more than a day or two to put things in order here."

"Do you think we ought to wait until your mother's visit is over?" she asked, with a note of concern.

"I think we ought to tell her of our plans. Likely she will insist on remaining here to look after things." Lucas chuckled and stood, reaching to help Virginia stand. "Though she prefers London most of the year, I know she misses the country from time to time."

Virginia left her hand in his as he spoke, her smile warming him. "And what of Marcus and Ellen? Should we abandon them?"

"Absolutely. He abandoned me in London, at the beginning of the season, to disappear into the country with his wife. It would only be fair I do the same to him." Though Marcus had escaped with Ellen under entirely different circumstances, and with a much more pleasant reason.

Virginia laughed and released his hand, holding her letter in both of hers. "Very well. I will send word that we are coming and I will make the necessary arrangements for the boys and Nurse Smythe to remain behind."

"And I will make the travel arrangements." Lucas half-bowed. "And speak to my formidable mother."

She curtsied, almost playfully. "Thank you, my lord. Shall we discuss the particulars after dinner?"

"I would like that." He watched her leave, her step noticeably lighter than when she'd entered, and his heart gave a joyful, and somewhat painful, thump. To see her happy, even for just a few moments, did something to him. It gave him hope for their eventual future, yes, but it was more than that.

He went back to his desk to begin making his own arrangements and the late afternoon sun broke through the clouds, bathing his desk in golden light. His eyes landed on his latest gift from Edward. It was a water-color this time, depicting a rose bush with a mix of pink and red blooms amid greenery.

He wanted *all* of them happy and whole again. Virginia, Phillip, Edward, and himself.

If only he could speed the process. There was just under eight months left for Virginia to mourn, but surely the healing she needed might begin sooner?

Lucas would do all in his power to make it so.

¤

"Why can I not go?" Phillip asked for the tenth time. "It isn't fair. It's my barony."

Virginia closed her eyes and counted to five before responding. When she opened her eyes again, she pulled the blankets up to his chin. "And when you are a little older, you will make every visit with me. For now, you need to stay here and look after Edward. I will not be gone long and you will have a great deal to keep you busy. You have your riding lessons, your new grandmother wishes to get to know you better, and your Uncle Marcus and Aunt Ellen have promised to keep you entertained as well."

Phillip's eyes grew stormier and he turned over, putting his back to hers. "It isn't fair."

Sighing, she reached up to run her fingers through his hair. What could she say to help him understand? "I'm afraid it isn't, darling. But if you came, that would hardly be fair either. I cannot stay long. My duties as the wife of the earl keep me here. You would not have time to unpack your things or see your old friends. The trip would be too short to satisfy you. I will speak to the earl about a longer visit. I know we sent for most of your things, but is there anything you left behind that you would like me to fetch for you?"

"I'd like my shell collection," Edward said from his bed.

Virginia turned to smile at him. "And where might it be hidden, Edward?"

"In the crow's nest," he answered. "I hid it there to keep it safe from pirates."

She nodded seriously. "Very wise. I will bring them to you." He had collected a jar's worth of tiny shells on his first trip to the beach, just before they went to Bath. Charles had told her some time at the seaside would be all he needed to feel more the thing. Weeks after that trip he confessed he made that excuse in order to take the boys on one last adventure.

Behind the well-constructed walls, her pitiful heart glowed with the memory. When Charles had admitted the truth to her, she'd been hurt and afraid to lose him. Looking back on their time at the seaside, she realized her husband had given his sons a beautiful gift. Their last adventure with him had been grand. They'd spent every morning combing the beach for treasure and every afternoon picnicking in the sand. They'd chased waves away from shore and been chased back in return. She could still hear Charles's laughter mingling with the giggles of their sons.

"You look happy." Phillip's statement interrupted her thoughts and she looked down to see him facing her again, a curious expression on his face. "You don't always look happy anymore."

Although her first emotion was guilt, Virginia shook that away. "I know, Phillip. Sometimes I am caught up in being sad or worried. But I was thinking of when we went to the beach with your father. Do you remember it?"

He stiff little body relaxed beneath the blankets, his eyebrows shot up. "I do. We found a crab and followed it to its home."

"And collected our treasure," Edward said. "That's why I need the shells back, Mama. I want to 'member it better." His words slurred and his eyes blinked heavily at her.

"Papa bought me a ship," Phillip said from beside her. "I left it on my shelf in the nursery. Could you bring it back for me, Mother?" His frown was gone and in its place was a gentler expression, a hopeful one. "I'd like to have it here."

Virginia's relief at receiving the request made her shoulders sag. "Yes, darling. I will bring back your ship and Edward's shells. I promise." She bent to kiss his forehead, then went across to give Edward the same token of her love. They said their goodnights and Nurse Smythe saw her to the door of the nursery.

"Don't you worry about a thing, my lady," the nurse said. "I'll look after the young masters. They'll be perfectly safe and sound until your return."

"Thank you, Nurse." Virginia gave the woman a grateful nod and left the room, her dinner gown swishing softly as she walked down the hall. She paused just before she reached the landing, looking at the table where Lucas had put the candle down to hold her. Had that been only three weeks ago? It felt far longer.

Continuing on her way, Virginia allowed gratitude for the earl to slip through her walls. Truly, he had done much for her and the children, and he continuously gave far more than he needed to. He halted his work once or twice a week to take her children riding. He laid down whatever was at hand to answer her questions about household matters. He conversed with her at breakfast, even if he'd been reading through correspondence. And Lucas always remembered to ask how her day had gone, if the boys needed anything, and if there was anything he might do for her.

Virginia had been relieved to find Lucas Calvert kind, but she did not entirely know what to do with someone who so consistently put her needs above his own.

Only Charles had ever done that before.

Charles. She missed their easy way of talking, she missed knowing what he would say almost before he said it. Would it ever be possible to feel such closeness to another?

Dismissing that thought, she went down the stairs and to the parlor adjacent the dining room. The adults in the household would go in to dinner soon. There would likely be more conversation about Virginia and Lucas's trip. They had discussed little else the preceding two evenings and tomorrow was the departure.

When she came down to the first floor, she saw Ellen preparing to descend the stairs to dinner. Her new sister-in-law smiled in her quiet, welcoming way.

"Good evening, Virginia," she said. "I am sorry it will be the last one we spend in company. I have enjoyed coming to know you better."

"Thank you, Ellen. It has been such a pleasure to meet you. Thank you for staying on while we're away, helping with the boys. Mother Calvert dotes on them, but I think their energy can be too much for her at times."

Ellen's eyebrows raised and her eyes glittered with amusement. "Best not let her hear you say such things. She will be terribly affronted that you've perceived a weakness in her."

They both laughed softly.

"I am glad to do it," Ellen added more seriously. "They are marvelous boys, and I am quite accustomed to being around children. My sisters have more than a few."

"You are well practiced at being an aunt. I think the boys could sense it the moment they met you." Truthfully, Virginia hadn't seen them take to anyone in such a short time, even Christine. "I hope you aren't spending too much time away from your own household."

Ellen lifted one shoulder in a shrug. "The wonderful thing about well-run households is that they are well-run even when you don't oversee them." She looked down at her dress, a beautiful pink evening gown with a dark blue sash, and smoothed her skirt. "Will this do for dinner?"

"It's perfect, and very lovely on you." Virginia tried to keep the note of longing from her voice. Charles had loved when she wore pink, but it hadn't been her favorite color. She much preferred the richer hues permitted married women. But anything would make her feel more alive, more like herself, than gray. Tonight she wore gray crepe, the fabric made in such a way that it didn't shine as a silk gown would.

Charles had told her once, when they first received the prognosis, that he would hate to see her in mourning. She had said he wouldn't have to, of course, and wore her most beautiful gowns every day she attended to him. He never saw gray or black upon her in those final days.

"If it is not too personal for me to ask, Virginia, are you in half mourning?" Ellen motioned to Virginia's gray dress.

"Not precisely." Virginia looked at her lavender gloves. "To tell the truth, I am uncertain where I am in mourning. It has been four months since Charles passed away, but I feel as though it has been so much longer. And as a newlywed, where does the duty to my late husband end and my present husband begin? It leaves me out of sorts."

Ellen didn't speak for a moment, but Virginia did not rush her. The other woman, she had learned, possessed a thoughtful nature.

"I cannot imagine your position, your feelings, on the matter." Ellen reached out and laid her hand on Virginia's wrist. "But I do know something of marrying into a rather impossible position."

"You?" Virginia couldn't contain her surprise. "Marcus is entirely devoted to you."

Humor sparkled in Ellen's eyes. "He is, isn't he? But it was not always that way for us. When we married, it was a matter of convenience. It took a little time for us to understand one another. Your situation is very different than mine, and I will not pretend otherwise. But I wish to give you hope, Virginia, that where we begin is not where we must end. Lucas is a good man, as I'm certain you know. If you are struggling, if you cannot find the footing you need in your relationship with him, speak to him."

Though she did not think herself able to follow such advice, Virginia appreciated Ellen's words. "Thank you, Ellen. You are a kind friend."

Ellen shook her head, deflecting the compliment before she spoke again. "You will be alone in a carriage with your husband for nearly all of tomorrow. Make use of that uninterrupted time."

A tiny prick of anxiety touched Virginia's heart. She had avoided thinking about the long journey by carriage. Why, she could not say, but with Ellen's words the truth came into her mind at last.

Their journey to Heatherton Hall would put them alone, truly alone, for the first time. Thus far, they had only spent snatches of time in each other's company, nearly always with a servant or family member present. Or else they spoke to each other with a very specific purpose, such as she checking menus with him and he asking if he might take the boys to their riding lessons. They never simply talked.

Oh dear. What if we have nothing to say?

Marcus appeared at the bottom of the staircase, looking up at them. "There you ladies are. You had better come down to dinner. Mother is convinced you are both having a wonderful time without her."

Virginia and Ellen shared quick smiles before saying, in unison, "Coming!" They laughed and descended together, going directly to the dining room. Ellen went in on her husband's arm, though he offered to take Virginia in, as was correct.

"It is a family dinner," Virginia had protested. "We need not be formal here."

When they entered, she saw her mother-in-law already seated and Lucas standing beside her chair, waiting to assist her into it. Their eyes met and his lightened with his smile. Virginia's heart gave an odd twist.

The carriage ride became all the more daunting.

Chapter Seventeen

If the roads stayed dry, Lucas calculated it would take ten hours on the road to reach Suffolk. They would travel for six, changing horses twice, and stay the night in Kentford. He had sent Randal and Virginia's maid ahead to prepare the way for them and sent letters to the stable yards along the way to ensure a speedy change of horses when they stopped.

It would be a long day of travel, but hopefully a pleasant one. His cook had provided them an excellent hamper, at his request. One never knew what sort of food they would find at roadside inns.

Lucas waited for Virginia in the entryway, the whole family lingering to bid them farewell. Ellen was speaking with the boys in a soft, lilting voice while Nurse Smythe smiled encouragingly at them both. His mother sat on a cushioned bench, dog in her lap, watching everyone around her with an indulgent look. And Marcus stood next to him, hands tucked behind his back, staring upward at the chandelier.

"I like your wife," his brother said, tone low enough that only Lucas heard him.

Lucas turned and raised his eyebrows. "Do you? I rather like yours, too."

Marcus's smile appeared, though crooked. "It would seem we both have an unusual amount of luck, to stumble into marriages with women who are rather perfect for us."

This gave Lucas pause. His brother's match hadn't begun with affection, but Marcus's own desperation. Eventually, Marcus had fallen in love with his wife, and had been perhaps the last to realize it.

"You needn't look at me like that," Marcus continued after Lucas stayed silent too long. "I think you know precisely what I mean. I've seen you, and the way you watch her."

Lucas cleared his throat and turned his eyes away, studying a faded tapestry hanging on the wall in front of him. "She's in mourning," he said at last. "And she would not have married if she hadn't needed to protect the boys."

"You're playing the gallant hero, Luc, as you always do. But I think you and she are rather meant to rescue each other. Those boys are already worshiping you, even if you won't tell them where the secret passage is." Marcus clapped his brother on the shoulder. "And what kind of man would you be if you didn't notice your wife's beauty?"

Lucas opened his mouth to protest, but his eyes caught movement on the stairs and he raised them to see Virginia. All thought went out of his head as he took her appearance in. She wore a travelling suit of soft gray, putting him in mind of a dove, with a matching bonnet. But she could've been dressed in a gown made from burlap and still looked lovely. The angles of her figure had softened in her time as his wife, the color in her cheeks more often a pleasant shade of pink.

Marcus had spoken truly enough. Virginia's beauty stole Lucas's breath away.

He waited to approach her, allowing Edward and Phillip to step forward first, slinging their little arms around her waist and legs.

"What's this? Darlings, I will be back in a week's time. There is no need for tears." But as she bent to return their embraces, Lucas caught the sheen of moisture in her eyes.

Lucas put a hand on Marcus's shoulder. "Excuse me. Duty calls." He stepped in behind the boys and crouched down to their level. "Gentlemen. I feel I need to speak to you both very seriously for a moment."

Phillip wiped suspiciously at his eyes and Edward looked up, not bothering to wipe at his tears.

"You see," Lucas continued, his mind reaching back to what would've soothed him as a boy. "We must exchange duties for a time. I am leaving my estate, and my guests, in your care."

"In *our* care?" Phillip asked, incredulous as always.

"Quite right." Lucas didn't crack a smile. It was important they knew he was serious, that they knew he held them in high esteem. "I expect you to be good hosts to my mother and your uncle and aunt. Treat them with respect and kindness. See to it the staff fulfills their duties. Be good to Nurse Smythe. And for the time we are away, I will look after your mother. I will protect her and see that she is safe and comfortable. When I return, I expect to confer with you both so we may report on our successes. Does this suit you, Phillip? Edward?"

Little Edward nodded at once.

Phillip regarded him with a frown and Lucas's heart dropped. He thought they'd been making progress, becoming closer, but maybe not.

"You will keep Mother safe? You promise?" the child asked, his voice quiet.

"I promise." No one who heard Lucas speak could doubt him. He wasn't just speaking to the boy, but to everyone in the room. "You have my word."

Phillip nodded. "I'll look after things here, too."

"Excellent." He reached out to shake Phillip's hand and the boy nearly smiled at the grown-up gesture.

165

Edward stepped forward, pulling a folded sheet of paper from the inside of his jacket. "I made you a picture of the house, so you'll remember it."

Lucas took the paper and tucked it into his jacket. "Thank you, Edward. May I share it with your mother?" Edward nodded and then, to Lucas's surprise, he launched his four-and-a-half-year-old body into Lucas's arms.

Looking up at Virginia, Lucas saw her cover her smile with one hand. He wrapped his arms around Edward, returning the embrace, and his throat tightened up. The little boy's complete trust, his innocent affection, had been given freely and completely. Lucas didn't feel worthy of it. He cleared his throat and Edward stepped away, smiling.

"Thank you, Edward." He smiled back. "I will miss you."

Then he stood and was swept up in the farewells of the adults, and Virginia with him. Somehow, they finally disentangled themselves enough that Lucas could escort Virginia outside into the warm morning sunlight. It felt like summer at last, and all the rain had turned the whole countryside green and vibrant. If they could have more days like this, the fields would turn gold and lush, and he would not need to worry so about his tenants and farms. But if the rains continued and weather didn't warm sufficiently, the harvest would be late.

It was a situation he would have to look over at the Heatherton estate as well.

Lucas offered his assistance, helping Virginia into the carriage. Her gloved fingers rested trustingly in his for only a moment, but it was enough for his heart to acknowledge the touch with a skittering beat.

As soon as he climbed in behind her, a footman closing the door, they were alone.

No family. No servants. Nothing to call them away.

He sat down beside her and took off his hat, tossing it on the seat across from them. The carriage would grow warm quickly and he preferred to ride in some comfort.

Virginia finished waving from the window, the equipage started forward, and then she sat back and noted his hat. "That must be pleasant," she said with half a smile. "I rarely envy the fashion of men, but today I do envy you your hat."

He chuckled and leaned into his corner of the coach, turned toward her. "You could cast off your bonnet nearly as easily."

She shook her head. "And spend hours shaking dust from my hair? Or straightening pins every time I step out when we change horses? I think not."

"It isn't solely my hat you envy, but my hair." His valet would have choked on his disapproval had he seen Lucas reach up and run his hands through his hair in such a way as to purposefully leave it a mess. But Virginia laughed, which was a rare enough sound that made it worth the ridiculousness of the moment. It set the tone for their time together, too, and Lucas would rather begin with a laugh than stiff politeness.

"I don't envy it when it looks like a nest made of straw." She folded her hands primly in her lap and pressed her lips together, obviously trying to regain a more proper manner.

He frowned as severely as he could make himself and put his nose in the air. "Madam, I have been told my hair looks like burnished gold."

Virginia's laugh came as a short burst this time. She covered it the sound with one hand. "Oh, dear. Who made that proclamation?"

"A very eager young miss, about eight years ago." He grinned and folded his arms across his chest. "But as someone with hair of a similar hue, you must've heard worse." Though her hair was brighter than his, more like the reflection of the sun on water. His was dark, burnished gold in need of shining. He'd never considered the beauty of such hair until he met Virginia.

Someday, he might tell her so.

"I certainly have." She raised a finger to tap against her lips, narrowing her eyes as she thought. "One of the worst was when someone compared it to a crown, only lacking acceptable jewels to adorn it."

That was the worst? "It sounds rather poetic to me."

"The man was a fortune hunter," she added with a shrug. "If seeing me made him think of tiaras and jewels, I had a fair idea of what he was really after."

"Ah, that does make more sense." Lucas let his eyes rest on her lovely face, taking in the beauty of her eyes. "And what have you heard about your eyes? Mine are usually compared to a stormy-sea."

"Emeralds, of course," she said, getting into the spirit of the game. She raised her chin loftily. "What other shade is there?"

He leaned forward and peered at her, pretending to study her eyes. Even in the darkened carriage, they shone. "I can understand that, for the unimaginative, it is the first thing that comes to mind."

"And for the imaginative?" she asked, raising her eyebrows.

"They are the cool green of a forest pool on a summer day, giving and reflecting the life around it."

Her cheeks went pink and her expression faltered. "That is more imaginative," she said, false levity in her voice.

He shrugged, maintaining his casual attitude. "You asked." He leaned back into his corner and lowered his eyes. "What did Charles say about them?" Lucas needed to make certain she knew, that she understood, he was not trying to turn their relationship into more. Not yet. No matter how much he wished it.

Virginia looked down at her gloved hands, adjusting the fingers of the light material. She was quiet long enough he thought he might need to apologize for overstepping. But just before he opened his mouth, she started to speak, her voice soft with memory.

"Charles compared them to any number of things. Summer meadows, I think, was my favorite. Mostly he just told me he loved them."

"Smart fellow." Lucas allowed his eyes to drift to the window on her side, looking out over the verdant fields they passed by. "How did you meet him? If you don't mind my asking."

It was the right topic for both of them. As she spoke of her first season, beginning slowly at first but then with more feeling, he realized how much she needed to talk of Charles. She apologized often enough for bringing up her late husband, but being without him likely made the memories the sweeter to hold. He listened, only making an occasional remark, as she told him how spoiled she had been before meeting the young baron.

Their love story drew him in, and he saw Virginia as she had seen herself. Young, naive, too proud, until love and tenderness softened the edges of her heart. But she credited motherhood with causing her true change.

"Charles adored the boys. He paid them so much more attention, from the start, than my father gave me. He was besotted with them." Virginia's posture had relaxed as she spoke, her hands rested in her lap.

"I can understand that. They are endearing children." He remembered Edward's drawing and pulled it from the inside of his coat. "Edward has been giving me artwork nearly every day for the last several weeks." He unfolded the paper and moved so they could both look at it. "He has an excellent eye for color."

Virginia held her hand out, taking one corner of the drawing to examine it. It was the house, drawn in red near the shade of the brick. He'd made the sky above it blue with gray clouds. There was green grass all around it, and too few windows. He'd added white, swirling blobs in the grass that must be his depiction of sheep. He'd written his name in the corner, the letters as well-formed as his unlearned hands could make them.

Lucas studied Virginia as she looked at the drawing, real interest in her eyes. They sat close, close enough that he could bend his head and place a kiss on her cheek if he were inclined.

He released his side of the paper and went back to his corner. "If I could frame all of his little masterpieces, I would," he said brightly, covering his retreat. The scent of oranges followed him.

"We would swiftly run out of wall space," Virginia said, her smile almost sad. "He used to do drawings for Charles, too. I think you have captured Edward's heart. I'm not surprised. He's a loving child and you've been so good to him. Thank you for that."

Lowering his eyes to the floor, Lucas didn't know what to say. Did it bother her, that Edward had so fully attached himself to Lucas?

"I do not mean to take your late husband's place. Does it trouble you that he—?"

"Not at all, Lucas. I want them to have someone in their life who is good and kind, who teaches them how to grow into good men." She reached out and laid her hand on his arm, her expression earnest. Though separated from her touch by the layers of her gloves, his jacket, and shirt, Lucas was supremely aware of it, and the gentleness in it.

He resisted the desire to lift her hand, to hold it in his.

Lucas could never have sent her on this journey alone, but he began to question how he would make it through the trip without revealing more than was appropriate of his feelings.

"I will do my best. I have my work cut out for me with Phillip."

Keep talking about the children. Being a parent. Just keep talking.

"He's always been a trifle serious. I think he is warming up to you, though. It was clever, giving him responsibility before leaving. I think putting trust in him will allow him to do the same for you." At last she removed her hand. Virginia began to fold the drawing in her lap.

Lucas kept on in that vein, asking her question after question about her sons. Virginia grew animated as she told him stories of their earlier childhood. Stories about frogs in gardens, sliding down banisters, their first words. She filled the carriage with her memories and Lucas took them all in, watching her all the while.

Her love for her sons knew no bounds. No wonder she had been willing to marry a stranger, on the hope that it would all work for the better. Virginia would do anything for Phillip and Edward.

And for her sake, and theirs, Lucas knew that he would too.

Chapter Eighteen

The sounds in the courtyard woke her. The inn's bell sounded loudly, signaling the arrival of a mail coach. Virginia laid still, staring up at the ceiling. Her body didn't ache as much as it usually did after a day of travel. Limiting the first leg of their journey to only a few hours had been wise, and Lucas's carriage was well sprung. Another two or three hours of the journey awaited them.

What would they talk about today? All the day before, Lucas had been content to let her prattle on about anything and everything. First Charles, then the boys, then her growing up. After changing horses the first time, he asked more about Heatherton Hall and the management of the estate. He asked about its tenants and her neighbors.

He knew nearly everything about her after one carriage ride.

Nearly.

She hadn't told him how nervous she was to return to her neighborhood. To meet old acquaintances and explain about her married state. Or how much she dreaded the moment when she would visit Charles's grave. She had not seen it yet. What would it be like to stand before a tombstone bearing his name? Would it make the pain fresh again?

When she'd spoken of Charles the day before, answering Lucas's questions, she had waited for the knife of loneliness to pierce her. She'd expected to feel her heart crumbling a little more with each mention of his name. But those feelings didn't come. There was an ache, an empty space, in her heart that Charles had once filled. But it was not as painful as it had been.

Months remained to mourn him. Ought she to hurt more as she had at the start?

Virginia turned her thoughts from there, ignoring the guilt creeping in upon her.

I will make Lucas talk today, she told herself firmly. She would ask the questions, she would learn all about him, come to understand why he felt the need to rescue her, a complete stranger.

Louisa, her lady's maid, entered the room quietly, holding a tray. Virginia sat up slowly and smiled when they made eye contact.

"Good morning, my lady." Louisa dipped a curtsy and hurried to put the tray down on a small table. "I thought you might prefer your breakfast here. The private parlor is full up with another party and the public room is frightfully loud." She opened the thick curtains and then the window.

"Thank you, Louisa. Is his lordship up yet?" Virginia ran a hand down her braid, checking that it all stayed in place. She still felt gritty from travel, but when she arrived at Heatherton Hall she intended to take a bath.

"Yes, my lady. He is taking his breakfast, too." Louisa brought over Virginia's tray, then bustled about to lay out what Virginia would need for her travels.

Virginia began nibbling at her ham and eggs, her thoughts on the carriage ride from the day before. "How was your journey yesterday, Louisa?"

"Quite lovely, my lady. But I don't know that we can hope for the same today. There are clouds in the sky." She pointed to the window and Virginia looked. She had thought it only to be early, but now she saw the gray skies.

"I had better hurry then, so you and his lordship's valet can get a good start." Virginia took a quick swallow of tea and set the tray aside, moving to begin her preparations.

"As you say, my lady."

Between the two of them, Virginia was ready in under a quarter of an hour. In her more youthful days, Virginia was known to take hours to get ready in the morning. She smiled and shook her head at that thought, then paused.

It was the most rushed toilette she'd had in a long while, yet when she looked in the mirror she felt she would do. The color in her cheeks was heightened, likely due to her rush, and her bonnet hid any deficiencies in her hair. And really, how could one fuss and fret over whether a gray traveling gown looked fashionable enough?

But it was more than that.

She was eager to begin her travels again. Eager to join Lucas in the carriage and begin her line of questioning. And, she told herself firmly, she was impatient to return to her home. Heatherton Hall was waiting, along with a great deal of work. The sooner she arrived, the sooner she could get things settled and return to her children.

"There you are, my lady." Louisa finished the last button on her glove. "Will there be anything else?"

"No, thank you. Fetch a porter and we can have these things packed."

"Yes, my lady." Louisa curtsied and left. Virginia went to the doorway and looked out into the hall. A woman and gentleman down the hall stood together, the woman lifting her chin, and the man tying her bonnet ribbons for her.

That lonely ache made itself felt again. Charles had helped her retie bonnets and adjust gloves. He'd buttoned a fair number of gowns for her, too. The easy intimacy between a husband and wife was something she had taken for granted. She had not even realized it until the night Lucas held her as she cried. A thousand little gestures and touches could take place between a husband a wife, just within the course of a day.

Would she ever have that again?

"Good morning, my lady."

Virginia pulled her eyes away from the couple down the hall just as the woman began to straighten the man's cravat.

Lucas stood behind her, in his own doorway, his hands busy with his gloves. "Nearly ready to begin again?" His easy smile helped ease her melancholy thoughts.

"I am, my lord."

"Excellent. I think we ought to enjoy a short walk, take some exercise before we are confined to the coach again. What do you think?"

Virginia nodded and took his arm when he offered it. She glanced behind her once more, but the other couple had gone.

Lucas led her through the inn, where guests and servants alike buzzed about like bees in a hive. They stepped out into the courtyard, the dull gray of the skies softening the morning light. Virginia managed not to shiver when a crisp breeze snapped along at her heels.

"Will summer never settle in England?" she asked aloud, then bit the inside of her cheek. She hadn't meant to complain. Bemoaning things neither of them could change, like the weather, would do little more than lead to more whining.

But Lucas's response was made with a serious expression. "I have been thinking on the strange summer as well. I cannot remember it being this cold. In the summer, just a few years ago, it would be abominably hot. My brother and I used to swim in the lake at Annesbury Park. I cannot imagine plunging into that water now."

"Every time Nurse Smythe asks about putting away the boys' winter clothes, we determine their warm boots and coats might still be needed." Virginia adjusted her hold on her skirt when they stepped onto a small dirt path leading away from the inn. She wore sensible half-boots and felt grateful for the exercise. Confinement to a coach or carriage had never been something she enjoyed. "How are the tenant farms faring?" she asked, keeping her eyes on the horizon and the tall, green grasses lining the path.

"Not as well as I'd wish. Fields have flooded, been cleared, and flooded again. The lack of sunlight is doing real harm to the plants. I fear the harvest will be late this year. I can only hope it yields well." When Virginia glanced at him, she saw his head lowered and his eyes upon the ground. The burdens of thoughtful landowners were many indeed.

"If the harvest is late, and poor, what will we do?" she asked.

He raised his eyes, meeting hers, and his expression softened. "We will do our best for the people under our care. Thankfully, my father taught me to always set a portion of our income aside for difficult times. We will need to see what comes of the harvest to truly plan, but we would certainly see to the needs of our tenants before worrying over any profits the land could yield."

Virginia realized, after he began talking, that she had included herself in his plans. But he had said "we" enough times to prove he didn't mind.

"I confess, I don't know what Charles did for the barony. I hope those lands have done well enough it will not be a concern, but will you show me how you determine what to set aside for such situations?"

"I will. And when Phillip grows older, I will teach him as well. We never know what the future will bring." His walk slowed and his eyes drifted across the land before them. She watched as his expression relaxed and she waited, silently, her hand resting on his arm.

Lucas's eyes were grayer today, like the sky above them, but where the clouds muted the sun his eyes were bright. The breeze flew by again, making the grass around them dip and ripple like water. He took in a deep breath and the faintest of smiles curved his lips upward. Any woman who saw him would find him handsome. That she knew him to be a kind man, an intelligent one too, gave her greater appreciation for what it meant to stand at his side as his wife.

Would he come to fill the empty places of her heart? Was it disloyal to think he might? He was not Charles, but his good qualities reminded her of her late husband. He was honest, generous, cared genuinely for those under his responsibility, treated her sons like they were his own, and appreciated the good things in his life.

And he looked at her, sometimes, like he could not have wished for another companion in her place.

As he did then, his gray eyes meeting hers, his smile growing.

"What are your thoughts at the moment, my lady? You are studying me closely enough, ought I to be concerned you've seen a fault to correct?" He was teasing her, but Virginia blushed to be caught staring.

She was worse than a girl fresh from the schoolroom. She couldn't remember feeling this disconcerted around a man. Not since her courtship days.

"I was actually thinking quite the opposite," she said, deciding on honesty. "I was thinking how fortunate I am to have been rescued by you. I think back on that day you proposed and I still cannot quite understand your motivations. You've accepted a great deal of responsibility with very little given in return."

Eventually, she knew he would expect more from her. That was clear from the time he had solicited her for her hand. But he could've married nearly anyone and had an heir sooner. His position in society, his wealth, were enough in themselves to attract a throng of women eager to wed him. Why choose a widow with two sons? Why take upon himself a woman who came with her own burdens and griefs?

Lucas didn't turn from her, nor did he tease this time, though his smile gentled.

"It might seem that way, I suppose. But in the time you've been part of my life, my world has changed for the better."

Virginia had to raise her eyebrows at that, not quite believing him. She took her hand from his arm and started to walk down the path again, clasping her hands behind her. A tightness in her chest loosened as she created distance between them, a tension she hadn't examined ebbed away.

"You don't believe me?" he asked, a step behind her, matching her pace.

"It is difficult to do so, my lord. In what way can a widow and her two sons have made your life easier?"

He spoke from behind her and she resisted the desire to look back, to study his expression and match it to his words. "For a long time now, my life has been rather hollow. I've seen to my duties, for the most part, but the responsibilities of my position cannot keep me company. With you, Phillip, and Edward, the days are less empty."

Here she stopped, the empty place in her heart echoing his words. Virginia knelt and picked a wildflower at her feet, more for something to do than a real desire to possess it. His words sounded much as she felt. After she saw to the boys at the end of each day, she had to avoid examining her feelings too closely. At first it had been her defense against the pain of Charles's lost, but of late it had more to do with avoiding what she might find in place of that pain.

Lucas bent and began to gather flowers as well, and he continued speaking. "My life has changed. I prepare myself for the day knowing I will see you at breakfast, that I will be presented a new drawing from

Edward, that Phillip might seek me out to ask questions about being a landowner."

"Phillip? Really?" Virginia's surprise couldn't be concealed.

"You didn't know?" Lucas asked.

"No. I thought he only saw you in passing, or during rides. He seeks you out?"

Lucas looked up at her, his gloved hands full of brightly colored flowers. "I thought you might've suggested it to him." He stood slowly, his height emphasized by the tall black hat upon his head. "He knows my schedule better than I do. It always seems to be an accident when we meet, usually in a hallway. Phillip bows and I ask about his day. Then he asks after mine. If I tell him I was looking at accounts, he asks how to know when the accounts are right. He always has a question or two. I've been wondering, actually, if I might begin some instruction with him. He's young, but he shows a real interest."

Phillip was young. But he would be seven years old before the summer was out. Perhaps it was time for more lessons than a nurse could provide.

"I think that would be good for him. If it isn't too much trouble."

Lucas arranged the flowers into a smaller bouquet, picking off leaves and shortening a stem. "Phillip and Edward are never any trouble. Neither is their mother. I am completely at their disposal, and under your command." The words were spoken softly, but with a feeling behind them Virginia could not name. Would not name. She told herself he was only being gallant. It was in his nature to be kind and even self-sacrificing.

He held the bouquet out to her, met her gaze again, and Virginia's heart rose into her throat.

No. No, it is too soon.

She accepted the flowers and added her own to the mix, their bright colors contrasting against the black gloves she wore today. "Thank you," she whispered.

"We had better return to the carriage." He turned on the path and offered his arm to her again. She took it, grasping the flowers in her free hand. In the distance, she heard a rumble of thunder.

The day's journey might be more difficult than she had anticipated.

Chapter Nineteen

The remainder of the trip to Heatherton Hall passed quietly. Lucas tried not to mind, allowing his thoughts to wander freely while he stared out the window. Virginia didn't speak often, but he watched from the corner of his eye as she began to weave the stems of the flowers he'd given her, turning them into a small braided loop. Once that had been completed, she rested her hands in her lap and stared out the opposite window.

The silence wasn't uncomfortable. He was grateful for that. He knew either of them might break it at any time, without anxiety for what might be said, but it had felt right to let it lie between them.

He'd said more than he intended on their walk that morning. But she'd been lovely, and sweet, and he'd wanted to reassure her of the place she held in his life.

Unwittingly, he'd nearly revealed to them both the place she, and the boys, now held in his heart.

"We are a mile from Heatherton Hall," Virginia said, just before noon. She sat up straighter and looked out the window with eagerness.

He watched her, thinking of what it meant to return to her home. "How long has it been, Virginia?" he asked.

"I've not been here since last autumn. October." She gave him a bittersweet smile, her eyes sad in the way they often were when she spoke of Charles Macon.

Lucas took himself in hand, putting off the examination of his feelings for another time. For now, he only reached out to her, offering his gloved hand. She put hers inside it, after a brief hesitation. He clasped it gently, giving her his support.

"It will be a good visit for you, to see everything still in place as you remember it." Then he released her and reached across the carriage for his hat, which he had discarded again as soon as the carriage door had shut that morning. He settled it firmly on his head and looked through the window.

The trees lining their path were younger, perhaps only twenty or thirty years old, with bright green leaves and ash-colored bark. The land was green and damp. The clouds seemed to have followed them from the inn. When they turned down a lane, iron gates standing open on either side, Lucas leaned forward to catch a glimpse of the house.

The driveway was not long, and Heatherton Hall sat nestled among tall hedges and little else. It was constructed entirely of gray stone, with a multitude of small, white-pane windows. It reminded him of castles he'd seen, ruins really, built when English land was forever being conquered by invaders and neighbors alike. But it was handsome, for all that it was imposing.

"It's impressive," Lucas said.

"It's an old pile of stone." He looked to see her smiling, though her face had lost some of its color. "But there have been improvements made to it in the last few decades. It is comfortable and will make Phillip a fine home someday."

The carriage slowed to a stop and a footman appeared to open the door.

Lucas stepped out first, nodding his thanks to the servant, then reached up to help Virginia down. He turned with her hand in his, facing a small row of servants. The expressions on their faces ranged from indifferent to curious. Randal and Virginia's maid were part of their ranks and neither of them looked particularly pleased either.

This will be interesting. Lucas barely kept the frown off his face. He would follow Virginia's lead. This was her home and Phillip's inheritance. He would help where asked and remain silent on the rest.

Virginia greeted the head servants, introducing him.

"My lord, I have a few things to discuss with the housekeeper, if you would prefer to go freshen up?" Virginia met his eyes, her smile gone and her lips thin.

"Of course, my lady." He gestured for Randal to lead him into the house, paying no mind to the other servants. In a matter of minutes, they had crossed the dark stone floors of the entryway, gone up the floating staircase, and down a hall carpeted in red. Very little light entered the hall, with only a window at the very end of it. Randal opened a door leading into a bedroom decorated in blues and greens.

The moment the door shut behind him, Lucas took his hat off and tossed it into a chair near a small hearth. "Out with it, Randal," he said, already stripping off his gloves. "Something has upset you and I want to hear what it is."

Randal cleared his throat and retrieved the hat. "It isn't my place to say anything, my lord."

"Hang your place. That was the most unpleasant looking line of servants I've ever seen and you look like you've swallowed salt water." Lucas thrust his gloves out to his valet, fixing the servant with his narrow-eyed glare. "What ails the household?"

Randal took the gloves and walked to a tall bureau in the corner, carefully laying the hat on top and placing the gloves in a drawer. His movements were stiffer than normal.

"You are in the guest wing, my lord."

Lucas thought that over a moment. "And the countess?"

"Her old room, in the family wing." The valet's cool tone conveyed little emotion but plenty of disapproval. "And I am uncertain as to who determined the arrangements, whether it was my lady the countess or the housekeeper, Mrs. Thackery."

He was a guest. His wife still the mistress. Interesting. If it was the housekeeper's doing, she showed a distinct lack of respect for him and her mistress. If it was Virginia's—

"It is best not to take offense, Randal. One room is very much like another, and we are here only a matter of days. Now, help me clean up for luncheon."

Randal nodded and said no more on the subject, but the valet's expression said he thought plenty.

By the time Lucas left his chambers in search of the dining room, tension had entered his body and shoulders. He descended to the first floor and found a footman standing as sentry in the hall. The stone-faced young man led him to the dining room.

A cold lunch was spread upon the table, but Virginia was nowhere to be seen yet. Lucas looked at the food with some longing, his stomach reminding him he hadn't eaten since he'd woken that morning. He walked to one of the windows, facing out into a gravel path disappearing between two tall hedges. The gray stone contrasted against the greenery.

Did any colors besides green and gray exist at Heatherton?

The door to the dining room opened. Lucas dropped his hands to his side and turned to face his wife. Her eyes snapped in a manner he'd only seen once before, when he'd upset her with the boys in the rain, and her posture vibrated with agitation.

"Virginia?" He stepped nearer her without hesitation, almost reaching out but resisting that impulse. Instead he met her at the head of the table, only needing to take a few strides to reach it.

She reached out and grasped the top of the chair, her green eyes full of sparks. "I am sorry, Lucas. I'm not sure what happened. I instructed that we both have rooms prepared for us, but apparently I was misunderstood. I meant for two rooms in the family wing to be prepared. I specified that the baron's room was to remain untouched, but somehow—"

Lucas put his hand over hers, on the chair. Neither of them wore gloves and the contact sent a current into his arm and directly to his heart. Years of training, of subjecting himself to the scrutiny of the *ton* and Parliament, kept him from giving any hint at the sudden jolt.

"It's of no matter, Virginia. My room is pleasant and well-appointed. If it was a mistake, it isn't a fatal one. We will not be here long."

Still, the fact that she hadn't made the arrangements eased his mind.

Virginia's shoulders slumped and she dropped her eyes to look somewhere below his chin as she spoke. "I don't think the staff quite approves of me at present. There have been other things that speak of resentment on their part."

Lucas removed his hand from hers and reached out to touch just beneath her chin, barely grazing her skin. His chest tightened when her eyes darted upward, meeting his with a measure of surprise.

"Then you will get to the heart of the matter and correct things, I am certain of it. And I will be here, should you wish for my company or assistance."

Did Virginia know how much he meant those words? Could she ever understand the emotions behind them?

"Thank you, Lucas." His eyes fell to her lips as she spoke his name. He backed away, pulling the chair out for her. Imagining what it would be like to kiss her did nothing for his self-control.

"You are most welcome, my lady. Would you care to partake of this excellent meal?"

A humorless chuckle escaped her. "Since when is cold ham excellent?" She moved to take her seat.

"Since I am absolutely famished," he answered, forcing lightness in his tone.

Lucas went to the opposite end of the table, grateful for the distance between them.

¤

Being slighted by her own servants had never happened to Virginia before. She could hear her mother's voice in her mind, repeating lessons of household management to her. But something such as this had never been discussed. Then again, Virginia couldn't imagine anyone daring to show so much as a hint of insubordination to Lady Vinespar. The woman likely would've routed Napoleon on her first entry into battle by doing no more than casting a glare in his direction.

At least Lucas hadn't seemed insulted. His calm acceptance of the matter had eased her irritation enough for her to enjoy the meal.

"Where would you like to begin our work here, Virginia?" Lucas asked when she put her fork aside.

"The steward should arrive soon." She dropped her hands to her lap and kept them still, though she felt more like rubbing them down her skirts. "I think the best place to conduct that meeting will be in the study."

"Excellent." Lucas stood and dropped his napkin on the table. He came to her side before the footman could move to assist her from her chair. Lucas took the task upon himself, then gestured for her to lead the way from the room.

Virginia showed him down the hall, pointing out closed doors to him, telling him what lay behind each. "That is the music room. There is the parlor. Here is the study." She put her hand to the handle and hesitated, thinking of the last time she'd been inside that room.

"You almost expect him to be there," Lucas said softly, standing close enough for her to feel his strength at her back.

She nodded, her eyes on the dark-stained wood, imagining the scene as it had been months and months before. Virginia had been summoned to the room by Charles, entered the door with a light step and a smile, and he'd been standing at the window behind the desk. He'd looked out over the courtyard at the rear of the house. The leaves had all changed color by then, beginning to fall.

It was in that room where he had told her they must go to Bath, for his health. Did he realize, even then, that he would never return to Heatherton Hall again?

Lucas's steady presence at her back gave her the confidence she needed to push the door open and step inside.

The curtains were open, the windows too, allowing a gentle breeze to freshen the room. Ledgers were stacked upon the desk, as she'd requested. The bookshelves lining one wall were in good order. The room felt and smelled clean, not abandoned and forlorn as she thought it might be.

Virginia went to the desk, her hand coming to rest on a stack of account books.

Lucas went to the shelves first, giving her a moment to gather her emotions. She took in a deep breath and moved to one of the chairs across from where Charles had always sat to conduct business.

"I wouldn't sit there."

Lucas's soft voice made her pause. She turned, raising her eyebrows at him in question.

"Your steward needs to understand who's in charge here. Sit behind the desk." He nodded to the tall-backed chair, bound in rich brown leather.

Virginia looked from the chair to Lucas. "But where will you sit?"

"I will stand behind you, my lady." His lips tilted, his crooked smile gentle and teasing at the same time. "That is my place here. You are Phillip's guardian, I am your husband. Together, we will see to it his inheritance is safe, but I am in an advisory role only."

She tilted her chin up and tried for some levity. "Unless someone needs to be punched in the nose?"

Lucas's smile grew, almost wickedly. "Of course, my lady. I will not hesitate should that become necessary." He nodded to the chair again. "In the meantime, make yourself comfortable. Your steward must see you there, where you belong."

She walked around the desk and sat down, feeling strange in the seat that had always been the baron's. But not for long. Taking in a deep breath, the familiar scents of the room settled her. She could smell the tobacco from Charles's favorite pipe, caught in the curtains most likely. The leather of the chair, the scent of books and furniture polish, hung around her in a comforting embrace.

Resting her hands on the desk before her, Virginia's eyes lingered on the ink blotter and the fresh pens laid out for her use. How many times had she entered this room to see Charles bent over correspondence, or reading? He would look up at her, his brown eyes lighting up, and put everything aside to speak with her.

Her eyes came up to meet Lucas's. He stood at the shelves still, watching her with a knowing expression.

"Will it always be like this?" she asked before thinking better of it.

"Does it hurt?" he asked in turn.

Virginia contemplated that question, studying her heart and it's slow, peaceful rhythm. To her surprise, she found no pain. "No," she answered. "But I miss his company."

Lucas's smile was sad, not quite making it to his eyes. "I missed Abigail for a very long time. Would you like to know what helped?"

"Yes." She dropped her hands from the desk into her lap, watching him come nearer. "What did you do?"

"You may think me a little strange for it." He stopped at the corner of the desk and raised a hand to rub the back of his neck. "But I spoke to her. Or, I spoke aloud, as if she were listening. It helped, to ease my thoughts, to express them and imagine what Abigail might say to me if she were present." Lucas shrugged and dropped his hand. "It made me less lonely for her."

Virginia did not have time to ask more questions, to tell him how often she'd wished to do that very thing, because a knock at the door announced the steward.

Lucas shared one more look with her, and a wink of encouragement, before moving to stand behind her chair, as he said he would. His support silent but firm.

She took in a deep breath and bid the steward enter.

Chapter Twenty

Lucas woke Sunday morning, early as always, his eyes on the dark blue canopy of his bed. He rang for Randal and then went through the motions of getting ready, though his thoughts remained on the day before. The steward's meeting with Virginia had gone well. The books were all in order, the correspondence adequate, and Lucas could find no fault in the man's conduct. The steward had been amiable and kind to the baron's widow, and he'd expressed his hope that he would one day work with Phillip as well.

The household staff remained stiff, but Lucas dismissed that as a real concern. If it became a problem, he knew Virginia would be ready to handle the situation. She was a supremely confident woman in matters of household management.

This morning, Lucas had another concern entirely. Church. Virginia had told him, as if in passing, that she had decided to attend in order to renew acquaintances in the neighborhood.

"You needn't come, if you'd rather rest," she had added. But the lack of care in her tone was not matched by the look in her eyes. She was worried.

What if the rest of the neighborhood had the same view of her new marriage as her household?

"I wouldn't want to miss it," Lucas had said. "When would you like the carriage to be ready?" And that was that.

Virginia met him for breakfast in the dining room, wearing all black. The stark color, the complete lack of embellishment on her gown, brought him up short when he saw her. Her gowns had been growing lighter—he mostly saw her in gray and even lavender at times—and if she wore black she usually had white lace or a cream-colored fichu at her throat. But not today.

Virginia met his startled look and a rosy hue grew in her cheeks.

At least that's some color. Lucas forced a smile.

"It's the first time I have attended since Charles's death. They should see— The people here liked him. I want them to know that I am respecting his memory." Her fingers fidgeted at the folds in her skirt while she spoke, her voice tight with anxiety.

"You do great honor to the baron," Lucas said, nodding deeply to her. "No matter what you wear."

She smiled and sat down to breakfast. He watched her eat, noting with concern that she barely nibbled at her food. It had taken him some time to coax her into a healthier appetite, but he supposed today would be an exception for them both. He wasn't all that hungry either.

The carriage came to fetch them at the appointed time. Virginia pulled her gloves into place before they stepped out into the cool morning. Only the barest hint of blue could be seen on the horizon, the rest of the sky was a dismal gray. Lucas narrowed his eyes at it, thinking of his wilting crops.

Climbing into the carriage, Lucas settled next to Virginia on the seat. Her hands were tucked in her lap, clutching a reticule.

"Virginia," he said, bending his head to catch a glimpse of her down-turned eyes. "You mustn't let the opinions of others worry you. They cannot know the full story."

She nodded. "I know." Her eyes darted up to his, their green depths drawing him in, making him wish he could protect her from all her fears. "I don't dread it for my sake. Not really. But for the boys. For our family's reputation and place in the community."

He nodded, then reached into his coat and pulled out the black band he'd asked Randal to procure for him. "Would you help me with this?"

Virginia's eyes went to his hand and widened. "Lucas, you don't have to—"

"Of course I don't. But I want to. Really, I think I should've been wearing one before now." He held the band, meant to be wrapped around his arm, out to her. "I didn't have a black cravat or ornament for my hat, but I thought this would do." It would stand out well on his gray jacket sleeve.

"Indeed." She held the material in her gloved hands, looking down at it. "Thank you, Lucas." Then he extended his arm and she tied the band, twisting it around so the knot would be inside his arm instead of out. Her eyes glistened, brightening them considerably.

"Would you like my handkerchief?" he asked. He hadn't meant to make her cry. He wanted to show he stood by her, he wanted the world to see that he respected her choices of both mourning and marriage. He wanted to save her from censure.

Virginia shook her head and breathed deeply, in through her nose and out again. "I think I will be all right. Thank you."

And the carriage stopped. Lucas reached out to clasp her gloved hand in his own, offering a quick squeeze of reassurance, before he stepped out. He had also ordered that they take one of the baron's carriages, emblazoned with the Heatherton crest. He had no intention of calling more attention to himself than necessary.

Virginia stepped down, her hand in his.

There were already people in the churchyard, conversing, watching. Some were going into the church and after a nod from Virginia, Lucas took her in that direction. It did not take long to find their seats, at the very front of the room. Lucas slid in beside Virginia, on the outside of the pew. She kept her gaze forward from the moment she sat until the end of the service, and he followed her example.

The moment the vicar stepped away from the pulpit, skirts rustled, whispers began, and Lucas readied himself to be whatever support Virginia needed. If she needed him at all. They stood and an elderly woman dressed in purple came forward, on the arm of a younger woman.

"My lady," the elderly one said, her voice loud in the nave. "My condolences, my lady. And my congratulations."

More than a few conversations stopped near them and Lucas could practically see ears stretching in their direction to hear Virginia's response.

"I thank you for both, Mrs. Carter. Please, allow me to introduce Lord Lucas Calvert, Earl of Annesbury. He has been most kind during these past months." Virginia hadn't so much as batted an eye as she spoke, her tone natural and gracious, as if it was the most normal thing in the world to mourn one husband and wed another.

Lucas inclined his head as the old woman curtsied.

"A pleasure, my lord. It is good to know our fine neighbor is being looked after. I did worry for her and those boys. But where are my manners? Here, this is my great-niece, Miss Tabitha Clark." Miss Clark curtsied and Lucas showed her the same courtesy he had shown Mrs. Carter.

"How is the rest of your family, Mrs. Carter?" Virginia asked. Others in the church shuffled around, and most went out the door. Lucas had no idea what significance Mrs. Carter held in Virginia's life, but he was immensely grateful that the woman chose to present herself immediately.

After a few minutes spent in simple niceties, the old woman took her niece and her leave.

Virginia's hand went to Lucas's arm. Had he not known the state of her mind that morning, Lucas would never believe her to be anxious about meeting her neighbors again. Her expression remained perfectly pleasant, her smile mild, and her posture relaxed.

As they walked down the aisle, Lucas leaned down just enough to speak in her ear. "You are a masterful actress, my lady."

She looked at him from the corners of her eyes. "Surely, as an earl, you can claim to have perfected your own outwardly displayed character, my lord."

He raised his eyebrows at her and schooled his features immediately, becoming no more than an impassive nobleman. He saw her smile but did not remove his mask to return it.

The vicar, a roundly-shaped man in his fifties, stood by the door to the church. "My lady, welcome home," the vicar said with a deep bow. "You have been greatly missed. Will you introduce me to your husband?"

Virginia made the introductions, the vicar bowed politely, then presented his next question to Lucas. "Will you and Lady Calvert remain in the neighborhood long, my lord?"

"Not this visit, Mr. Andrews. After some business is seen to, I'm afraid we must return to Annesbury." Lucas darted a quick glance at Virginia before adding, "Though I do hope we will visit often, and for longer, in future."

"Excellent, excellent." The vicar's warm smile turned uncertain. "My lady, I do offer my condolences on the baron's loss. And if you have any need to speak of it, or if you would like me to show you to his resting place, it would be my honor to assist you."

Virginia's cheeks paled at the mention of her late husband's grave, but to Lucas's surprise she shook her head. "That will not be necessary, Mr. Andrews, though I appreciate your thoughtfulness. I will visit another time, perhaps."

Because I am here? She must want to see it for herself, to make certain all is right with it.

Lucas would broach the subject with her later. For now, he bowed to the vicar again and led Virginia into the yard, where they were soon met with more fluttering women and stoic gentlemen, all casting him curious glances. No one asked outright about Virginia's speedy marriage, of course, and more than a few people cast their eyes at his armband. Let them make of the situation what they would; he hardly cared, so long as they remained civil to his wife.

And they did. No one spoke an unkind word to her.

The neighborhood held her in high enough opinion, and honored her late husband's memory, enough to trust her actions.

Then why was the household so unwelcoming? Perhaps he ought to see if Randal had learned anything on the matter.

When he handed Virginia back into the carriage, Lucas saw her shoulders slump. He climbed in next to her and as soon as the vehicle started moving, she untied the bonnet's ribbons and pulled the whole thing off her head. She cast it onto the seat across from them and turned to face him, her genuine smile back in place.

"You're quite right, Lucas. It is rather freeing to take that thing off in the carriage."

Lucas couldn't help it. He laughed, the tension from the morning gone. Perhaps the rest of their visit would go as smoothly. For Virginia's sake, he hoped so.

¤

Monday morning came, and Virginia's first order of business was to meet with the housekeeper and go over the household expenses. Without the family in residence, some of the servants were extraneous as well, but Virginia wanted to find a way to retain them without incurring unnecessary expense.

Mrs. Thackery came in at the requested time, moving stiffly, her expression sour. Virginia had never had reason to complain about the woman before, but now she wondered if it was wise to continue working together.

"My lady, here are the accounts." She put the book on the table and took her seat.

"Thank you, Mrs. Thackery." Virginia opened the little book and began going through the expenditures, asking the occasional question, making notes in her own little book. She paused over one notation. "What is this order for beef here, Mrs. Thackery? That is a higher amount than I would expect. Was there a celebration?"

"Mr. Macon was in residence that week, my lady."

The blood drained from Virginia's cheeks and lay cold in her heart. "Mr. Macon? Here?" She checked the date again. "Two weeks past? Why was I not informed?"

Mrs. Thackery straightened her shoulders and raised her chin. "He is family, my lady. I thought you knew and, if you did not, it would be a little matter. He has always been welcome here."

The cold treatment, the disrespectful attitude, all of it made sense. Mr. Macon had been present and likely filled the staff's ears with his complaints and slurs against her and Lucas.

She would set the matter right at once.

"Mrs. Thackery," she said, her tone strong. "That man is to never enter this house again unless I give express permission for him to do so."

Mrs. Thackery's eyes narrowed behind her spectacles. "But he is family—"

"Not anymore, Mrs. Thackery. Family does not threaten a mother's children, nor does it call a woman a harlot before her husband."

Mrs. Thackery's cheeks pinked. "Whatever are you speaking of?" she asked, the words half-whispered. "Mr. Macon informed us that you had been coerced, forced, into your new marriage. He said that your family poisoned you against him. That—"

"Enough. Please." Virginia raised a hand to her brow, trying to sort through the lies, wondering how much she ought to say to a servant. She had to make it right, but she did not wish to lay her private affairs at this woman's feet. "I chose to marry Lord Calvert, after his kind and generous proposal, in order to protect my sons from Mr. Macon. My late husband's brother wanted guardianship of the children and access to the estate funds. He is a greedy, conniving, unfeeling man. He is not permitted in this house or on our land again. Do I make myself clear?"

Mrs. Thackery, her eyes now the size of dinner plates, started nodding. "Yes, my lady. My apologies, my lady."

Virginia dropped her eyes to the book as she spoke. "You gave great insult to the earl and to me when you disobeyed my orders for our rooms, Mrs. Thackery. I would demand an apology, but I feel it is best if we let the matter alone."

Mrs. Thackery nodded again, lowering her eyes to her lap. "Yes, my lady. As you see fit."

They went through the remainder of the accounts without further incident. Virginia added to her notes and suggested a few minor changes in expenses. Then she pointed at a staff member's name. "How is Mr. Brennan doing as first footman?"

"Very well, my lady. He has held that position for three years now."

Virginia nodded and bit her bottom lip, thinking on Gresham's position at Annesbury. She would need to speak to Lucas, but perhaps it was time to pension the butler off, give him one of the cottages, and put a younger man in his place.

"Thank you, Mrs. Thackery. That will be all today."

The woman stood to leave but hesitated before offering her departing curtsy. "My lady, I am truly sorry for my foolish mistake."

Charles would've forgiven her. Virginia must as well. She nodded but said no more.

Her next item of business would, of course, be to meet with the steward again in the afternoon. This time they would be discussing the tenants' needs.

Virginia made a few more notes in her book before standing, trying to stretch the stiffness from her back and shoulders. It was nearing time for lunch. She ought to find Lucas.

A knock on the door, and the earl's blond head popping around the door frame, made the search unnecessary. "Would you care for a walk?" he asked.

Virginia looked down at her charcoal gray gown, then put a hand up to the twist of her hair. "I don't know—"

"Just around the hedges," he said. "You hardly even need a bonnet. The sun is being shy again."

A smile tugged at her lips and she made a show of sighing. "Oh, very well. But only a short walk, Lucas. Luncheon will be served soon."

He pushed the door all the way open and waited for her to join him in the hall. Once he had her tucked against his side, Lucas steered them down the stairs and out the front door. He took her to a path that wrapped around the back of the house, neither of them saying a word, but the silence was not uncomfortable.

Virginia appreciated Lucas's ability to converse with ease or allow quiet between them. He never tried to fill the space between their conversations with inane comments, nor did he make small talk. When he spoke to her, it was with purpose and thoughtfulness. His intelligence and kindness made him the rarest and best sort of company.

"I discovered the motive behind the staff's discouraging behavior," Lucas said after they'd entered the rear courtyard.

"Did you?" She raised her eyebrows at him, studying his composed expression. He did not seem upset or offended. What had he learned? "How did you achieve that knowledge?"

"Servants gossip. Randal asked a few questions." Lucas shrugged, his eyes remaining on the hedges and the scenery beyond them. "I learned your brother-in-law came for a visit."

"That corroborates what I have learned of the situation," she said, still studying his profile. His strong, angular features, the confident tilt of his head, was something she knew many women would admire. How many ladies in London had cursed her name when they learned of his marriage?

"You are not upset?" he asked, turning at last to look at her, his eyebrows lifted.

"I am disappointed in my staff's behavior, but I cannot say I blame them. They don't know the whole story. Nor will they. It's quite personal, after all. But I have corrected the assumption and I do not think it will be long before things are set to rights." Virginia turned away, taking in the rolling hills as far as her eye could see. It was a different view from what she had become accustomed to at Annesbury Park, yet she found she loved them both. Trees or open fields, red brick or gray stone, each place held distinct beauty and charm.

"I've missed being here," she said, then drew in a deep breath. "I never appreciated country living until I came here."

"It's beautiful," he said quietly. Virginia turned to smile at him and realized his eyes were on her, not the distant hills.

Heat rushed into her cheeks and she cleared her throat, stepping away from him. "I've just recalled, I promised Edward to retrieve something from the children's crow's nest. It's in the trees, south of the gardens."

Lucas nodded and turned in that direction. "Do you think we can fetch it and return before luncheon?"

"Yes, of course. But you needn't come if you are busy—"

He laughed and looked sideways at her, a twinkle in his eye. "Virginia, my whole purpose for being in Suffolk is to assist you. Whether it's meeting with the steward or climbing a tree, I am at your service. Now, will you lead the way to the crow's nest?"

Virginia smiled back at him, despite the strange flutter behind her heart's walls.

It is flattering, and would be in any situation, for a man of his standing to offer such aid.

She started down the path, tucking her hands behind her. He did the same, rather than offer his arm again.

"Who built this crow's nest?" Lucas asked when their path veered down a small hill.

"Charles's father had it built, years ago, for his boys. When Phillip came along, Charles had it repaired. Phillip was barely out of leading strings the first time Charles took him there. I stood beneath them, certain something terrible would happen and Phillip would fall." She shook her head, her eyes going to the small grove of trees that marked their destination. "I should not have worried. Charles would never allow harm to come to those boys."

Lucas said nothing, and when she glanced at him from the corner of her eye, she saw a look of serious contemplation on his face. What was he thinking? Was she speaking of Charles too much? Too warmly? Had she said something wrong—?

"He sounds like the very sort of father I hope to be," Lucas said, his words quiet but firm.

Did he mean for the children he fathered someday, or for Phillip and Edward too?

When he looked down at her, the warmth in his expression answered the question. "And I hope he would approve of my endeavors on behalf of your sons."

"I'm certain he would."

Virginia's attention focused on the trees again, and she pointed at the one with boards nailed to its side to create a ladder. "Just up there. Edward left his seashells somewhere inside."

Lucas looked upward and nodded, then stripped off his jacket and handed it to her to hold. Virginia watched as he pushed his shirtsleeves up and took a rung in hand.

The bottom of the crow's nest, which was really a rounded wooden box, was at least ten feet off the ground. Lucas made short work of the climb, pushed the hatchway open and hoisted himself inside with little effort.

She heard his boots on the boards and then the top hatch swung open, and his head popped out of it.

"This is incredible," he said, looking down at her. "If I'd had something like this as a boy, I never would've come inside for lessons." His grin was wide and impish, his eyes alight. "Do you think we ought to build something like it at Annesbury Park? Perhaps two such constructions, so battles may be planned by opposing field commanders."

His obvious delight made Virginia laugh, picturing him running about under the trees with Phillip and Edward, enacting grand battles.

"Lucas, you have proved something I have long wondered."

He folded his arms on the rim of the crow's nest and looked down at her, his head cocked to one side. "And what is that?"

"Inside every gentleman, there is still a little boy looking to turn pirate."

He laughed, but he did not deny it. With his grin still in place, he ducked back down and a moment later he was coming down the ladder with a jar tucked under his arm.

"I can see why Edward would miss these. They are quite the treasure."

She hesitated a moment, looking at the jar in his hands, before deciding to explain it to him. "His father collected those shells with him, last autumn, when we went to Aldringham to visit the seaside."

"Then they are all the more precious." He held the shells out to her and she exchanged them for his jacket. He shrugged back into his coat, buttoned it, then bowed and offered his arm to her again. "Might this pirate escort you to luncheon, my lady?"

Virginia put her hand on his arm and an unlooked-for tingle shot from her ungloved fingertips straight to her heart. Her eyes shot to his, wide and uncertain. Did he feel the curious sensation as well?

But Lucas was looking up the hill, the way they'd come. "A morning's work of discovering treasure has given me quite the appetite." He looked down just long enough to share his grin, then started up the hill.

Stop being foolish, Ginny, she chided herself. *Lucas respects your situation as a widow. He feels nothing but responsibility for you.*

That might've been so, but it seemed her body was not entirely certain of her status as a bereaved woman.

Chapter Twenty-one

Their third day at the estate, Lucas arose early and made his inspection of the stables. Horses had always held an interest for him, and he wanted to see if the stables had any mounts he might bring back with him to Annesbury Park, for the boys' use.

Measuring his time between his own holdings and the barony would take consideration. He needed to be fair to his new family and the people of the estates. Annesbury Park was his principle home, but there was also the house in London and three other properties held by the title for him to consider.

Perhaps it was time to lease out one or two of the smaller holdings, allowing someone else to maintain the responsibilities of the local landowner. Lucas would discuss it with Virginia first, then consult his financial adviser in London when next in town.

He paused, midway through his admiration of a butter-colored stallion. When had it become a natural thing, to desire to speak to Virginia about his business practices?

"Do you fancy King Lud, my lord?" the stablemaster, Mr. Ritter, asked.

Lucas came back to himself and looked the beast over again. "I do. I imagine his lines are excellent?"

"Aye, my lord. And he was a favorite of Lord Heatherton's. The baron always intended to breed him, too. He's a fine hunter."

Lucas nodded, examining the animal with a more critical eye. "I can understand that. His coloring is unusual."

"His line goes to the continent, my lord. A Spanish Dorado is in his ancestry. It's in his papers."

"*Palominos*," Lucas murmured, looking at the dazzling animal with greater appreciation. The honey-colored mane and light coat was striking. "And his name is King Lud?"

"Yes, my lord." Mr. Ritter grinned, scratching his forehead beneath his cap. "The king part I agree with, but Lud I never could figure out."

Lucas chuckled and stepped away from the stall. "When we leave, I'd like to take His Majesty with me. King Lud might sire a suitable mount for the Lord Phillip Macon."

Mr. Ritter's eyes took on a different quality, his face plainly showed his surprise. "Aye, my lord. I can't think of a better thing to do for the lad. I'll make certain King Lud is ready for travel."

"Wonderful." Lucas crossed his arms, taking in the stable. It was all in good repair and tidy. The staff knew their work.

"Will there be anything else, my lord?"

"Yes." Lucas took his pocket watch from his jacket. "In an hour's time, Lady Calvert and I would like to ride out and visit her tenants. Would you make ready a gig?"

"Yes, my lord."

Lucas bid the man good morning before heading back to the house. He and Virginia had agreed to the outing the night before. She had three families who worked as tenant farmers, and a pension cottage, to visit.

The day was fine for the errand, too. The sky was bluer than gray, the clouds wispy and white. Lucas planned to ride later in the afternoon to inspect the fields now that the household matters were well in hand.

When the hour to meet Virginia came, Lucas waited in the hallway, gloves in hand and hat on his head. The black band was around his arm, as it had been every time he'd left the house since Sunday.

"I hope you've not been waiting long."

Lucas's gaze went to the stairs as he heard Virginia's voice. He never tired of seeing her. She'd changed clothing since breakfast. Now she wore a walking dress of light gray, black gloves, and a straw bonnet with a black band. It was less embellished than her other dresses, appropriate for visiting tenants. She carried a parasol, too. Her cheeks were rosy again, her step lighter. It was easy enough to tell this was an errand she looked forward to. Lucas didn't dare allow himself to think that her pleasure stemmed from spending time with him.

Ignoring the way his heart's rhythm increased at her approach, Lucas pulled on his gloves. "Not at all. I am only eager to be outdoors again, and the day is very fine."

What an inane thing to say. Am I a boy of sixteen or a peer of thirty-three? He nearly huffed at himself, but schooled his features and instead offered her his arm.

Virginia smiled up at him, not at all put off by his remark on the weather. "I have been glancing out the window all morning in anticipation. It's wonderful the sun has made a reappearance."

It was more wonderful how her smile lit up his whole day. But he refrained from saying so.

I am *no better than a schoolboy.*

A footman appeared from the hall with a basket. "My lady. From Cook."

"Ah, thank you, Stephan." Virginia took the basket and, at Lucas's questioning look, lifted the cloth from the top to show him its contents.

"Biscuits," he said. "And a great many. I hope those aren't for us."

She laughed and lowered the cloth. "No, though if you wanted one I might spare it. They're for the tenant children. I always take them sweets."

"A joyful task indeed. Shall we?" Her tender heart was yet another reason his feelings for her strengthened daily.

In minutes, they were outside and he was driving the gig, following her instructions to come to the first of the tenant cottages. They were well-built and appeared no more than a few years old.

Children played in one yard, kneeling beneath the shade of a tree, while a woman sat outside the door working a butter churn. The woman stopped her work and came to her feet when the gig came to a stop.

Lucas jumped out. He tipped his hat to the woman before reaching up to help Virginia descend.

The woman used the corner of her apron to wipe perspiration from her forehead as they approached.

"Hello, Mrs. Martin. How are you this fine summer day?" Virginia asked when they were steps away.

"Very well, my lady. Thank you."

"My lord, may I present Mrs. George Martin, wife to one of our tenants. Mrs. Martin, this is my husband, Lord Calvert, Earl of Annesbury."

Mrs. Martin dipped a curtsy. "A pleasure, my lord."

"You have all the children here today? Except the older boys, I see." Virginia nodded to the gaggle of little ones who watched her with rapt attention, their eyes directed at the basket on her arm.

"Yes, my lady. Mine and Mrs. Simmons's, and Mrs. Johnson's eldest girl is helping me mind them. Mrs. Simmons is helping to nurse Mrs. Johnson's children today to give the poor lady a rest. There's illness in the home. It's all the poor weather, my lady. It doesn't give a body time to get well."

"Dear me. I didn't realize the Simmons family was ill." Virginia looked to the children and waved over an older girl, probably no more than twelve. "Sarah? Would you come take this basket? It's terribly heavy. If you and the other children could see to lightening it by a cookie apiece, I'd be grateful."

The little miss hurried forward, a smile on her face. "Yes, my lady." She took the basket and curtsied before hurrying back to the others, all their little faces split in half by their grins.

But Lucas stayed focused on the topic of conversation. "What is it that ails the family, Mrs. Martin?" he asked, concerned. Summer was not usually a time for serious sicknesses. Perhaps the difficult weather did have something to do with it.

"The apothecary's been to see them," Mrs. Martin said, creases appearing on her brow. "He said it's not too serious, but suspects the scarlet fever, only he used a fancier name for it."

Lucas's blood went cold. His muscles stiffened, and his eyes went to the children. If there were members of the infected family in that group, might they not carry it with them? The basket was passed around from one child to another, and he watched each of them carefully. Did that little boy appear to move more slowly? Did he look pale?

"That's terrible. The little ones are all right?"

"Yes, my lady. They're keepin' everyone covered in cool cloths and drinking good broth. I sent some over myself with Mrs. Simmons."

"Do they have any needs you know of? I would like to take them a basket of things to help." Virginia's kind voice, appropriately serious, brought Lucas's attention back to her as the crack of a whip would.

"Perhaps more herbs to make the broth palatable? But you would know best, my lady. You take such care with us." Mrs. Martin smiled and reached out to touch Virginia's hand. "We're all glad to see you, my lady. It was a shame, to lose his lordship. But it's good you have someone else to look after you now."

And look after Virginia he would.

Lucas didn't say another word, waiting for the visit to end. He could hardly give ear to what the women said, so focused was he on his thoughts and the desire to be on their way. When Virginia at last said her goodbyes and moved to retrieve her basket, Lucas sprang into action.

"Let me tend to it, my lady." He steered her to the gig instead, barely registering what she said to him. He handed her up, then turned to see the young girl had followed, basket in hand. There were still biscuits inside, likely for the other children Virginia anticipated seeing.

"Thank you," he said. She bobbed a curtsy as he took it.

Lucas went to the gig and shoved the basket beneath his seat, climbed up, and stripped his gloves. He dropped them on the floor and lifted the reins. Virginia watched him, brow furrowed in confusion, but he turned the gig around to go back to Heatherton Hall.

"Lucas, we ought to go the other way to see the Simmons family—"

"We aren't seeing any more tenants today," he said firmly, keeping his eyes on the horses. "Nor during the remainder of our visit."

Virginia jolted and turned, eyes wide. "Lucas Calvert, you do not make those decisions on my behalf! What has come over you?"

"Actually, I am within my rights to make *those* decisions, my lady," he said. Her eyes were snapping dangerously, but he didn't care. "As your husband, I must insist you heed me. No more visits."

"Lucas, these people are under *my* care until Phillip comes of age. You cannot simply—"

"I can and I have." He turned to her long enough to make certain she saw his determination, that his will must be obeyed. She'd gone red in the cheeks, her lips pressed tightly together. "Your tenants have managed this long without your interference, they will keep a little longer."

Virginia threw her hands up, her frustration evident in the movement. "They aren't preserves on a shelf to *keep,* Lucas. These are people. Good people. They've been neglected, they need to know—"

He pulled the reins, more harshly than his usual manner, and when the horses stopped he turned fully in the seat to glare at her. Why did she have to be so stubborn? He never asked anything of her. He saw to all her needs, made certain she and the boys had everything they could want, and she wouldn't acquiesce to this single request?

"I need to know that you will obey me in this, Virginia." He'd lowered his voice, realizing he'd been shouting before, but even he heard the edge to his tone. He was nearly growling at her. He didn't care.

"Obey?" Virginia's head reared back on the word. "*Obey?* Lucas, you are being completely unreasonable. I have tenants that I have a duty to, and that duty is also to my son. There is illness among them, and—"

"That's precisely why I need you to listen to me," he said, a note of pleading in his words that he could not help. Anger was easier. Frustration was easier. But if he must beg, he would. "You cannot risk yourself. Not with the fever—" And there his voice cracked and Lucas turned away, studying the reins in his hands.

"Scarlet fever is serious, Lucas. And the tenants cannot afford the care we could." She huffed, sounding as if she was reprimanding a child, explaining the obvious to him.

"Then pay the apothecary to make another visit, to take them more concoctions." He swallowed and his hands tightened on the leather straps. She didn't understand. "Send a basket, send a cart full of things for them, but do not go yourself. Please. Please, Virginia." Then he closed his eyes, his heart aching with memories and fear.

Virginia's hand on his arm, her touch gentle, made him shudder.

"Lucas, what's the matter with you? I know scarlet fever is contagious. Everyone knows that. I will be careful. I promise."

That wasn't the promise he wanted. He opened his eyes to look at the black glove she wore, reminding him of too many things at once. His loss, and hers. The reason he could not tell her everything he felt, how much her safety mattered. What was at stake for him, should she fall ill.

"Abigail died after complications with scarlet fever," he said at last, the words nearly choked from him. "And I cannot lose you too." Let her make of that what she would. It was the truth. If he lost Virginia now, with his feelings new and undeclared, if she fell ill and did not recover, Lucas did not think he would either. Ever.

He didn't look at her. He couldn't. He didn't want to see her reaction to his words, to what they implied. She wasn't ready for him to bear his heart to her.

Silence hung between them. He could feel her tense beside him. Her gloved hand at last moved, sliding from his arm.

Lucas sighed and took up the reins, slapping them lightly against the horse's back. The gig moved forward, to the Hall, and Virginia said nothing to halt their progress. She remained silent, and he dared to glance at her from the corner of his eye.

Her face was pale, her lips white and clenched tight. Her eyes unfocused, her thoughts obviously turned inward. Was she thinking over what he said, or how he had said it? Would she speak to him of Abigail? Promise not to go on her visits?

When they returned to the stables, Lucas stepped down without a word to the groom who came forward. He held his arms out to help her down, and Virginia stepped into them. The fabric of her gown against his ungloved hands was soft and smooth, her waist trim and an excellent fit to his hand. But he thought little on that and more on how she kept her eyes averted.

"Please see to it the basket is returned to the kitchens, and the gloves to my man for cleaning," Lucas said to the groom, then offered his arm—as always—to Virginia.

She took it and walked with him. Mere steps from the side door, she spoke at last.

"I understand your concerns, Lucas. Thank you for telling me."

That was all. She didn't say another word. Virginia released his arm and went ahead at a quicker pace, leaving him to stand in the doorway. Lucas watched her go, a piece of his heart going with her and leaving the rest to beat painfully inside his chest.

Chapter Twenty-two

D inner was a strained affair that evening, though Virginia did nothing to alleviate the tension between them. She barely said two words to Lucas, and he remained silent as well. She excused herself as early as possible, intent on gaining her bedroom and its blessed peace.

What happened between them regarding visiting her tenants, though she could not accurately explain it, had strained their relationship. She could feel it between them, as if they had been holding on to opposite ends of a string and, pulling in two different directions, waited for it to snap. His demands, his fears, couldn't rule her actions.

Virginia shut the door behind her, in the room that had been hers since Charles brought her home as a bride, and leaned back against the cool wood. Though the summer sun should have kept the room lit, even at the after-dinner hour, the clouds had moved in again and everything was dark as night.

She found her way to the lamp on the mantel and the tinder box. Once she had light, she pulled the chord to summon Louisa.

When Charles's illness became severe enough he could not leave his bed, Louisa had assisted in her undressing every night. But before, when the room adjoining hers had belonged to Charles, it was he who saw to that task. He'd never minded.

Her cheeks warmed at the memories that came with that thought. Virginia hurried to her dressing table and sat, pulling pins out without regard for gentleness. It was better to distract herself, to move with haste and purpose. Just as she'd done all things since the morning after her husband's death.

The boys needed her to be strong. The people around her needed to see her as capable and practical. It was up to her to keep her children safe and—

"Good evening, my lady." Louisa entered the room, a smile on her face. "Turning in early for the trip tomorrow?"

Tomorrow? Virginia bit her bottom lip and glared at herself in the mirror. In the morning, they would start back to Annesbury Park. Lucas and she had agreed that matters were well in hand and they could return earlier than expected. At the time, she'd been glad she'd rejoin the boys sooner. However, with the rift between the earl and herself, and a long carriage ride before them, Virginia wished the journey could be put off.

She met Louisa's curious eyes in the mirror and swiftly nodded. "Yes. I thought it would be wise to rest well tonight. One never knows about the coaching inns, after all."

"Yes, my lady." Louisa went about her duties efficiently, chattering about seeing old friends and the news of the community. Virginia smiled and murmured a response when required, but attending to the conversation was difficult with her thoughts flying in several directions.

"My lady," Louisa began, brushing out Virginia's hair in preparation to plait it, "I was wondering if there is anything you would like me to bring back to Annesbury Park. Any of your personal items."

Virginia pulled herself from her thoughts at this question. She had considered it herself a time or two in the preceding days. "Yes. I have a list." She looked down at her dressing table and opened a drawer. "I think just a few things. But I have gone this long without them, they obviously are not essential. If we haven't room, take one of the trunks from the attics."

"Yes, my lady." Her maid took the list and read over it. "What of your gowns?"

Virginia started and met the maid's eyes in the mirror. "I have no mourning clothing here, Louisa."

The woman ducked her head. "I know, my lady. If you will permit me to say, we aren't certain when we will return again, and it may be practical to keep a few gowns in reserve, for after."

There would come an after, Virginia knew. One day, the mourning would be put off. It was sometimes difficult to remember that color would be part of her life again. Often, she tried not to look at herself in the black and gray ensembles she wore now. They were a stark symbol of her loss, meant as a reminder for her and the world.

"What would you suggest we bring, Louisa?" she asked, curious. Her maid was thinking far into the future, it would seem.

"There were a few gowns you had made for the London season that you haven't even worn. A few day dresses, an evening gown or two. I could put them up nice in a trunk for the right time, my lady."

Virginia rose and went to the wardrobe, opening it slowly. Her things had been stored in the dressing room for the visit, but she knew her favorite gowns, the newest gowns, were here. She looked inside, studying the shining fabric of a gown she had commissioned nearly a year before. A celestial-blue evening gown, which glimmered with different shades of blue and green depending upon the lighting.

When she had been fitted for it, by her favorite seamstress in London, she had thought it the most beautiful dress she'd ever owned. But after Charles became ill, it hardly mattered if she had a pretty gown or not. She'd left it behind, and all the memories she had meant to build while wearing it. The gown was like a wished-for dream that had never come to pass.

"Bring this one, too," Virginia said, laying her hand on the fabric. It would do her well to remember to dream, once in a while. Charles would not want her to give up on dreaming.

Louisa took her leave at last, promising to be up early to finish packing, and Virginia was left alone in her bed.

Alone. In Bath, when the doctor required she take a room separate from her husband, it had been an adjustment. Though they kept their own chambers, they were rarely without one another at night. To find herself apart from Charles had been difficult, but she'd adapted. The past several months, first with Christine and then at Annesbury Park, she'd not struggled too often to fall asleep. Not really.

But here, at Heatherton Hall, where she had spent less than a dozen nights in a bed without Charles, things were different.

She'd hardly slept at all.

Perhaps that lack of sleep had led to her argument with Lucas. Had she been more rested, more herself, would she have responded to him the same way?

She tossed from one pillow to another, squeezing her eyes closed.

Did she owe Lucas an apology? If he'd said right away why he didn't wish her to make visits to those afflicted with the fever, if he'd explained first, they never would've had reason to argue in the first place. Didn't that make it his fault?

Virginia pulled the blankets up to her chin.

Lady Abigail Calvert had succumbed to scarlet fever. That didn't mean Virginia would. She had a strong constitution. She'd nursed her own husband through consumption without falling ill even once.

But the fear in Lucas's eyes, the sorrow in them, had not been for *Abigail*.

Virginia dismissed that thought by sitting up in her bed. Sleep would not come swiftly. Her agitation with the situation remained too great.

Pacing from her bed to the window, Virginia tried to think on other things. Knowing she'd see the boys in two days' time comforted her. She had rarely been apart from them since their infancy. Her mother claimed it was unnecessary sentimentality, that servants were employed to allow mothers to go about in society. But Virginia had never understood how people could wish to be parted from their little ones. When the day came for her sons to go away to school, she was not sure how she would get through that time apart.

She had found Phillip's model ship and secured it well for travel. He would be pleased to have it back again. Edward would likely spend a great deal of time studying all his rescued shells, talking over where he had found them and what he thought of each crack or colorful line upon them.

Lucas had been kind to retrieve the shells for her. And his idea to build a similar structure to the crow's nest would likely give the boys a topic of conversation they would not soon exhaust.

Lucas's thoughtfulness, such a key trait in his character she'd noted from nearly their first meeting, was a wonder to her. He remembered every detail of import when a person spoke to him. Having watched him as they settled accounts and went through the steward's notes, she could appreciate that part of him even more. He recognized discrepancies, even small ones, and could remember different aspects of reports she had only glanced over. His assistance had proven invaluable, though he'd tried to stay in the background, acting as an adviser. Managing without him would've been difficult.

Virginia froze mid-step and folded her arms tightly about herself. *Why does every thought lead back to Lucas?*

She fought away the answer before it could fully form in her mind. She turned on her heel and went to the door linking her room to the baron's chamber. To Charles's bedroom. She touched the handle and took in a deep breath. She had not been inside his room yet. She'd wanted to ignore that it even existed.

Yet she knew his room as well as she knew her own.

Virginia turned the handle and pulled the door open.

It still smelled like him. Like lemons and leather, like his favorite soap, like a thousand days of love and laughter. Her heart lifted but almost immediately the fissures left by his loss broke open again. Virginia stepped inside, knowing her way in the dark. She went to his bed and sat on the edge, breathing deeply, each precious memory cutting into her more deeply. She reached out to his pillow, knowing it would be empty, but needing to remind herself of how it had been when he was there.

He would nevermore stand in that room, before his mirror, asking for her to adjust his cravat. He would never throw the door open, startling her and her maid, as she prepared for dinner or a night at a neighbor's home. He wouldn't watch the rain fall, standing at the large curtained windows that overlooked their rolling hills and the boys' crow's nest in the trees.

Charles would never hold her again.

A broken sob tore from Virginia's throat before she realized she was weeping. Covering her mouth, trying to mute the sound, another cry slipped past her lips. Like a child, Virginia shuddered and wept, laying down and burying her face in Charles's pillows. She sucked in a ragged breath, breathing in that scent that comforted her and tore her apart.

Her already broken heart cracked further. She curled herself around the pillow, embracing it tightly, weeping. Longing enveloped her; when was the last time she'd felt as safe and protected as she had in Charles's arms? She could lay her cares at his feet and he would make the world right again, or else hold her until it *felt* right.

Virginia had not allowed herself to cry like this since the night Charles had died. Her circumstances would not allow for it. She had to remain strong, for herself and for the boys, for the world to see she was capable of carrying on.

The world wasn't watching now, and the boys were far away. No one would know. No one would see her. The boys would not witness her breaking down. This moment would be hers and hers alone.

Alone. That word had never felt heavier than it did in the darkness, in a room she had never been alone in before.

Virginia cried until her tears and body were exhausted. At last she fell into a fitful sleep, and dreams troubled by a longing she couldn't name.

¤

Rising with the sun, though it was a dreary dawn that greeted her, Virginia didn't call for Louisa to help her dress. She left Charles's bedroom after straightening the coverlet and smoothing the pillow. She closed the door quietly behind her, determination driving her. Though her head pounded and her body was weary, there was something she must do.

Her hands searched the back of her wardrobe and pulled out a drab brown gown, more worn than the rest, reserved for the less delicate work of her life. Whether it was caring for her plants, working in the still room, or visiting the ill tenants under her care.

She didn't expect to do any such thing today, but her finer gowns required help to do up their buttons. Today, she wanted to slip from the house as quietly as she could, without fanfare or notice.

She twisted her braid into a knot at the back of her neck and pulled a black bonnet over it. Her gray shawl went over the whole and she left her room. Tip-toeing through the house, she saw no one, and slipped through a side door into the damp morning air.

The church was a mile and a half away. Cutting across country, Virginia knew she could make good time there and back to Heatherton Hall.

She didn't wish to tell anyone of her going to avoid their looks of understanding, their words of half-meant sympathy. She wanted no questions before or after. Seeing Charles's grave for the first time must be something she experienced on her own terms.

The grass was damp along the path she walked, brushing against her skirts to soak them with dew. Or had it rained in the night?

All the heavens do is weep this summer. Virginia looked up at the sky. Lucas worried over the amount of rain. It was too much, too frequent, and not enough sun to dry it up again and wake the plants from slumber.

Virginia passed over the bridge where Charles would stand to fish with the boys. They rarely caught anything, but Phillip had loved to lean against the rails with his fishing pole.

She swallowed a lump in her throat and kept going, through a stand of trees and across another field. The church's bell tower came in sight and her steps slowed.

Could she make it any farther? Did she truly need to?

Yes. Charles's memory kept her moving forward. She loved him. She wished to pay better respect to his memory, to see his final resting place, to do her duty by him.

In the distance, a rooster crowed. The world was otherwise very quiet when she entered the churchyard.

The Heatherton barons had not been nobility long, in the way England measured time. Their small church did not have room or the ability to bury people within its walls and under its floors. But the family had a generous portion of land near the eastern wall of the building. It was there she went, steeling herself against seeing the new gravestone.

It looked like all the others. Rows and rows of them, rectangles set low to the ground, with curving tops and deeply-carved names, to stand the test of time and the wear of weather.

Charles Macon, Baron of Heatherton. August 1780 - February 1812.

His life, everything he was, noted in the coldest and most formal manner. Her eyes pricked with unshed tears. After all, he was not here. His immortal soul was gone home to heaven, if she believed what she heard the vicar preach from his pulpit. And she did. She must. To think of Charles as gone forever—it would be too much.

She laid a flower down on his grave, plucked from the meadows as she came. It was a meager offering, but Charles had never been one for flowers.

Lucas's words came back to her, from days ago. Before their argument.

"It helped, to ease my thoughts, to express them and imagine what Abigail might say back to me if she was present."

Dare she try the same?

Virginia glanced up, looking around to ensure she remained alone in the cemetery. She took in a shaky breath and whispered words she had not spoken in months. "Hello, Charles."

Her heart burned within her, behind the walls she'd built to protect it.

"I miss you." Her voice cracked and she swallowed, composing herself. She could not break. Not here. "The boys do too. They are well. Happy, even. They are learning to ride, and you would be so proud of them."

Closing her eyes, imagining Charles standing beside her instead of somewhere beneath the earth on which she stood. He would stand near her, his head tilted to one side as he listened to all she said, his expression tender.

"Phillip is struggling with his place in the world, I'm afraid. He has taken burdens upon his shoulders he shouldn't bear. Edward only wants to make the people around him happy. They both remind me of you, every day. They remind me of what I've lost."

"*You will never lose me, Virginia.*"

She kept her eyes closed. The words came from her memory, from weeks before Charles had passed, when she held his hand and they spoke of what was to come. The doctor had given them no hope, had left them with a promise to return. Virginia's heart had fought against the prognosis while her head knew it must be true. Her husband had been failing in strength and health for a long time.

What else had he said that day?

"*I will remain in your heart, and the boys are a part of me and a part of you. They will be here, they will be a comfort to you. Watch them grow and know I will watch them, too.*"

That was a different day, a different conversation.

Truly, she had been blessed to have time with him. They planned together, spoke of what her life would be when he was gone. Of course, he hadn't known what his brother would do. He hadn't known Virginia would have to wed another.

"What would you think of me, marrying the earl?" she whispered, keeping her eyes closed, his image in her heart. "He's a good man. He is kind to the boys, very respectful and understanding of me. He asks for little in return. He is even here, helping me—helping Phillip."

What *would* Charles think of Lucas?

"*You can tell a man's character by how he treats those beneath him in society. Does he hold the lives under his care as cheap? Does he use his influence and means to better his own standing or to lift others? That is how I measure a man.*" He'd told her those things when she asked why he was so particular about his friends. That had been years and years past, when they were still courting.

"Lucas is good, Charles. He is the best of men." Virginia smiled to herself, a tear slipping from beneath her eyelids.

The memory of Lucas's fear when he learned of her visiting the sick, his plea for her to stay away, came to her again. He wanted her safety and health; he could not bear to think on her falling ill.

Because that's how he had lost Abigail. Because he would not lose her too.

"I think he cares for me, Charles. As more than a responsibility."

"A man would have to be deaf, blind, and dumb not to love you," Charles had said, more than once. Was it possible that Lucas could hold her in such regard? He had loved his first wife dearly, had mourned her loss deeply, and still held her memory close. And was it right, to love another as she had loved Charles?

Did she wish to?

"I love you, Charles," she said, the tears silently falling from her eyes. She opened them, looking down at the grave marker again.

"I love you, Virginia." She could never tally all the times he had spoken those words to her, and they were a balm to her aching heart even now. She had been loved, treasured, cared for in a way some women would never know.

And you need to love again.

Virginia gasped and raised a hand to smother the sound, her eyes darting around to discover the source of those words. It had sounded like— Charles had never said such a thing to her. Even in all their discussions before he became too ill to speak. He'd never—

Her heart thrummed, as it always had in his presence. A breeze drifted across the grass and around her, skimming against her cheek, bringing with it the scent of summers past, the warmth of the sun, the scent of newly-mowed hay and wildflowers.

Peace settled upon her, calming her whirling thoughts and weary heart.

Could it be possible that Charles would speak to her in such a way?

Virginia breathed deeply, trying to clear her head, to make sense of the moment. Charles was gone. Surely, she'd been imagining the words. Yet why did she feel such peace come over her so suddenly? Peaceful thinking on loving another man, while standing above the grave of her beloved? Could such feelings coexist? Grief and peace?

Tucking the moment into her heart, determining she would examine it later, Virginia looked to the sky to try and ascertain the hour. It was early yet. She had time to return to Heatherton Hall without drawing notice to her departure from it.

She started back, casting one last look behind at the graveyard before entering the trees and losing sight of the church. She would be able to come again, she knew, and it would be easier.

"Virginia."

She spun around, her hand going to her heart. Leaning against a tree, his jacket unbuttoned, cravat loosely wrapped around his throat, stood Lucas Calvert. Dark half-circles under his eyes, the shadow of stubble lining his jaw; she'd never seen him so exhausted.

"Lucas." She lowered her hand, tangling her fingers in her shawl. "What are you doing here?"

"My window faces the eastern meadow." He slowly pushed himself upright, but he did not approach her. "I was waiting for the sun to rise. I saw you leave, all alone, and after last night—" He lowered his eyes to the ground. "I wanted to be sure you were safe. I followed you. But when I realized your destination, I waited here. I had no wish to intrude upon your privacy."

Virginia studied him, from the top of his uncovered blond head to the boots on his feet. Obviously, he'd come after her in great haste, his appearance less than appropriate. It reminded her of the night Edward had started coughing, when Phillip had sent Lucas to check on the little boy.

"Thank you for your concern." She adjusted her stance, trying to understand the man before her. "You thought I would go to the Johnsons' home?"

She saw him swallow, thanks to his poorly tied cravat, before he nodded. He raised his eyes, his expression contrite. "Yes."

"I told you I would not," she reminded him, and though her tone was gentle he winced.

"Yes." He ran a hand through his hair and looked about them, taking in the empty field and the gray skies, anything but her. "You are a very determined woman, Virginia. I wasn't certain you would hold my concern as valid enough to humor me."

She ought to be angry with him, that *he* didn't hold her word as assurance enough. But instead, the peace from the churchyard lingered about her. This man, an honorable and good soul, genuinely cared for her. Cared enough that the thought of her falling ill, the idea of her succumbing as his first wife had, brought him out of the house to follow her in the early hours of the morning.

"Why couldn't you sleep?" she asked.

His eyes finally met hers again, the gray dominating them in the overcast light. The emotion in those eyes deepened the color in them, drawing her in, speaking to her in a way his words never had. The truth was there, easy enough for her to see, and she could not pretend otherwise.

But he didn't say anything.

Lucas came forward, moving with deliberate slowness, and extended his arm to her. "May I walk back with you?"

The barriers around Virginia's heart remained. Still impenetrable, she told herself. But with what Lucas's eyes revealed, she would have to work all the harder to keep herself well-fortified.

At least for now.

She took his arm and they went back the way they had come, Lucas's hand steadying her when she stepped over logs and around crumbling stone walls.

Chapter Twenty-three

L ucas didn't regret going after Virginia, even though she was silent the whole way back to Heatherton Hall. He'd never moved with such speed as he had upon seeing her in that field, moving in such a determined manner. Going after her had been the right thing to do. But he wished he had the strength, the ability, to tell her *why* it mattered so much that he protect her.

After their argument, he'd had no peace. If his mind was not going over their discussion in painful detail, it was recounting Abigail's last days on earth. Pulled one way and another, his heart did not allow him rest.

He'd been waiting for a new day, ordering his thoughts, trying to find a way to make things right between them. Dawn had come upon him, with his mind hardly better off than when he'd begun. He'd given up on rational thought the moment he saw her leaving the estate.

No one saw him return Virginia to her room in the family wing. She barely whispered a farewell to him before he sought out his own chamber, the physical distance between them suddenly seeming twice as far as it had before.

Did she guess his feelings for her?

He was the worst sort of man to wish she knew, to wish he could tell her.

Randal found him still pacing. The valet, arriving at the customary time, looked from the rumpled bed sheets to Lucas's clothing and raised an eyebrow. But Randal was too well trained to do more. He simply went about gathering Lucas's clothing for the journey back to Annesbury Park.

Virginia would be with him in the carriage for several hours.

Lucas didn't know if he could stand it. They would have to pretend nothing had happened, because he certainly couldn't speak about his actions that morning. His emotions were still too new, too close to the surface of his thoughts. Confined to a coach with Virginia, he may very well say more than he ought.

Virginia, his extraordinary wife, remained beyond his reach in more ways than one. There were nearly seven months of mourning left.

He closed his eyes at the thought, listening to Randal pack his things.

"Leave out my riding clothes," he heard himself saying. "I will go ahead to the inn. You will take the carriage with our things, and Lady Calvert's maid will travel with her. If her ladyship wishes."

Randal stilled, but when Lucas turned to see the man's reaction, his valet nodded.

"Yes, my lord. I'll send to the stables for a horse to be readied. Will you go after breakfast?"

"Send a tray up." Lucas had no desire to eat alone in the dining room, as he had little doubt Virginia would stay in her room today. "And be quick about it. I want to leave within the hour." He would then be several hours ahead of his wife's carriage, and hopefully the ride would allow him to clear his head.

His commands were followed, and at such a speed that Lucas found himself on the back of King Lud, the horse's finer qualities of less importance than his speed to carry Lucas away.

Then he moved the horse along, away from the stables, around the house. He'd left a message for Virginia, explaining that he would ride ahead. The short note was impersonal, direct, without all the details a face-to-face conversation would necessitate.

Having never taken the coward's way out before, Lucas did not make the decision lightly. It would be best for them both to be left to their thoughts.

Virginia mourned her husband deeply. Seeing her venture out in secret to visit Charles Macon's grave had crushed Lucas's heart. The sight had reminded him of her grief, of her inability to truly belong to *him.* She still loved her first husband, as was right and best, and Lucas was a dishonorable cur to even entertain the idea of caring for her in a manner beyond that of a friend.

And truly, even after her year of mourning was spent, what would he do then?

He passed through the countryside without much notice of it. The horse was obedient, the turns in the road easy enough to remember, which left him all too much time to think.

When Virginia's first husband had been gone a year and a day, when society's strictest members would not whisper at her casting off her mourning, what did he expect to happen? He had mourned Abigail, in his heart if not in outward appearance, for longer than a year. He couldn't be sure when he had put those feelings away.

An arbitrarily appointed amount of time passing would not propel his beautiful countess into his arms, or open her heart to his love for her.

It could be years before she was ready to accept him as more than her rescuer.

Perhaps she never would return his feelings.

His heart cracked, and with it his hope for the future.

Lucas arrived at the first coaching inn where the horses would be changed. It was the same one he and Virginia had stayed at overnight, then spent the morning walking and gathering wild flowers.

He dismounted, allowing a boy to run up and take the reins from him. The horse would be good for hours yet, going at the easy pace he had set. But he gave the boy extra coins to rub the animal down and see to its food and water.

Lucas didn't enter the inn. He wasn't hungry. He had no wish to be near people. He checked with the stable, ensuring the horses would be ready when his carriages arrived. After half an hour, he mounted and was on his way again.

The break from thinking of Virginia helped. He came back to his thoughts with a better mindset. His chest ached, his heart reaching for something it could not obtain.

I cannot remain near Virginia. Not like this. Sick at heart, without respect for her position as a widow.

What was the alternative?

Lucas began to form a plan, and a plausible way to put it in action, and tried to put aside his feelings.

Virginia and her sons must come first. Their feelings, their trust in him to do the right thing, were of paramount importance. The best way to take care of them and protect them would be to leave. At least for a time, to get his emotions back under control.

He'd spent years schooling himself for a public life, never giving away his thoughts and feelings, remaining aloof and above personal attachment. He must use those skills in his personal life as well. It was a lonely way to live, but it was better than pursuing a relationship with a woman who mourned another man. Even if that woman was his wife.

Chapter Twenty-four

When the carriage came to a stop in front of Annesbury Park, Virginia successfully composed her expression into a pleasant one. Louisa, sitting across from her, began gathering their things together in her basket. Keeping up a cheerful pretense with her maid had been difficult, but Virginia in no way indicated that her husband's decision to travel ahead of them both days, riding King Lud, was a surprise to her.

Lucas obviously had no wish to see her. She had thought he understood her visit to Charles's grave, but that had been the last conversation between them. The look in his eyes, the emotion in their gray depths, had haunted her the whole day long. But at the inn, she'd been informed he arranged a private dining room for her before going himself to bed, exhausted from the day's ride.

It was with difficulty that she masked her surprise when it was Lucas who opened the carriage door, still wearing travelling clothes, and extended a hand to help her down.

Virginia met his gaze, searching for some hint as to his emotions, his thoughts, but there was nothing there. No spark of happy light, no smoky anger, nothing. He looked as impassive and unaffected as she had ever seen him.

She opened her mouth, not quite knowing how to greet him, but was saved when a small body hurtled into her legs.

Edward hugged her tightly, his face lifted to look at her and a grin stretching across it.

"Mama, you're back!"

"I am," she responded, going down to her knees to return his embrace. She held him close and looked up at Lucas again.

He smiled, but the expression was tight and did not appear in his eyes.

"Mother," Phillip said, stepping forward from his place next to Lucas. "I missed you." Edward stepped back and Phillip took his place. Though his embrace was somewhat less exuberant, it was nevertheless affectionate.

"I missed you too, darling." She kissed his forehead as she stood, then held her hands out to each of them. She raised her eyes briefly to Lucas, and seeing him unchanged, decided she must break the silence between them. "How was your ride, my lord?"

"It was excellent exercise." His words were even, his tone polite. "And the carriage, my lady?"

"Satisfactory." She bit her bottom lip. "Lucas, I—"

Edward tugged her forward, pointing at one of the footmen carrying her trunk. "Are my shells in there, Mama? Did you 'member them?"

Lucas's smile returned for an instant, but it was there. Very well. She would wait until they were alone to speak to him and try not to worry over it in the meantime.

"Yes, darling. Let's go inside. Phillip, I remembered your boat, too."

The boys fairly dragged her forward, and Lucas fell in behind them. Her new mother-in-law stood in the doorway, hands folded primly before her.

"Welcome home, Virginia," she said, her eyes sparkling. "I must say, I have enjoyed the boys' company excessively. I am afraid I rather spoiled them."

An honest smile lifted Virginia's lips and she laughed. "I am glad to hear it. The best grandmothers always spoil children, or so I understand."

"Thank you for sharing them with me." Then Lady Pamela Calvert stepped forward and embraced Virginia, the boys' releasing her to allow her to return the gesture. "I am very glad all of you have joined the family," she said low enough for Virginia's ears only.

A lump formed in Virginia's throat. Bother. She'd thought she'd finished crying at last.

"Thank you."

"You had better come in. When Lucas arrived and told us you were just behind him, we postponed luncheon. The boys will join us today, of course, and Marcus and Ellen."

Virginia had nearly forgotten she had house guests still. She nodded and started for the stairs.

"You too, Lucas. Tidy up. We will wait for you."

Virginia's heart fluttered when Lucas followed her, stepping up beside her on the stairway. They walked up together, not touching.

Without a word they attained the landing of the first floor, then the second. Virginia made to go down the hall to their rooms, and Lucas finally spoke.

"Virginia?"

She turned hesitantly. He was staring at her, his brows furrowed and his manner serious.

"Yes, Lucas?"

"I am needed at the estate in Aylesbury." The words spilled out quickly, Lucas hardly pausing. "And I thought, since I will be travelling, to extend the journey to the other houses under my care. I will be gone some weeks. You and the boys ought to stay here and enjoy the rest of summer. I won't go before speaking to someone about their tree fortress. And Marcus said they finally found the passage. It's in the music room. I'll make certain you know exactly, so they cannot hide themselves there forever."

Virginia stared at him, her heart racing inside her chest as he spoke. He was leaving? And all he was concerned about was a secret passage and a place for the boys to play pirate?

"When are you going?" she asked, tucking her hands behind her back and clenching them together. *Is this my fault?*

"In three days. Mother is returning to London. I will escort her partway." Lucas looked down at the carpet beneath their feet, at his dusty Hessians. "I will write and keep you informed of where I am."

She opened her mouth, closed it, then turned away. "I hope you travel safely."

"Thank you."

Virginia closed her eyes against the feelings trying to break free of her carefully molded facade. Lucas was not abandoning her. He was seeing to his duties. Nothing more.

But it felt like more. Like he wished to escape, to be free of her. Why would he want such a thing when she had seen so clearly into his heart but yesterday morning? Had she imagined the look in his eyes?

Virginia went to her room and shut the door behind her without looking back. She stood against the door, her mind whirling, trying to remember. He'd looked at her with such an expression, such exposed longing and misery, that she felt certain he had feelings for her which she *must not* return. In her pride and pain, had she imagined it? Perhaps it was only pity?

She straightened and stormed forward into the room, stripping her gloves off and throwing them at her chair. *Pity?*

Lucas's haunted eyes, blue and gray constantly shifting for dominance, came into her mind more clearly. She hadn't imagined anything.

The walls around her heart gave a shudder.

"No," she said aloud, firmly.

Perhaps it was best he went away. For both of them.

¤

Edward delivered a stack of drawings to Lucas's office the morning after their return.

"What have we here?" Lucas asked, coming around his desk where Edward stood.

"I kept thinking about our house," the boy said, looking up at Lucas with deep brown eyes. "Our old house. I drew some pictures. Nurse said you prob'ly don't want *all* of them. But maybe you might like one so you can remember it too?"

Lucas drew the two chairs on that side of the desk together and gestured for Edward to take one of them while he sat in the other. "Show me. Nurse may be wrong and I may lay claim to each and every one."

Edward raised his dark eyebrows high. He began speaking eagerly. "This one's first. I drew the whole house. From the front." He held a drawing in grays and greens out to Lucas, who could very well see the similarity between it and the castle-like Heatherton Hall. "I see. This is very fine. A good likeness."

"And this is the fountain in the back garden. It's not as nice a garden as here. There aren't as many flowers. Mostly hedges." He held out the drawing for Lucas to inspect the blue shoots of water coming from the top of the fountain.

"You've done a credible job here. Do you like the fountain?"

"Yes. Phillip says we used to play in it, but I can't remember that." The little boy's shoulders dropped. "Last time I remember being there, it was too cold to play."

"And this drawing?" Lucas pointed to the next, though he had a fair idea of what it was. A brown cylindrical object had been drawn in at the top of a tree.

"That's the crow's nest. We used to climb up there to play with my papa." Edward's eyes lit up as he pointed to it. "There's a hatch in the bottom you can climb through and then close so your enemies can't get up. There's one on top, too, so you can open it and look out. I had to stand on a box to look out, though." He sighed and went on to the next picture, depicting his nursery, and another, showing the large oven in the kitchens where his favorite biscuits were made.

"Your drawings are very good," Lucas said when he finished, now holding the sheets, looking through them. "Did you show my brother your pictures?"

"Yes. He liked them, too. Then he showed me his."

Lucas's attention focused on that detail. "Did he? He doesn't show those to just anyone. He's very private about his drawings. He must like you a great deal."

Edward nodded and folded his arms across his chest. "He says I can call him Uncle Marcus, if I want."

Laying the drawings down on his lap, Lucas stared into the boy's serious expression. "That is a special thing, I think. Do you want to call him Uncle Marcus?"

"Yes. And his wife is Aunt Ellen now. But I like having a Grandmother, too. I have one, but she says children shouldn't talk to grownups. But Grandmother, the grandmother who's your mother, she likes my drawings too." The boy studied Lucas intently. "Phillip even calls her Grandmother. I asked Phillip what we should call you."

"Did you?" Lucas was all ears now. He told himself he shouldn't care so much. Especially since he intended to leave. He would be parting from the temptation to love Virginia and parting from the boys. "What did Phillip say?"

"He said we could call you *my lord*, but he wasn't sure you'd want to be called Papa. Phillip says you can't love us the way our papa did before, because we aren't yours." Edward leaned forward, furrowing his brow. "Is that true?"

Oh, to be a child, without fear of saying the wrong thing.

"Your father loved you with everything in him," Lucas said solemnly, taking in Edward's earnest expression, recognizing in the boy a yearning Lucas had experienced himself. It was the desire to be accepted, to be loved, though the fear was there that it simply could not be. "And he loved you from your very birth. I've not known you as long as he did."

Lucas bent closer, maintaining eye contact. "But I love you very much, Edward. I would do anything for you. To protect you, to care for you, to see you healthy and happy. If you wish to call me Papa, you may."

It was as if a fire kindled in the boy's eyes and in an instant he was kneeling in his chair and leaning over to Lucas, wrapping his arms around Lucas's neck in the fiercest hug the earl had ever received. Lucas pulled the boy into his arms and hugged him back.

"Thank you," Edward said softly. Then he pushed back and looked into Lucas's eyes, a triumphant grin on his face. "I can tell Phillip he was wrong."

"Yes, I suppose you can." Lucas grinned and set the boy back upon the ground, standing with him.

"Thank you, Papa." Edward half-bowed and darted to the door, Lucas watching him tear across the carpet and then right past his mother, who stood in the doorway.

His breath hitched. How long had she been standing there? What had she heard? Had he done the right thing?

Virginia barely stepped into the room, her gray skirts floating around her like the clouds at the forefront of a storm. "Marcus and Ellen are leaving," she said, not coming further into the room. "I thought you would wish to bid them farewell."

"Oh. Yes. Thank you." She nodded and made as if to turn away. "Virginia?" he called after her, his traitorous tongue speaking when he ought to do everything in his power to avoid her. "I should have consulted with you before answering Edward. I hope I've not offended you."

Her hands came before her, her fingers laced together. "Lucas, my sons are coming to care for you a great deal. They look up to you, and I am depending upon you to help me raise them to be the best of men. Of course, they can call you papa, or father, or anything they and you agree upon." Her expression remained neutral, as it had since dinner the day before. "Thank you for being kind to them."

Then she walked out. He waited a moment before following, giving her the distance from him she seemed to want. The sooner he left, the better.

Chapter Twenty-five

Lucas left, escorting his mother's carriage on horseback. From the looks his mother had given him, Virginia knew he was riding to avoid conversation with Lady Pamela Calverton as he had done on their return trip from Heatherton Hall.

Phillip held her hand, not something he had done a great deal of late, as his new grandmother and step-father disappeared down the lane. He squeezed her fingers, bringing her attention down to him.

"Do you think he'll be back before our fortress is built?"

Lucas had kept his word and hired a carpenter from the village to begin construction on the little hideaway for the boys, at the trees by the lake. But the carpenter would likely be done in a matter of days, not the weeks that the earl would be away.

"I doubt he will return that soon," Virginia answered with what she hoped was a cheerful tone. "But I am certain he will want to see it the moment he returns. He was quite taken with the crow's nest."

Phillip nodded, a thoughtful expression on his face. Edward had been at the bottom of the steps when the carriage pulled away, then became distracted by the activity of a beetle crawling along on the ground. He spoke a trifle absently from where he was crouched, making his study.

"He really did like it. He took my drawing of the crow's nest with him. I think he took all my drawings."

Virginia raised her eyebrows. Lucas had told her he'd been keeping Edward's artwork. But why take it all on his journey? "He must've wished to keep them close," she said.

"Yes." Edward stood, having finally lost interest in the beetle. "Can we go feed King Lud a treat?"

The boys had been delighted to see their father's favorite horse again. How had Lucas known what it would mean to them? How did he always know what they needed?

Dismissing that thought, Virginia smiled at the two little hopeful faces turned up to her. "I suppose you may, but only a vegetable each this time. You're going to spoil that horse and he won't be fit company for anyone."

Phillip grinned and turned to run through the house.

"Walk like gentlemen, if you please," Virginia called after them. Both boys slowed only a few steps into the entry hall, but not by much. Entering the house, Virginia took one last look down the empty lane before shutting the door behind her.

¤

Three weeks, which felt more like three-hundred years, had gone by. Lucas had finished visiting his properties. It hadn't taken as long as he'd hoped, due to the very efficient men he had hired to manage the estates in his stead. There wasn't as much for him to do as he'd hoped. It didn't help that every place he went, within hours he was longing for Annesbury Park. He missed Virginia's company at breakfast and in the evenings. They didn't speak of profound things, but their conversation on the household, the day's events, and the boys had been something he looked forward to.

The boys. Had the carpenter completed his work? Were they even now up in the trees, spying on the world beneath them? He would wager his finest horse that Edward would have created a number of masterpieces for him in his absence. He would likely need to restock the nursery's paper supply.

Which was as good a reason as any to return to London. He had sent Edward's drawings to town with his mother, and the project he'd given her was likely completed. Lucas could pick up paper, Edward's drawings, and find gifts for the boys. Of course, he didn't know when he might see the children again. He'd believed a few weeks would be enough to gain mastery over his emotions, but every time he thought he had made progress, the simplest thing would fill his thoughts and heart with Virginia.

That day, before leaving for London, it had been a peacock. His neighbor kept the dreadfully loud creatures, but one had wandered onto the lawn beside Lucas's carriage. It had fanned its tail and promenaded about, as if to dare Lucas's staff to remove it. The feathers had glistened in a brief burst of sunlight, blues, browns, greens, creating a beautiful display of color. Lucas thought immediately of Virginia's beautiful green eyes, a color so rich and dark he understood the comparison to precious stones. But her eyes were more alive than an emerald could be, and never as cold.

He wanted to be by her side to catch a glimpse of those eyes when she laughed.

Lucas shut his heart away again and again, determined to ignore its pining.

Perhaps being in London for a time would distract him sufficiently.

Did they miss him at all? He'd kept his word, sending a letter to Virginia every time he left one property for another. She hadn't written back. That should indicate fairly well that she did not at all care for his company, as was right. She was a grieving widow. Even society expected her to continue her mourning.

When the carriage rolled into London, his mind was still miles away, along with his heart, at Annesbury Park.

Chapter Twenty-six

For the fifth time that day, Virginia closed her eyes and silently counted to ten.

Her mother had come to visit, arriving on August first. She had been present for a week. Lucas had been gone for four weeks. Counting the days after counting to ten was sometimes necessary as well.

"Really, you ought to change the whole house, especially since he's gone, for he cannot object." Lady Jacqueline Crawlton, Dowager Countess of Vinespar, had a decided opinion on everything. But Virginia had never witnessed her mother's Machiavellian instincts manifest themselves this plainly. "Not a single stick of furniture that *she* chose ought to remain."

The she, of course, was Lady Abigail Calvert, Lucas's first wife.

"I see no reason for that, Mother," Virginia said, calmly dipping her pen in ink as she wrote an invitation to Christine. Again. She'd begged her cousin to visit as often as possible during her mother's stay. "I rather like most of the furnishings. I have thought of refreshing the rooms by moving a few things around, but nothing so extraordinary that would require a complete redecoration."

"I like the rooms, too," Rebecca Devon said from her place on the settee across the room. Rebecca was Christine's younger sister and had been given into her Aunt Jacqueline's care. The hope was that Rebecca would be molded into the young woman her father expected her to be. So far, Virginia doubted her mother was having much of an effect on the girl. "They're bright and cheerful."

Virginia could well imagine the frosty glance *that* comment earned from her mother.

"Rebecca, mind your tongue and your stitch. Your embroidery is atrocious."

Sighing, Rebecca murmured her "Yes, Aunt" very dutifully.

"And I do not mind if Lord Calvert is reminded of his late wife," Virginia continued, signing her name with a flourish. "I would not want him to attempt to erase all evidence of Charles."

"It is surprising he has not. Really, most peculiar of him." Virginia's mother crossed the room to the window. "Perhaps the earl is soft-headed. I have heard he is an eccentric sort. Or maybe he truly means to give you the year before he expects you to forget the baron."

Virginia glanced at Rebecca, wondering what the young woman thought of the decidedly intimate topics under discussion. Her young cousin met her eye and offered a commiserating smile.

"I cannot imagine that to be so, Mother. Lord Calvert is an exceedingly thoughtful man, and his business dealings ought to show his intelligence." Virginia folded her letter and rang the bell at her desk.

Gresham appeared, instead of the footman she'd expected. The butler was a wonder. He always did his work excessively well, especially given his advanced age.

"Gresham, see to it this message is carried to the Gilberts. Thank you."

"Yes, my lady." He took the missive and bowed.

"You ought to change the staff, too," her mother said before the butler had even left the room. Gresham, bless him, didn't even react to her words.

"Mother, your suggestions have been noted, thank you." Virginia came to her feet. "I have invited the Gilberts to dine with us this evening. Since Cousin Christine and I spoke of the possibility yesterday, I am certain they will come. If you will excuse me, I intend to rest."

Her mother flicked her wrist in dismissal, as though it were her morning room they sat inside and not Virginia's. Virginia gritted her teeth, curtsied and shared one last look with Rebecca, then hurried out.

Visits from her mother were never easy. Lady Vinespar knew exactly how to deliver barbed compliments, when she was in a good mood. But she was especially adept at offering advice with a tongue sharp enough to clip a hedge.

Virginia determined to search out the boys. Had it not been raining outside, she would've started her search at their completed castle in the trees.

The carpenter Lucas hired had done a masterful work with nothing but boards and a few small embellishments. Using two of the large chestnut trees down by the lake, the carpenter and his young apprentice had created two towers joined together by a small, but sturdy, bridge. Each boy had his own parapet to sit inside and watch the world around them. Their favorite thing to do was run from one side to the other, which would've been frightening had not the rails installed by the carpenter been very secure.

Several tenant children had watched the work progress for days, and it had pleased Virginia when her sons invited anyone who wished to "visit the castle."

Her mother, upon seeing the structure shortly after her arrival, declared it a waste of resources, funds, and time. She also disapproved of the boys mixing with children beneath their station. Of course, Virginia shouldn't have expected any other reaction.

She walked along the gallery hall, pausing before Lucas and Abigail's wedding portrait.

Her mother's words regarding that had been less acidic. "And when will you replace it with a wedding portrait of your own, Virginia?" she'd asked. Virginia had changed the subject.

Standing before it, regarding the woman's laughing eyes and a younger Lucas's hopeful smile, Virginia took in a deep breath. "I'm sorry she's so insulting," she said, her voice too soft to be overheard. "She has always been thus. Please don't take it personally."

Did Abigail know, from where her soul had gone, what went on in Lucas's life?

"Your things aren't going anywhere and your portrait will always be right here where it belongs," Virginia said firmly.

In truth, she'd come to regard the woman in that portrait as a friend. Though they had never met, they shared a very common interest. Lucas. Though she had never spoken to the portrait before, Virginia had often stopped to examine it and wonder about the bride. What would Abigail have thought about Lucas's marriage? Would she have been disappointed in how Virginia drove him away from his own house with her cool treatment?

Virginia sighed and lowered her eyes. "I didn't want him to leave. Though it did seem best when he mentioned it."

Yet it hadn't been for the best. Virginia had found herself constantly thinking of Lucas. Each time a letter arrived from him, she'd started one in reply. But every time she sat down before the blank sheet of paper, her heart had stilled her hand. No words seemed right. Anything she would say would look trite on paper. Why couldn't he return, so they might speak face to face as they'd done every day since their wedding?

She hadn't been so lonely since Charles's death.

The words she'd heard in the churchyard haunted her. *And you need to love again.* What did it mean? Had it been her heart or her head speaking to her? She longed to believe it was Charles. But how could that be? She didn't believe in the supernatural, beyond what she found in scripture.

Charles would not want her to be lonely, to seal herself off from love and happiness. She knew that. He had loved her with his whole heart and soul. He'd not liked the idea of her mourning for him. Would she have expected him to never love again? Would it wound her to think of Charles remarrying had she been the one to die?

It didn't. In fact, in the private thoughts of her heart, when she'd carried both boys, she'd wondered what would become of him if she died giving birth. It was a natural fear any number of women had. Death in childbirth was too commonly experienced for a woman to dismiss the idea entirely.

Virginia took a step closer to Abigail's portrait. Tipping her head to one side, she regarded the woman's likeness with curiosity. "Would you be hurt to know he loved again?" Virginia asked quietly.

It would be a selfish love, to wish that kind of loneliness on a person. Abigail hadn't been a selfish person. Charles had been the opposite of selfish.

"My lady?"

Virginia nearly leaped back from the wall, her heart racing. She'd been so intent on her thoughts she hadn't heard Gresham's approach. She turned to him, trying to look unstartled.

"I apologize, my lady." Gresham bowed, his bushy white brows furrowing in a contrite manner. "I did not mean to alarm you."

"It's quite all right, Gresham." She tapped her chest, drawing in a deep breath. "I'm afraid I was rather occupied by my thoughts. What is it you needed?"

"My lady, I wished you to know the message has been sent on as you wished."

"Oh." He never bothered to search her out to confirm such a thing before. "Thank you. Is that all?"

"Not all, my lady, but I do have a personal matter I would like to discuss, if it is convenient?"

"Of course, Gresham. What is it?"

"As his lordship is not present, and I believe he would have a difficult time understanding, I wish to ask my lady if I might retire from my duties in the house."

Virginia blinked at him, her heart sinking. "Gresham, if this is because of what Lady Vinespar said—"

He shook his head. "No, my lady. I have been thinking on it for some time. I have been a servant in this household since his lordship's grandfather was its master. It is time, I believe, for me to allow a younger man to look after the family. It has been my greatest honor to serve in this house."

Virginia nodded. "I understand. Very well. We will look into a replacement. Thank you for coming to me. I will make certain his lordship arranges your pension as well. You have served this family with great loyalty. Thank you. For everything."

He bowed. "Thank you, my lady." Then he took a step back, as if to leave.

"Gresham?" Virginia asked, bringing his attention back to her. She would never, ever confide the private matters of her marriage or family to a servant. She knew better than that. But Gresham was loyal to the family and had been for three generations.

"Yes, my lady?" He waited, his expression all politeness.

"You knew the Lady Abigail Calvert?"

The old man nodded once, his eyes softening. "I did, my lady. Before and after her marriage."

"If you do not think me bold to ask it, what was she like?" Virginia asked.

Gresham turned to look at Abigail's portrait, his posture straightening a touch. "She was kindness itself, my lady. Young, but thoughtful. A good mistress. She loved the family, and his lordship, with her whole heart." He turned back to Virginia and met her eyes squarely. "But what is it you really want to know, my lady?"

Virginia felt her smile waver. Dare she ask? "I want to know what she would've thought of me. Of Lucas marrying again. But I don't suppose you would know the answers to those questions."

The butler's shoulders relaxed and he returned her smile, his small and gentle, but genuine. "I can answer that, my lady, easy as you please. Lady Abigail, as we called her when she was a child, would have adopted you at once. She would have seen what my lord sees: a good woman in need of friendship and support, someone who took a burden upon herself to protect others. She would have liked you a great deal."

Virginia's eyes watered and she looked down, tempted to disbelieve him. But his words rang with sincerity. He had no reason to lie. He could've easily agreed he couldn't answer such a thing and been on his way.

"But as to the other matter, of his lordship marrying again, I know the answer to that too. I was there the night she passed. Me and Mrs. Hail, so you can ask her if you don't trust the word of an old man." When she looked, he was still wearing that gentle smile, and his eyes glistened too. "One of the very last things she said to my lord was to bid him to find happiness again. She knew as well as any of us how much heart he has. She knew it would nearly kill him to lose her. So she made him promise."

The young earl in the portrait, his smile and pride, had been a man very much in love, with all his life ahead of him to adore the woman at his side. He'd achieved happiness, and then bliss with the knowledge of her pregnancy, only to have it all snatched away by scarlet fever.

"How long did it take him to be happy, Gresham?" she asked, staring at Lucas's portrait.

"I'd say he didn't really find his happiness again until May of this year, my lady." Virginia's eyes widened at his words. "When he met you," he added, unnecessarily driving the point into her heart.

Virginia took half a step back. "Gresham, I am not searching out compliments."

He nodded. "I know that, my lady. But the morning that he decided to ask for your hand, I found him here." Gresham pointed to the place beneath the portrait. "He'd slept there all night. I imagine he had many concerns. Perhaps he worried it would seem unfaithful of him to love another." He shook his head, his smile fading before he continued.

"Lady Abigail, she would never wish for him to be alone or unhappy. My lord has always had a kind heart, but for so long, he kept much of himself locked away. In the weeks since you married, he has smiled more. Laughed more. Your sons bring him joy."

He paused and met her eyes again, his look becoming more serious. "My lady, it is not my place to speak my mind, but as I am old, and since you began this conversation, I must ask something. Would your baron want you to spend weeks, months, or years weeping over his loss, or would he hope your days would be filled with joy and laughter?"

She ought to be offended. She knew she shouldn't even entertain the thought of answering such a personal question. The division in their class, between servant and employer, created an enormous gap that ought never to be breached by a conversation of such intimacy.

But Virginia found herself speaking, a hand covering her heart, feeling the truth behind each word as it left her lips. "Charles was a vibrant man, kind and generous to all he knew. It would hurt him to think his memory prevented that for me." She sucked in a deep breath, meeting Gresham's steady gaze with surprise. "But it hasn't even been six months, Gresham."

He straightened his shoulders; his face became impassive once more. Gresham was her butler, not her confidante.

"My lady, where are the rules of grief written? And who do we offend when we write our own?" he asked. Then he bowed, turned, and walked away as though nothing out of the ordinary had happened.

Virginia stared after him, her thoughts spinning.

Society dictated she mourn her husband for a year. But society was already likely offended by her hasty marriage.

But here in the country, at Annesbury Park, what care did she have for *society*?

Virginia shook the thought away and continued to the nursery, hoping the boys would have need of her and she might count on them for distraction.

Chapter Twenty-seven

Lucas exited the printer's shop with a book wrapped in brown paper. He couldn't wait to see Edward's face when he showed the boy what he'd done with his drawings. He hoped it would be appreciated, perhaps even inspiring for the young artist. No one had ever encouraged the artistic endeavors of Lucas's brother, Marcus. Not as they should have. If Edward truly loved to draw and paint, and he did show a great aptitude for it, Lucas would do all he could to encourage the talent to grow.

He took in a deep breath of London's humid air, for once appreciating the cooler weather. It wouldn't help anyone's crops, but it kept the stench of the great city bearable. Like many of London's wealthy citizenry, he preferred the country to the city in the warmer months.

Longing for Annesbury Park had become Lucas's permanent state. There was little to occupy him in London that could not be accomplished elsewhere, especially with Parliament out and most of his friends gone to their own homes. He would rather be in the countryside, visiting Thomas Gilbert, riding about the countryside…

Lucas sighed and quickened his pace, trying to outrun his own lies.

He wanted to be fishing with the boys, inspecting their castle in the trees, taking them on the picnic he had long ago promised and never delivered. He missed Edward's delivery of drawings. He missed Phillip's serious questions and rare smile.

But it was Virginia he missed the most.

He took the steps two at a time when he arrived at his townhouse, which was now his mother's permanent residence. She had begun talking of setting up house elsewhere, before the season began, so as not to be in Virginia's way. The idea of her leaving, of hearing the queer echo of emptiness in another grand house, settled like a stone in Lucas's stomach.

The butler took his hat and gloves. "My lord, there is a gentleman here to see you. He has been waiting a quarter of an hour and said he would wait until you arrived."

Lucas raised his eyebrows. "I am not expecting anyone. His name?"

"A Mr. Ewan Snowley, my lord."

Tucking his package for Edward beneath his arm, Lucas gave a nod. "In my study?"

"Your mother is with him, my lord, in the morning room. She rather insisted on giving him tea." The butler's eyebrows twitched, a near-enough sign of disapproval. This butler had been engaged by his mother years ago, but he never had accustomed himself to her somewhat unorthodox manners.

"Thank you. I'll see to him at once." Lucas only just restrained his smile. His mother wouldn't care that she hadn't been properly introduced to someone. If they came to her home, she'd still be the best hostess they'd ever had the privilege of meeting.

Lucas went up the stairs, puzzling over the visitor's identity, pushing thoughts of the children and Virginia to the back of his mind. Any diversion would be a welcome one, truly.

He entered the morning room, a comfortable chamber obviously stamped with his mother's unique sense of style. She had turned the room into a Grecian oasis, or at least the English version of it. Pillars, urns, pastoral scenes in paintings, and furniture with scroll-work and Ionic columns supporting them all.

The gentleman rose when he entered, his hat in one hand and a cup in the other. He was nearly as tall as Lucas, though perhaps several years younger. The cut of his clothing was fine enough to mark him as a successful member of the gentry. He bowed.

Lucas returned the gesture, but went to his mother's side before speaking, dropping a kiss to her cheek as he always did when greeting her. "Mother. You look well this afternoon."

Her eyes sparkled up at him. "I look well every afternoon. Most of the day long, in fact. Lucas, may I present Mr. Snowley. I met him today in our entry hall. He says he must speak with you but will not tell me why."

"Is that so? Mr. Snowley, as we have never met before, I find myself very curious as to why you've come."

Mr. Snowley's expression remained neutral, giving nothing away. "I beg your pardon, my lord. It is not my habit to call on people in such a manner, but I felt you would wish to speak to me straight away. We are not in the same social circles, so I could not beg an introduction anywhere else. But I come on a most important matter, my lord, concerning your wife."

Virginia? Lucas nearly blurted her name aloud. "How do you know Lady Calvert, Mr. Snowley?"

The man, still standing, hastily put the cup down and held his hat in both hands. "I am from Suffolk, my lord. I am—I was familiar with the late baron's family. I—" He broke off and looked to Lady Pamela Calvert, hesitating.

"You may speak freely, sir. The dowager countess will torture whatever information you impart from me if you do not." Though he said the words lightly, Lucas knew his impatience was hardly masked.

Clearing his throat, Mr. Snowley spoke again, more rapidly. "I was spending an evening out with friends, my lord, when I recognized a member of the baron's family, Mr. Macon. I thought I had better go and do the polite thing, but as I approached him I became aware that he had been in his cups. He was saying things I will not repeat before a lady." He nodded at Lucas's mother briefly. "Mr. Macon, apart from deriding you and your family, also uttered threats. I gathered that he owes a great deal of money to someone and he seemed to think he could make your wife give him the money to pay it."

Lucas clenched the back of his mother's chair in both hands. "What did he say, Mr. Snowley? The man attempted to take my wife to court to obtain control of his late brother's estate, but he did not succeed."

"I cannot swear these were his exact words, my lord. He said something like, 'If I get hold of the little brats, she will pay me anything I like.' Then he laughed, and he said, 'I'll have the money by next week.' Then he left."

Sparing a quick glance down at his mother, Lucas met the man's eyes again. He saw no deception, no mark or reason to suspect Mr. Snowley told anything but the truth. In fact, the man's expression betrayed his worry.

"This was last evening?"

"Yes, my lord."

His mother reached up and covered his hand with hers. Lucas looked down at her, his blood running cold.

"Go, son. At once."

Without hesitation, he scooped up Edward's package and left the room, calling over his shoulder, "Thank you, Mr. Snowley!"

Hurry. The word reverberated through his very soul. *Virginia needs you.*

¤

Standing in Lucas's study, staring out at the gloomy skies, Virginia took in a deep breath. The room smelled like him. She'd never allowed herself to notice before, to think about it. But Lucas carried with him the scents of sandalwood and cinnamon, and sometimes a hint of leather to him, too, after he'd been riding or working at his desk for long hours. It was a unique blend of warm, comforting things, which really quite suited him.

Leaning against the window pane, Virginia stared down the road, willing him to return.

They were halfway through August. Why had he been gone so long? More than a month. She needed him to come back, to stand before her. Virginia needed to look him in the eye, to see again what she now told herself had been imagined. She needed to know, to really understand, how he felt about her.

She suspected she knew his heart. If she could see him again, if she could stand before him for just a moment more, she might finally understand her own.

Virginia had entered the study with two purposes in mind. The first was to take refuge and bask in the silence of her mother's absence. The woman's visit, her continual insistence that Virginia conform to her opinion on every subject, had exhausted Virginia completely. Bidding farewell to her that morning had been a relief.

The second reason for being in the study was to write Lucas a letter. She hadn't received anything from him in well over a week, which was all her own fault for not writing sooner. She wanted to rectify the situation.

The paper she held bore her rather pathetic attempts.

To My Lord, Lucas Calvert,

All is well at Annesbury Park. The rain continues to fall, my mother at last concluded her visit, and we miss you.

After that, the pen had rather gotten away from her.

Edward asks continually when you will come home. Phillip wonders whether we ought to come to London to see if you need help. They both want to show you the beautiful castle you had built for them. They both now call you Papa when my mother is not near enough to hear them. She disapproves, of course. But I do not.

I miss you. I cannot lie. I miss our conversations over breakfast when you always try to make me take one more bite than I intended. I noticed, Lucas. Thank you for looking after me. I miss when you find me in the hall, or in the sitting room, or in the music room. You always have something to discuss, but I wonder now if half those things were made up. I think there were several times I sought your opinion on matters when it was not necessary, making excuses to speak to you.

I miss sitting across the table from you at supper, talking of our day. You always make certain that the boys are happy, that I am content.

For so long, I thought I was the strong one. I thought I knew what was best for my sons and for myself. But as I look back over my time as your wife, I have realized something. I have realized—

She had stopped writing then, rather horrified by what she almost put on paper. What she had to say to Lucas, she must say in person.

But she could only do that if he returned.

Her eyes went to the driveway again, to the chestnut trees that looked rather like they were holding up a sky full of gray clouds.

Would he ever return? Was Phillip right, and they ought to go and search him out?

Virginia thought she knew why he left. She knew it must be her fault, somehow. She had to have said or done something terrible to discourage him so. That morning, at the churchyard, everything had changed. Or had it been before that?

She didn't know and she didn't care, though the outcome left her wondering how she might repair the damage done.

A flash of color appeared from between the chestnut trees—a dash of deep blue against the browns and greens of nature. She took in a deep breath and leaned closer to the window, her nose touching the glass.

But no. Even from this distance, she knew it could not be Lucas. The rider had dark hair and hunched over his mount in a way she had never seen Lucas sit. Who could it be?

Virginia stepped away from the window, folding her letter. She dropped it atop the desk, noting Edward's ever-growing pile of sketches waiting for Lucas's return. Edward had asked to post his artwork to his new papa, but Virginia convinced him it would be a greater surprise for Lucas to have them all waiting upon his return.

Why hadn't she recognized that she needed the same thing as her children? Edward had been quick to embrace Lucas in his life, to depend upon him for protection and care. Phillip, though he'd been slower to accept Lucas, hadn't hesitated because he didn't want to be loved by his stepfather, but because he didn't know if he would be loved in return. Lucas proved himself to Phillip by not giving up and allowing the boy to come around in his own time.

Virginia had held herself apart. Yes, she still missed Charles. She would always miss Charles. He was a part of her, the father of her sons, the man she had loved for several precious years and who would always hold a place in her heart.

But Charles had also been the man who would tell her now, with a tenderness she could feel within her heart, that he would want her to be happy, to find someone to care for her as he had.

Walking to the front door, preparing to greet the unknown visitor, Virginia became distracted by a sound on the stair. She looked up and saw Phillip and Edward, their faces looking over the rail. She smiled, realizing Edward would be on his toes to manage it.

"Is it Papa?" Edward asked.

Had they been watching the windows too? Her heart sunk. When would Lucas return?

"I'm afraid not. But stay just there and your curiosity will be satisfied shortly." She smiled up at them, listening for the knock that would come—

The door burst open upon its hinges. Virginia whirled about, her mouth opening in a shout of surprise. Who would dare—?

Gerard Macon rushed in, wild-eyed, and came directly for her. She readied a scream but stopped when she saw his hand waving at her, gripping a pistol.

"Where are the boys?" he demanded, his voice a hiss that carried through the entry hall and blew up the staircase.

Dear God, let them keep still, she prayed, even as she started shaking her head. "What are you doing here?" Her voice trembled but the words came out strongly. She lifted her chin and stood straighter. "Take that gun out of my house." Only her sons' safety could make her so bold as to demand such a thing.

He laughed, an angry, sharp sound. "Your rank doesn't scare me, Virginia. I want the boys. Now."

"Why?" she asked. He must be out of his mind. His eyes were bloodshot, his face bright red, sweat shone on his forehead. What devil had possessed him to take up arms against a woman and two children?

"Now," he said, his voice becoming shrill. He raised the pistol and pointed it at the center of her chest. "Or I shoot you and find them myself."

Virginia's mind had been spinning even as she spoke, going through what must be done to protect her sons from their obviously insane uncle. How could this be happening? She could not doubt the reality of her situation, though she wished it was but a nightmare from which she could wake.

The boys on the stairs hadn't made a sound, but they might if they believed her to be in danger. Surely a servant had heard the commotion. Help would come, but would it be soon enough?

She needed to ensure the safety of her sons and the household.

Time. She needed to stall for time.

"Outside. It hasn't been raining. They will be in their tree castle." She lifted her chin. "By the lake."

He took a step to her, and another. "Lead the way."

Heart racing, Virginia nodded and went to the front door. She had to get him out of the house. Had to protect the boys. They would go for help, or they would hide.

She lifted her eyes slightly, looking over her shoulder, to see if Edward and Phillip were still at the rail. She saw no sign of them. Good.

"Eyes ahead," Mr. Macon said, his voice cold.

Virginia didn't look back again. She walked down the steps, lifting her skirts as she planned her route. Around the house, between the stables and out buildings? No, around those too. It would put her in the path of fewer people, but would take more time. She doubted Gerard would let her walk into a public area. Then down the hill. She would fall, trip, stumble, whatever necessary to make the time last longer. She wasn't dressed to walk through the long grass; clumsiness would be plausible.

Then to the lake. But after that, what?

Her stomach rolled, sweat broke out on her brow. Giving in to the physical need to fall apart was not possible now. She had to keep her wits about her. Had to control herself.

She bit her lip and threw pleading eyes up to the dreary skies. She invoked every prayer she knew, every angel, to keep her sons safe and deliver her safely back to them.

Chapter Twenty-eight

L ucas rode hard, changing horses twice and travelling with more haste than care. He didn't know if Gerard Mason was blustering in a drunken fit or would have already left to commit whatever terrible act he'd planned. All Lucas knew, all he could think upon, was that his wife and children needed him *now*.

He never should've left.

Lucas spurred his horse onto greater speed when he turned into his own lane, riding beneath the chestnut trees, but he pulled the animal up sharply when he spotted another horse idly eating grass and the front door to his home standing open.

What should he do? Assess the situation or go straight in?

He thought carefully, then determined it would be best to go around to the rear entrance. If Mr. Macon had a weapon, Lucas didn't want to walk in blind.

He tamped down his fears as best he could, knowing if he allowed himself to dwell on the possibilities of what he might confront, what might've happened if he arrived too late, he would be useless to them.

Calm. I must keep calm. Going in panicked is worse than going in blind.

Skirting the property as best he could, Lucas took the foaming horse around the house and began to loop back around.

A footman appeared, running toward the stables. It was such an out of place thing to see, Lucas knew with certainty the scene had been caused by Macon. He rushed his horse through the grass and whistled. The footman stumbled and turned, looking in Lucas's direction, then he ran straight for the earl.

The man nearly ran headlong into the horse, but Lucas pulled up in time and bent down.

"He took the countess! A man, the one we took from the house. The boys saw him. He has a gun and he said he would shoot her if she didn't give the boys to him."

"Are the boys safe?" Lucas demanded first. "Where is the countess?"

"The boys are hidden in the passage," the footman said. "The house is ready to defend them. But my lady—to the lake. He took her to the lake. I was going for the stables, to send for help. Gresham went to your guns, my lord."

Lucas's eyes went back to the house. "Go to the stables. Send a man to the Gilberts and another to the magistrate. Tell the rest to wait for me." He hadn't finished speaking before spurring the horse to action again, going for the back door of the house. He arrived at it just as Gresham stepped out, a shotgun in his gloved hands.

"Have you a revolver?" Lucas asked, halting his horse again. The animal's sides heaved. He had nearly pushed it too far.

Gresham immediately reached into his coat and pulled forth Lucas's favorite pistol. "It's loaded, my lord."

"Stand guard over the boys," Lucas said, accepting the revolver. "I've sent for help." He kicked the horse's sides, promising himself he'd make it up to the borrowed animal later, and went for the stables. He didn't know how much time had passed since Macon had taken Virginia, or why they were going to the lake, but *hurry, hurry, hurry,* thrummed through his mind at the same rate as his pulse.

He rode through the stable yard and saw two men climbing onto the bare backs of horses. He didn't bother to address them. They would know their assignment. The stable master and two younger men remained, and a gardener came forward with wide eyes and trowel.

"A man has taken your countess captive at the lake. Come as quietly and swiftly as you can, with whatever you have at hand. I will confront him but I want everyone ready, should I fail, to rush him. He has a pistol and the most he could have is two shots. We must save the countess at all costs." The men nodded their understanding.

Lucas didn't wait for more but turned the horse's head to the lake.

He hoped he had not delayed too long.

¤

The third time Virginia feigned a slip in the grass, Mr. Macon grabbed her upper arm and held onto it with bruising force, leaving her no choice but to keep her feet beneath her. He dragged her down the hill and to the water. There was only one stand of chestnut trees near the lake and that was where they went. Every foul word imaginable was growled at her, but Virginia ignored his vitriol. Her hastily constructed plan had several flaws she must attempt to repair before he realized what she'd done.

Obviously, the man wasn't thinking clearly, but that could make him more apt to shoot her should he become overly agitated.

Before they were at the trees, he started yelling for the boys. "Phillip. Edward. Come here." Nothing about his tone was friendly. Virginia kept moving, propelled forward with him behind. They passed beneath the trees and stood under one of the turrets.

Thunder rumbled in the distance, the morning air heavy with the scent of rain.

"You little brats, come down!"

"You've frightened them," Virginia said loudly, her voice desperate. She made each word tremble, forcing her limbs to do the same. Let him think her helpless and weak. "They won't come down if they're afraid. They're little children." Adding another dry sob for good measure, Virginia bent her knees, going limp in his hand.

Mr. Macon shook her. "Stand up, you—" He derided her in every way, but she kept her face turned away and sobbed.

"I'm hurt. I've turned my ankle."

He shoved her away, against a tree. Good. Virginia leaned heavily against it, turning her eyes up to the castle in the trees. "You must go up and get them." She sank down, making a show of her weakness. They had only been walking for a short time, but he was frenzied enough he might not stop to consider how such a short journey could do her in so terribly.

Fouling the air with his language, Mr. Macon pointed the pistol at her, the barrel nearly touching her nose. "If you move from this spot, I swear I will kill you."

She didn't even dare nod. "I understand," she breathed. Was he a good shot? She couldn't remember ever hearing. But once he discovered the boys were not hiding in their castle, would he leave her alive? She stood a better chance running from him, but she had to time it correctly. "There is a bridge connecting the towers," she said quietly.

He raised the pistol and Virginia began to hope. If he climbed into the fort, she could run. He would catch her too easily if she ran up the hill. Would he pursue if she went around the edge of the lake? The ground was even, which gave her a clearer path to run, but it would be an easier shot for him.

The side of his pistol came down, crashing into the top of her head. The world went bright in a flash of pain, then dark again. She tasted bile in her mouth. Smelled the earth beneath her. Her cheek was pressed into the grit and grass beneath the trees.

She came to laying on the ground, watching his boots walk away from her. Dazed, but not unconscious, Virginia's determination became fuzzy with fear.

She heard his boot hit the first rung of the wooden ladder, and the rain started falling against the leaves. It would mask the sound of her departure.

Pushing herself up with her hands, Virginia tried to pull her knees beneath her. Her head swam, the world spun, but she gritted her teeth.

If I can stand, I can walk. If I can walk, I can run.

Keeping her head down, she moved her hands to the side of the tree and used its strength to gain her feet. Then her eyes went to the hill. No. She had decided against the hill. Then where—?

A flash of brown and blue. Had Mr. Macon not gone up the ladder? Was he around that tree instead? But why?

A hand on the trunk of a tree opposite hers appeared, and then an arm and shoulder, and then she saw him. It wasn't Mr. Macon. It was Lucas.

Lucas! She nearly shouted in her relief. Not caring how he arrived, or how he knew to come to her, Virginia took a step in his direction. He reached out to her, but her eyes stayed on his beautiful gray eyes, swirling with his worry. If she could reach his hand, she would be safe.

"I said not to move." Mr. Macon's voice came from above and she knew he must be on the bridge, looking down at her. She had precious seconds before he discovered her lie. Was he pointing his weapon at her? Did she risk the mad dash around the tree to Lucas?

Standing at his full height, Lucas stepped around the tree, arm raised and a revolver pointing upward. "Get behind me," he said.

Virginia moved without looking, hurrying to do as he said, ignoring the way the world began to grow black around the edges. Lucas had come. Nothing else mattered.

"If it isn't his lordship."

"You raise your weapon and I will shoot you where you stand. You won't get a shot off. Drop your revolver to the ground. Men are coming to secure you. Do it, Macon, and I'll help you avoid the noose."

Gerard Macon laughed, and it was a sound that sent chills running through her spine. "And go to prison?"

"Deportment. We'll send you to the colonies. That's a better life than prison." Lucas kept his arm outstretched, his aim steady.

Virginia lifted her eyes to look up, to see what Mr. Macon would do. His face had gone white and he stood deathly still, his arm at his side. He appeared, for a fleeting moment, like Charles had. The brothers were similar in some physical ways, but she'd never thought them alike in character. Still, the resemblance smote her heart.

"Please, Gerard," she said, her voice barely loud enough to be heard over the rain. "Charles loved you. Don't throw your life away."

"I think I already have." When he uttered those words, Virginia's heart dropped.

But he didn't fire. He turned away and lifted his arm slowly, showing he would not shoot, then dropped it over the bridge's rail and to the ground. It landed with a thump.

From around the tree one of the groomsmen appeared, startling Virginia, but he went directly to the revolver and picked it up. Another man appeared, and another. Did she hear horses coming too?

Lucas finally lowered his weapon and turned to her, his heart in his eyes again. This man loved her, had done nothing but put her and her sons first in his thoughts since they met. She had only been a widow six months. But how could she dictate to her heart that it must wait, when he stood before her ready to give her everything?

Spots appeared before her eyes and she sucked in a sharp breath, nearly whimpering.

"You're hurt." He turned and gestured for another man to come take his weapon. Gerard was climbing down the ladder with one pistol trained on him already. Lucas took off his coat and wrapped it around her shoulders. It had turned cold, hadn't it? Virginia opened her mouth to thank him, but then his arms were around her and he dipped down to hook one around her knees. He lifted her up, cradling her in his arms.

"I came as soon as I could," a familiar voice said. Virginia turned her startled gaze to Thomas Gilbert, sitting astride a fine bay horse. "I was riding this direction when your man spotted me. What can I do?"

"Give me use of your horse and keep an eye on Macon until the magistrate comes."

Thomas swung down from his horse and held it steady. Lucas lifted her up first and she gripped the front of the saddle, still addled. An instant later, Lucas was behind her, his arms around her again. She sighed and leaned against his chest, tucking herself against him.

"You're safe now," Lucas said, pulling the horse around and taking her back up the hill to the house. "The boys are in the passageway. I'll take care of you, Virginia."

She closed her eyes and smiled. "I know." She felt his lips press gently against the top of her head, near what must be a rather impressive bump by this time. "I'm glad you're home," she whispered. His arms tightened around her and they said nothing more until they reached the house.

The first person she saw when Lucas led her into the front door was a harried looking footman, who was obviously relieved to see her. His wig was askew and his shirt untucked. Gresham would not be pleased.

But then Lucas took her up the stairs and she saw Gresham standing in the gallery hall, a shotgun in his hands. His posture was perfect, his old face the proper mask of a butler. He bowed when he saw them. "Welcome home, my lord. My lady, I am pleased to see you are safe. Shall I put this away then?"

"Yes Gresham. And when everyone has returned, see to it all the men get a good, strong drink and whatever food they need." Lucas met her shocked expression and grinned. "He's very loyal."

"I know." She kept moving and saw Nurse Smythe stick her head around a doorway.

"Oh, thank the Lord," the nurse said, then disappeared. Virginia hurried forward and entered the music room just as the panel concealing the secret passage slid aside and her sons tumbled out. "It's all right, boys. Your mother and father are back."

Virginia dropped to her knees and opened her arms, tears burning behind her eyes. The boys came out, shaking and talking all at once, running into her embrace. Virginia looked up at Lucas.

His eyes were shining and as she watched, tears escaped. He knelt next to them, hesitating, asking her for permission with the look on his face. Virginia nodded, offering him what must've been a tremulous smile. Lucas's long arms opened and he wrapped them around them all, holding the boys, holding her.

"Papa's back," Edward whispered loudly into her ear. "Did he save you?"

"Yes, darling." She met Lucas's gaze over the children's heads. "Again."

He chuckled and shook his head, holding them all tighter.

"Next time you go to London, you better take us with you," Phillip said, his voice muffled as his face was still pressed into Virginia's shoulder.

"I won't leave you behind anymore," Lucas said firmly.

The walls around her heart had been crumbling for weeks, but now they fell to the ground at last. Lucas was a man of his word. He wouldn't leave again. And finally, she would have the chance to tell him what she could never have put in a letter.

Chapter Twenty-nine

"Papa?" At Edward's quiet greeting, Lucas looked up from his desk, a smile already on his face. "May we come in?" Edward had put his face around the door, an earnest look in his eyes.

"Please, do." Putting his pen down, Lucas stood. Edward pushed the door open and came in, Phillip directly behind him.

"How are you this morning, Phillip? Edward?" Lucas gestured to the chairs on the other side of his desk. "And does Nurse know you're here?"

"Yes, Papa," they chorused, taking their seats before him.

"I have wanted to speak to you both since yesterday. It was a very hectic afternoon, wasn't it?"

They nodded and Phillip started talking rapidly. "I was frightened for Mother, but I knew she wouldn't want us to make a sound." After the initial heightened emotion began to wear down, Lucas had received a full account of all that had happened from everyone.

No one had heard Macon enter the house aside from Virginia and the boys. The servants had all been called to their hall for special instruction. Gresham had been most apologetic, though no fault could be laid at his feet. Phillip had pulled Edward away from the rails when he heard his mother's fright and listened to everything, then took Edward to the secret passage before running to find the servants. He told them what he heard and Gresham took over like a general. Two maids escorted Phillip to the secret passage, then told Nurse what had happened. Lucas had been astounded by Virginia's quick thinking to lead the villain away from the house, but she had not allowed a single compliment to be given. She insisted she did what any mother would, and that was to lead danger away from her children.

It could have gone terribly wrong when Macon realized her trickery. Lucas tried not to think on it, afraid of what he might do, what acts he might commit against the man for threatening his family.

It was done. Gerard Macon was in custody and would stand trial. Lucas would do all he could to have the man transported, as he promised, but he would never lose sleep thinking on the man's fate.

Lucas looked between Phillip and Edward, two of the most important people in the world as far as he was concerned. "You both did very well. Your bravery is commendable, and I rather think it deserves a reward."

The brothers exchanged a glance, then Edward tilted his head to the side and narrowed his eyes. "I thought the cake was our reward."

Lucas chuckled. In light of the disturbing events, Cook had presented the family with an enormous lemon cake, covered in lavender frosting, *before* dinner.

"I think the cake was Cook's way of saying she was grateful you two were safe," he said. "But I had another thought. Long ago, I promised you both a picnic. And if you will look outside, you will see we've been given a blue sky and sun. Would you two join me?"

"And what about me?" another voice asked. Virginia stood framed by the dark wood casing of the door, her summer-gold hair worn half up in a bandeau, the other half loose across her shoulders. She wore a dress of pale lavender, almost white, which Lucas found caused her eyes to appear darker, like the depths of a pool in the forest. "May I join you?"

"Oh, yes, please. Can Mother come too?" Phillip asked.

Virginia's smile grew slowly as she kept his gaze and only then did Lucas realize he was staring.

Taking hold of himself, Lucas turned his attention to the boys and nodded. "Of course. As she wishes to, and as we must honor a lady's wishes, she will come. I thought, as luncheon would normally be about now, we should leave right away."

Edward didn't need to be told twice. He leaped from his seat. "Can we picnic by the lake, at the castle?"

"That would be lovely," Virginia said, before Lucas could suggest another location. He met her eyes again, looking for any sign of distress, but there was nothing in her expression to hint that going to the scene of yesterday's drama would upset her. Virginia's strength and courage, her level-headedness in the face of danger, gave him further cause to admire her.

"Phillip, would you please tell Gresham? The staff will prepare our picnic for us while you both get ready."

Phillip nodded. "Come on, Edward." The two boys walked out of the room, bowing as they passed their mother, but the instant they were in the hall the sound of their feet pounding away at a run echoed behind them.

Virginia laughed and turned, meeting Lucas's eyes with that tender, gentle look he had noticed the day before. Something was different about her smile, too. Yesterday, in the midst of all the chaos and calm, he told himself it was only gratitude he saw. Perhaps she had been euphoric in her relief. But that was all. Allowing himself to read more into it would drive him mad.

"I will see you shortly. I'm afraid I'm not dressed for a picnic." She gestured to her morning gown and he nodded his understanding. Then she disappeared and he sat down heavily, feeling his strength leave him.

Would it always be this way in her presence? When she left a room, it was as though she took all the light with her.

Lucas shook his head and dropped his face into his hands, trying to clear his thoughts.

I'm stronger than this. I will control myself. So saying, he stood and went to make himself ready for the walk to the lake. He imagined he would be climbing into a tree as well.

By the time he was ready, the boys were in the entry hall chattering at Nurse Smythe. Virginia met him on the landing, her dress a more sensible one for a walk out of doors. It was pale blue. Had he ever seen her in blue? Was blue a mourning color now?

He cleared his throat and tried not to notice, offering his arm to escort her down the steps.

When they stepped outside, the boys were a great deal like pups. They ran forward only to come back, jumped through the grass, and walked in circles around Virginia and Lucas. The whole while they laughed and chattered away about all they had done with Lucas gone, and about their castle in the trees. He couldn't help smiling as he watched their antics, a sense of contentment entering his heart. Their happiness, their safety and ease, gave him more joy and more purpose than any endeavor of his life had yet to bring.

Virginia, on his arm, trusting him so completely with her life and the lives of her sons, sharing them with him unselfishly, completed him.

He risked a look down at her just as she laughed, watching Phillip spin in circles ahead of them. Hearing her laugh, seeing her eyes dance and sparkle, the pleasant flush in her cheeks, made his heart swell. He loved her, with everything he was, and if all he could ever receive from her in return was this unfettered happiness, he could be content. He *must* be so.

Virginia looked up at him, smiling wide. "I never thought I would see Phillip so happy again. But this summer, with all you've done for him, and in this beautiful place, he is the child I remember. Edward is more full of life than ever, too. Thank you, Lucas. For everything."

He pulled his gaze away from hers, his heart pounding in his chest. "You have all given me a greater happiness than I had before, too. Thank you for that, my lady."

Two liveried footmen were at the bottom of the hill, putting finishing touches on the picnic. Cups, plates, and cold food had been laid out. The boys pounced on the food and Virginia pulled away from Lucas to hurry after them, calling out instructions to mind their manners as she went.

Lucas paused, standing still on the rise, admiring his family. Watching Virginia call the boys to order, listening to them giggle. They sat nestled on the ground beneath the trees, the lake behind them glimmering in the afternoon sun.

Never had he imagined he would have so much in his life. But even with all his wealth, his titles, the grand estate at his back, Lucas knew what meant the most to him in the world, and it was right before his eyes. His family. His wife, his children.

"Are you coming, Papa?" Edward's voice called.

"Of course. I cannot let you lot eat all this food without me," he answered, joining them to laugh beneath the trees.

¤

With a folded piece of paper in his hands, Lucas paced in the parlor. He wore his evening clothes to go into dinner with Virginia. He'd found the letter an hour previous, while going through Edward's stack of artwork on his desk. He'd been surprised to recognize Virginia's hand, to see she had written him a letter, but it remained unfinished.

Why hadn't she finished it? And why had she left it on his desk in such a manner? Was she trying to tell him something?

The letter expressed her gratitude, which he understood, but it ended on such a different note. She had *missed* him. She'd longed for him to return, if he read the letter correctly. She'd written in detail about his absence. Why hadn't she sent the letter? When did she write it? If he would've received even one line of such expressions before, he would have come home much, much sooner.

But the last lines, those were what confused him, and gave him the most hope. *For so long, I thought I was the strong one. I thought I knew what was best for my sons and for myself. But as I look back over my time as your wife, I have realized something. I have realized—*

What had she realized?

Could she possibly feel for him as he did for her?

Lucas attempted to quell that thought. It wasn't appropriate for him to even speculate on the matter before her mourning period was over. Until then, he must keep his hopes silent, his emotions in check, and his heart resolute. Virginia might already suspect something, after the rather difficult exchange between them at Heatherton Hall. But with a month between those events, maybe she had forgotten—or at least would pretend to forget.

The door opened and Lucas fixed a calm smile to his face before he turned. He moved to tuck the letter behind him. It might not be wise to ask her about it after all.

His breath caught.

Candles and the light from the fading sun bathed the room in a soft glow, and Virginia stood there, eyes luminous, vibrant, and joyful. Jewels were in her hair, making it look like a celestial crown of stars had nestled in the golden waves. Her cheeks were a dusky pink, her smile gentle. And she wasn't wearing black, or gray, or lavender, or brown.

The gown was shades of blue and green, shining in the gentle light, encasing her form in silk swaths.

Virginia smiled and his heart nearly burst from his chest, so rapid was his pulse and strong his desire to step forward and take her in his arms.

"Good evening, Lucas," she said, her voice wrapping him in its spell.

"Virginia," he said her name with awe. Could this truly be her? Was he dreaming?

She came forward slowly, her skirts swishing and her eyes never leaving his. What could he say? What could she possibly mean for him to know? It took everything he had not to ask, not to reach for her.

She stopped when she was an arm's length away from him. "I have something I must say."

Lucas's ability to speak had apparently completely left him. All he could do was nod.

"I have decided that following my heart takes precedence over the expectations of society. I didn't mean for it to happen, but now that it has, I do not feel that Charles would see the matter with anything other than approval. He was a very good man and would want all of us to be happy. And he never cared for mourning customs very much anyway. He hated black." She spoke clearly but quickly, her eyes searching his with each word, but he didn't entirely understand.

"You don't wish to wear black?" he asked, his brow drawing down, his hope fading.

"No. Yes." She narrowed her eyes at him. "This was supposed to be easy."

Lucas shook his head and reached out, to take her hands, but he stopped, remembering he held her letter still. "Does it have something to do with this?" He raised the paper for her to see.

The pink in her cheeks turned red. "I'd forgotten about that."

"Oh." They both stared at the paper, then Virginia did the unthinkable and stepped closer to him.

Her fingers went to his cheek. Lucas met her eyes.

"I loved Charles. I have no wish to forget that or to forget him. But I have every intention of living a life of happiness and filling it with love."

Hope burst free of its chains and took flight in his chest. "You do?" he whispered. He dropped the letter and raised a hand to her cheek. "Virginia?"

"Yes," she said, her eyes reflecting back at him the words he didn't know if he dared speak. But Virginia saved him. "I love you," she said, and then again when he froze. "I love you, Lucas. Please don't ever leave me again."

Lucas's answer was to bring his lips to hers, brushing against them in a gentle, tentative kiss.

Is this real?

Virginia responded, her lips caressing his, her hands resting against his chest. Lucas slipped his hand from her cheek gently to her jaw, then to cradle the back of her head. Her kiss tasted like fireworks, and long summer days in the sunlight, and oranges, and every good thing he could remember. His free arm wrapped around her waist, pulling her closer, and she sighed as she deepened their kiss.

They parted for breath, her eyes opened, and Lucas could see the rest of his life in their deep green depths.

He was *married* to this beautiful, intelligent, brave woman.

"I love you," he told her, dropping his forehead against hers, the tips of their noses touching. "I have loved you for so long, but I didn't think— I didn't want to presume anything."

"Because you are good, kind, and noble." She punctuated her words with a quick kiss on his lips, but as she pulled away he bent to capture her lips again, more tenderly. She responded in kind, sliding her hands across his shoulders and around his neck. She fit perfectly in his arms, her lips against his, and Lucas had no intention of ever letting her go.

A quiet cough interrupted them. Lucas looked up over her head.

"It's Gresham," he whispered, bending to speak closer to her ear.

"Ah. Does he look pleased?" she asked, not stepping away from his embrace.

Lucas hadn't thought to look that closely. He could feel his cheeks reddening. He glanced at his butler, who wore a supremely smug expression on his wrinkled face. "Yes."

"Good." She pressed a brief kiss to his jaw and turned to face the butler. "Gresham, is dinner ready?"

"It is, my lady." Gresham then did the most absurd thing Lucas had ever seen him do. He winked. At Virginia. Then stood aside for them to go into dinner. Lucas glanced at Virginia in time to see her wink back at the old man.

"I think it's time to give Gresham a cottage and his pension. A very generous pension," she said cheerfully, looking up at Lucas as if it was the most normal sort of conversation for them to have.

"You do?" A smile tugged at Lucas's mouth.

"Yes." Then she stopped beside her chair, dazzling him with her smile and the light of love in her eyes. "I love you, Lucas."

What could he do, but kiss her again?

Chapter Thirty

May 1822

Virginia lifted her skirts and ran down the gallery hall, two squealing little girls running before her. They raced by their ancestors hanging on the wall, but just before they reached the stair, Lucas jumped from around the corner.

"Ah ha! Found you at last!" The girls halted too quickly and stumbled.

"They were in the passage," Virginia said, trying not to laugh as her daughters grabbed hold of each other to stay upright.

Lucas turned to call down the steps. "Phillip, we found them! Call off the search."

Phillip's voice, still changing but promising to settle into a rich timbre, came up the steps. "All right, I'll tell the others. And remind the girls that the passage is cheating!"

Lucas turned back to his daughters, crossing his arms over his chest. "You heard him."

"It was Emma's idea," the younger of the two said loudly, pointing at her nine-year-old sister. Amelia was only six.

Emma folded her arms in a near perfect imitation of her father. "No, it wasn't. It was Amelia's."

A shout came from upstairs. "Did you find them, Papa?"

"Your mother did," Lucas called up. "It's time to come down and have luncheon."

Amelia's lips stuck out in a pout. "I always get found. I thought the passage would work."

"Because it's out of bounds?" Virginia asked, raising her eyebrows.

A loud thump made them all turn to see four-year-old Rupert grinning, laying on the floor at the bottom of the stairs. "I jumped four steps."

Lucas laughed and assisted the boy to his feet. "Well done. But let's not try five steps until you're five years old. Will you do that for me?"

Rupert nodded, his grin still wide.

Phillip and Edward appeared on the steps, laughing and talking together. Phillip would start at Cambridge soon and Edward was doing well at Eton. They were both tall, handsome young men. Virginia looked her children over, from her elder sons, to her daughters, and her youngest boy. And there was one more in the nursery, their baby Frederick, called Freddy by the whole family.

How she had the energy to keep up with them, Virginia could not say. Lucas told her it didn't take so much energy as it did patience and love. He must've be right.

"All of you, go clean up for luncheon and then pretend we haven't spent the last hour running about the house." She tweaked Emma's braid and her daughter grinned up at her.

"Yes, Mother," the group chorused, and a moment later there was more pounding as the children went upstairs and down the hall to their respective rooms. Lucas caught her eye and grinned, raising his eyebrows as they listened to their children chatting and giggling with each other.

"And what about you, Lady Calvert?" he asked, reaching for her. "Have you a need to freshen up before luncheon?"

"Indeed." She placed her hand in his and walked with him down the gallery to their rooms, her heart full. "Do you think it will always be like this?" she asked, her voice quieter. "Children running every which direction and us right behind them?"

Lucas snorted and shook his head. "Of course not. Eventually, you and I will sit comfortably in our chairs and laugh while our children chase our grandchildren about the house."

Virginia laughed and stopped, standing before a pair of portraits on the wall. "And how do you think those two feel about our antics?"

Lucas turned to look with her at the portraits, his and Abigail's, and hers with Charles. Another hung in the parlor downstairs, of he and Virginia.

"I think they would both be pleased with the way everything is turning out," he said at last, his tone more serious. "Aren't you?"

Virginia stood on her toes to place a kiss on his cheek. He turned and captured her lips with his.

"Thank you for saving me, Lucas," she whispered when they parted.

"Ginny, we saved each other." He squeezed her hand, his heart in his eyes, and Virginia agreed. They'd filled their home and hearts with love, children, and laughter. Charles and Abigail would've been happy for them both.

"I love you."

The world could not be more wonderful.

Author's Notes

Thank you for reading *The Earl and His Lady*. When *The Gentleman Physician* was published, I started receiving emails and messages from readers asking if Virginia would ever find love again. When I wrote my first book, *The Social Tutor*, I had Lucas and Virginia's story all mapped out. I hope it's proved as satisfying for you to read as it was for me to write.

Writing about grief is such a difficult task. I read the accounts of people who had lost loved ones and then remarried, both modern and historical. I consulted my critique partners, trying to make sure the emotion was written accurately and respectfully. Everyone mourns differently. I am in no way suggesting Virginia's story is meant to tell others how to go about this process. I do hope her story was moving and emotionally satisfying for readers.

On another note, historical accuracy is important to me. If you noticed any errors, I apologize. I do my best to stay true to the era and remain accessible to modern readers.

Thank you to all my friends who helped me polish this story. Thank you, Joanna Barker, Carri Flores, Michayle Hales, Arlem Hawks, Shaela Kay, Heidi Kimball, Megan Walker, and everyone from the LDS Beta Readers.

Thank you to my readers for all your kind comments, your lovely reviews, and your encouragement.

About the Author

Sally Britton lives in the desert with her husband, four children, and a black dog named Cherry. She wrote her first story on her mother's electric typewriter when she was fourteen years old. She knew romance was the way for her to go fairly early on. Reading her way through Jane Austen, Louisa May Alcott, and Lucy Maud Montgomery, Sally also determined she wanted to write about the elegant, complex world of centuries past.

Sally graduated from Brigham Young University in 2007 with a bachelor's in English, her emphasis on British literature. She met and married her husband not long after, and they've been building their happily ever after since that day.

Vincent Van Gogh said, "What is done in love is done well." Sally has taken that as her motto, for herself and her characters, writing stories where love is a choice each person must make, and then go forward with hope to obtain their happily ever after.

All of Sally's published works are available on Amazon.com.

Made in the USA
Monee, IL
12 October 2022

15747187R00164